Famous Last Meals

Famous
Last Meals

— *novellas* —

RICHARD CUMYN

ENFIELD
&WIZENTY

Great Plains Publications gratefully acknowledges the financial support provided
for its publishing program by the Government of Canada through the Canada
Book Fund; the Canada Council for the Arts; the Province of Manitoba through
the Book Publishing Tax Credit and the Book Publisher Marketing Assistance
Program; and the Manitoba Arts Council.

Pages 215 to 223 of "Famous Last Meals" first appeared as "Perennial"
in *I Am Not Most Places*, copyright Richard Cumyn 1996. Published with
permission of Dundurn Press Limited

Design & Typography by Relish New Brand Experience
Printed in Canada by Friesens

LIBRARY AND ARCHIVES CANADA CATALOGUING IN PUBLICATION

Library and Archives Canada Cataloguing in Publication

Cumyn, Richard, 1957-, author
     Famous last meals / Richard Cumyn.

3 novellas.
Issued in print and electronic formats.
ISBN 978-1-927855-17-1 (pbk.).--ISBN 978-1-927855-18-8 (epub).--
ISBN 978-1-927855-19-5 (mobi)

     1. Title.

PS8555.U4894F34 2015   C813'.54   C2014-907245-7
                                      C2014-907246-5

ENVIRONMENTAL BENEFITS STATEMENT

Great Plains Publications saved the following
resources by printing the pages of this book on
chlorine free paper made with 100% post-consumer
waste.

TREES	WATER	ENERGY	SOLID WASTE	GREENHOUSE GASES
7	3,310	4	222	610
FULLY GROWN	GALLONS	MILLION BTUs	POUNDS	POUNDS

Environmental impact estimates were made using the Environmental Paper Network
Paper Calculator 3.2. For more information visit www.papercalculator.org.

FSC
www.fsc.org
MIX
Paper from
responsible sources
FSC™ C016245

Didymus,
ghostly father

"He had always been an actor, the call had never come."
—JAMES SALTER, *SOLO FACES*

"She was by nature an actress of parts that entered into
her physique: she even acted her own character, and so well,
that she did not know it to be precisely her own."
—GEORGE ELIOT, *MIDDLEMARCH*

"In a mad world it always seems simpler to obey."
—GRAHAM GREENE, *OUR MAN IN HAVANA*

CONTENTS

Candidates

WHEN ASKED, HE COULD THINK OF ONLY ONE personal interest or hobby that might be applicable to the job as he imagined it. Thinking, rightly, that it sounded thin, he added, "I write pretty well."

"Excellent. We need people who can write." Nothing marred the blank steel purity of the woman's desk. "What kind of puzzles, then?"

"Crossword?"

"Is that a question?"

"Crossword."

"Cryptic?"

"Until I solve them, yes."

"Try this: characteristic on the alternative tergiversator. Seven letters."

He shook his head.

"Starts with T."

"I'm sorry."

"That's fine. Aside from English, what languages do you speak, read and write?"

"French." He could fill the car with gasoline, order bacon and eggs in a restaurant and give passable directions to his house from most points in the city.

"We're looking for people who can speak Russian. Also Arabic and Urdu."

"I could take lessons."

"Couldn't we all."

After the interview she escorted him to a room where a man took ink impressions of his fingerprints. Then the man took a photograph of his face and led him back downstairs to the front desk.

He had parked in a spot reserved for visitors, not far from the building's gatehouse, a squat concrete building that looked like a World War II pillbox. A high steel fence topped with razor wire enclosed the complex. When he got to the car the doors would not open. He pressed his forehead against the damp glass of the driver's window. The keys were hanging from the ignition. To compound his defeat, he had left his overcoat in the interviewer's office.

He smelled exhaust. At the end of the row, in a numbered parking spot reserved for employees, a car was idling its engine. A green plastic garden hose ran from a point behind and under the car, along the driver's side and in through a gap between the top of the window and the doorframe. The interior of the car was opaque with smoke. A darker mass seemed to fill the driver's seat. He stepped towards the car, stopped, turned and went back to the guardhouse, where only minutes earlier he had returned his temporary identification necklace.

"Yes sir, back again," said the uniformed man on duty.

"Yes. It's—okay, three things, actually."

"Three."

"Right. In no particular order: one, I think somebody's trying to commit suicide in the parking lot; B, I've locked myself out of my car; and lastly, I left my overcoat in the building. Come to think of it, that's descending order of importance, isn't it?"

"What building would that be?" The guard looked both blankly menacing and cheerfully clueless.

"Is there more than one? Where I had my interview."

"Give me that name again."

Reading upside down, he put his index finger on the line, the most recent filled, in the ledger where he had signed and printed his name. "You should really take a look at that car. It's full of exhaust."

"Adam Leaner. And your reason for returning would be...?"

"My overcoat. And it's Lerner."

"As in lifelong."

"Please."

"Yes?"

"I can go back in?"

"Not without authorization."

"Whose?"

"That's a Need-to-Know. Who did you say was in your car?"

"Nobody. I'm locked out of it."

"No person or persons is trying to kill him or her self in your car."

"Correct. That's a different car."

"Myself, I always duck-tape a spare key to the inside of my wheel well."

He wondered how the man had ever got hired and how he got his hair to stand straight up like that. He wanted to place a book atop the level plain of the guard's perfect brush cut.

"Is it possible for you to phone the woman who interviewed me? I forget her name."

"They say the devil's in the details."

"I really need my coat."

After the guard made a phone call he told Adam, as he had earlier that morning, to return to the fortress by its main entrance (he could see no other door) and report to the desk. He did and waited for ten minutes. When his interviewer appeared she came down the central stairway, his trench coat draped over her arm. He couldn't tell if she was amused or annoyed.

"I guess this blows my chances," he said, expecting her to contradict him. He said thank you, which she echoed, and they said a simultaneous goodbye, their voices creating a brief choral harmony.

When he returned to the guardhouse and began to ask about his car, the uniform waved him through. The doors were now unlocked, the keys still in the ignition, but the suicide car was gone. Had he imagined seeing a body inside the vehicle? Had it all been a dream?

He phoned his interviewer, whose name was Hannah Pachter, once a week for the next five. All she could say was that he was on a short list of eight.

"It was the coat, wasn't it?" he said, the last time he phoned to inquire about the job. Communications Security Officer. He could do that. He could be a Silent Sam. "It was because I forgot it in your office."

"Yes," said Hannah Pachter in a voice that could have been serious or wearily playful, he couldn't tell which.

"I thought so."

"We'll let you know as soon as we've made a decision, Adam. In the meantime, keep your options open."

"I figured out that word, by the way."

"Excuse me?"

"The word you were looking for the day of the interview. It's "traitor." It took me a while, but I got it."

"Really. You're probably right. I'm sorry, I don't remember."

The Prime Minister's principal secretary was leaving his post, and Adam's father knew a man who had been the incoming PS's roommate at university. A call was made, as calls are made on behalf of recent graduates who have few skills other than the ability to feed themselves without developing scurvy, clean their clothes, and write sensibly on the theme of fidelity in *Henry IV Part I*. A dozen or so of the children of the Party faithful had been hired to fill summer research positions in the PMO and in some federal ministers' offices, and such a position was created for Adam.

When he reminded his father that he was on a short list for the communications security job, Lerner said that a man could not sit around on his duff waiting indefinitely. Things were happening. Adam wanted to wait, he wanted the spy job, but sensed that his chances were not good. He considered challenging his father's definition of acceptable string pulling, but let that pass, too. Paid or not, secret operative or not, the beneficiary of nepotism or not, he was going to be occupied for the summer. And, as his father was wont to point out, repeatedly until it numbed, it would be "quite the choice plum for the old *curriculum vitae*."

Adam found the address on Sparks and walked past the entrance at street level twice before deciding to go in, the first time because he was looking for something grander and the second because he saw no identifying sign or plaque either outside or on the wall inside as he peered through the glass door. He looked at the street number stencilled on the transom window again, checked it against the one he had written on the back of a used envelope, and saw that they were the same. The nondescript unidentified building stood between a formidable stone bank headquarters on one side and a newer glass-and-steel office tower on the other. Its entrance had room for one person at a time to step in before having to turn immediately right.

Entering, he was startled to see an aged commissionaire seated at a little desk just out of sight of the street. Reminded of the brush-cut guard at the Bureau of Secure Communication, he thought that in contrast it wouldn't take much to get past this little fellow. More puzzling about this obscure back way into the office of the country's most important elected official was the apparent absence of a door or hallway nearby, for he could not yet see what was around the corner to his left and kitty-corner to the guard: a small elevator and, near it, a fire door leading to a stairwell.

He showed the old man his driver's license and social insurance card and told him that he was meeting a Ms. Castelli, the summer-student co-ordinator. The commissionaire spoke Adam's name, seemed to listen a few seconds, and told him to get off on the fourth floor.

The elevator opened onto a room filled with wooden desks, steel filing cabinets piled with bulging manila folders, wooden swivel chairs with armrests, and three sturdy coat stands. A woman who looked not much older than those she was addressing stepped forward to welcome him. The meeting had just begun. She wheeled a desk chair over for him to sit on. He nodded to those who met his eye, and listened as Ms. Castelli introduced him.

"Adam comes to us with a background in journalism." He had in fact a second-class-honours degree in English and geology and had published one article, about the men's varsity lacrosse team, in the university newspaper. "He's going to be our expert on water." The congregation made appreciative noises that were echoed when she repeated the statement in French.

When the meeting ended she led him to the desk he would be using, one of two in a small office with windows overlooking the Sparks Street pedestrian mall. He shook hands with his office-mate, Eugène Racicot, who sported an air and a mode of dress decades older than his age. A fan of Frank Sinatra, he told Adam that his favourite song was "New York, New York," adding an extra syllable to "York" and making it seem as if he were evoking a replacement for Hamlet's poor, dead, ultra-spare jester.

"I am working since three summers for Robert Lavallée in his office while I am the student. Do you know about Monsieur Lavallée?"

Adam knew that the man was a Party warhorse, first elected twenty years earlier, and that he was a cabinet minister in the present administration, but could not say which portfolio Lavallée carried.

Eugène made it clear that Adam should bother him as little as possible, that he was in the capital of English Canada to learn as much as he could about the way the Anglo mind worked, so that he might return, after graduating with a degree in politics from *l'Université de Montréal* to work full-time on the Hill and bring a new ethic of Quebecois verve and savvy bilingualism to the moribund federal government. Robert Lavallée was one day going to be PM. Did Adam not realize that?

"Better you arrange your canards in a row according to the Ps and the Qs," he said, index finger extended and pointing skyward for emphasis, "if you wish to stay yourself dry, that is. *Comprenez, monsieur?*"

Adam did not, but nodded his head all the same. After all, he thought, it was his first day on the job. For all he knew, this was a highly specialized from of political jargon. He made a note to learn more about Robert Lavallée.

His first project was to gather information about water in and around the town of Feeney, Manitoba. Monica gave him a list of names and phone numbers to call. She warned him not to discuss his work with anyone outside the office and to keep his files locked in his desk. She did not tell him the reason why he was compiling an encyclopaedic array of facts about water, its sources, uses, purity, erosion caused by, rainfall amounts, groundwater flow, sewage, drainage and flooding. The scientists he talked to were usually happy to share what they knew about their subject. Sometimes they answered his questions with a tone of caution. What did the PM want with their obscure studies of wetland depletion in the Red River watershed? Did this have anything to do with the time they had worked as a guide for that group of California businessmen who said they were up north on a fishing expedition, chartered plane and all, but who never changed out of their suits and ties? No, said Adam, it didn't.

He took the job seriously. Once he had mastered the art of sounding at once official, non-threatening and interested, he began to relax. Every day or so a package came by courier and he added its contents—reports, maps, charts, schemata—to his files.

And every day he walked to and from work along the same route, quietly exulting in his newfound sense of importance. At university he had bought a green blazer to wear on special occasions, and, with a white shirt, pale yellow tie and grey flannel trousers, it became his uniform while he worked at the PMO. The sleeves were a little short and it pooched across the shoulder blades, making it look as if he had won the Masters golf championship some years before and was loath to doff the symbolic jacket. It being the height of the tourist season in the capital, people took him to be a guide and began stopping him on the street to ask directions to the Library of Parliament and the Supreme Court and the spot where you caught the double-decker sightseeing bus.

One day, after Adam had returned from the Langevin Building, a young woman came in and sat on the edge of his desk. She kept one foot on the floor and darted her eyes between him and the pen she rolled back and forth across his blotter. She looked as if she could laugh at any minute. Her dark curly hair was a snaky halo. When she smiled, her eyes almost disappeared. He decided that it was the smile of someone just this side of mad. She was dressed in whimsical layers: a long full peasant skirt, sandals, a man's loose white dress shirt unbuttoned over a tight black T, an oatmeal-coloured granny shawl draped at an angle off one shoulder, and a fine blue floral scarf tied loosely at the neck like a western bandit's ready disguise. When she smiled her lips spread, melting into her face, and he wanted either to run his tongue lightly around their periphery or look away.

"I'm Pookie."

"Sorry to hear that." He wished Eugène, who was talking loudly on the phone, would leave. Still seated, Adam leaned across to shake her hand.

"Penelope, but don't you dare. Not if you ever want to speak to me again."

Was she this happy all the time? Perhaps her outward hilarity hid deeper sadness. He decided on the spot that it would be difficult to love someone like Pookie, for the very reason that she was distracting and probably disturbed. He came to this conclusion about her mental state quickly and intuitively, as he did about most things. Life with someone like Pookie Pereau would be unpredictable and spent too much in large groups. Even as he was imposing this personal ban, he craved the spontaneity she promised, the way the body craves a missing nutrient.

None of this precluded their having the occasional lunch together. Daily and with heartening regularity does the stomach supersede the heart. She led him down Sparks to a sandwich shop she had found in the bottom of a green-tinted tower inside which glass-bubble elevators rode the airy verdant space. The sandwiches, made with whole-grain bread, overflowed with bean sprouts, thickly cut vegetables (cucumbers with the rind still attached, zucchini, sun-dried tomato) and pungent spreads of chickpea-and-tahini hummus.

While they ate she told him about the survey she was conducting. She asked her respondents, residents of a riding in Halifax, about their ethnic background, household income, number of children, extended family, spending habits, religious affiliation, moral beliefs, what they thought about various social issues, and how they felt about authority. Her goal was to get five hundred replies. She assured those who answered that their names would not be recorded, that she was compiling aggregate data only, and that it was for use in a wider study of the impact of federal policies on their community.

"Do you tell them where you're calling from?"

"I say I'm doing an independent survey for the Kent Hulse Tackeberry Institute for Policy Studies."

"What if someone calls your bluff or traces the call?"

"One, I hang up. Two, the lines we use can't be traced. Do you want to know where the name comes from?"

"A law firm."

"No, my first boyfriend was Kent Bradley. Hulse was my dog when I was but a wee thing. He got smushed by a bus. And when I was learning to skate I wanted boys' hockey skates, so my mother bought me a second-hand pair of Tacks. Top drawer!"

"You should tell people the truth."

"Lorne and Monica want their answers to be as free of authority-taint as possible. The minute you tell them you're PMO you've lost the unguarded response. We don't want them second-guessing themselves. 'What does she want me to say? Why is the PMO interested in this?' And so on."

She told him that she had been the new PS, Lorne Childs's star pupil at Brown while he was the Stanley Knowles Distinguished Visitor lecturing on parliamentary procedure. Born in Canada and raised in the States—her parents still lived near Duluth—she had dual citizenship. She was living with an aunt and uncle in Sandy Hill for the summer. Lorne knew bright, talented, delightful and easy-on-the-eyes when he had it beaming at him from the front row of the lecture hall, thought Adam.

When he returned from lunch he had a note from Monica asking him to see her in her office. Monica Castelli looked like a ballerina, a principal dancer who, at the age of 30 and because of injury or stiffening joints, was moving into the next stage of her life, a new career built upon the foundation of her beauty and poise. The way she carried herself and the way she spoke came from what he thought of as a refinement now rare even among those who purported to be the ambassadors and purveyors of culture. Her style and sense of self were Old World. That she presented herself with such quiet grace was all the more remarkable given the world she worked in, the single-malt, leather-upholstered, Cuban-cigar club in which power was bought, or snatched, then wielded, subtly, in the pursuit of more, or crudely like a bludgeon in Question Period and the committee rooms. Monica Castelli was either shrewder than she let on or, as Pookie believed, she had caught the eye of an old Party rainmaker.

Monica asked him how the work was progressing. Was there anything he needed or needed to know, anything that had come up in his research? No, he said, he couldn't think of anything just then, but would be sure to ask.

"You're doing a great job on Water, by the way."

"I am? I mean, thanks. There's so much more I—"

"In fact, you're doing so well that we want you to take on something new. Switch over, actually, to work on exclusively. Do you think you can handle it?"

I don't even know what it is. How can I say? "Sure thing."

"Good. We want you to do a study of the federal presence in the riding of Halifax Citadel. What government programs are in place there, how effective they are, how long they've been going, that sort of thing."

"What about Water?"

"Move it to the back burner for now. We need this information very soon. Day after tomorrow. Are you up to it?"

He told her that he was, but left without asking why she needed the study and without making the link between what he would be doing and the survey Pookie was working on. Halifax. It might as well have been one of Jupiter's moons.

He returned to his desk and tried to see himself as others in the office did, but nothing gelled. Even Beverley from Lethbridge, who had quit after the first week to work for Greenpeace, seemed to belong there more than Adam did. Everything Beverley said had a political component. She had seen what sour-gas well contamination was doing to ranchers like her father and uncles.

He wasn't like Alberta Bev and he wasn't like the Quebec contingent, either, who approached their internship at the PMO the way a member of Hamas approaches training with Mossad. They huddled in each other's offices, intently debating the question of their province's sovereignty. He wished there was something he could love as much as Eugène loved the crooning songs of Old Blue Eyes or his compatriots loved their province-nation or Beverley loved the West and the natural world. Everyone seemed committed to something: Pookie to the pursuit of pleasurable social intercourse; Emma Henry, a politics major, to making as many career contacts as possible before the summer was over; and Isaac Koehler, the son of a deputy premier, to making as few mistakes as possible. Isaac was sure that his father was aware of everything Isaac did.

"He's got my phone bugged, I just know it."

"It's not your dad who's listening," said Emma. "Trust me."

Emma had nothing in excess. It wasn't that her face was tired looking or drawn. She had no dark circles under her eyes or crow's feet at the corners. The skin of her face looked as if someone had stretched a fine thin parchment over a delicate frame. She made Adam think of bone china, ivory in colour with gold edges in a precisely scalloped line.

He was sitting by himself on a bench, eating a sandwich and reading John Fowles' *The Magus*, when Emma sat beside him. She lit a cigarette. Her teeth and the fingers of her right hand were discoloured but in a gilt-edged sort of way. She inhaled furtively, blowing the smoke upward and away from him. He had yet to see her eat anything. A protective urge overcame him, a strange feeling because he knew almost nothing about her.

"I'm keeping an eye on you," she said. "We don't quite have a bead on you yet."

"A bead?"

"They're not sure who you are and what you're doing here. Can't be too careful, you know: spies, infiltration from the other side." He pondered her shift from "we" to "they." "I'm almost a hundred percent sure you're harmless."

"Oh? I'm kind of disappointed. And how do you know I'm harmless?"

"Well, for one thing, you haven't gone to see Lorne yet."

"Are we supposed to?"

"No, not officially, but everyone else has. Lorne paves the way. He writes the exit letters."

He hadn't thought of this. He remembered his father mentioning something to this effect, but had assumed that, like a teacher putting end-of-year comments on a report card, Lorne

Childs would automatically write recommendations for everybody in the "class" and that there would be an egalitarian flavour to the process.

"This is what I was saying earlier. You all have a sense for this kind of thing. I don't. It's like I'm missing a piece of clockwork in my head. Every day I come to work, make my calls, write my reports, but I can't wait for lunchtime so that I can read some more of this book."

He thought about Fowles' main character, Nicholas Urfe, the young Englishman caught up in the mysterious world controlled by Conchis, the Magus, and about the women in the story, the way they were unpredictable pawns, erotic functionaries in the puppet master's elaborate psychological game. In a way, he imagined, Pookie and Emma were like these Gemini, except that there was nothing similar about them. They were like two opposite halves completing a whole: Emma, watchful, calculating, efficient, bold: rumour had it that she had slipped into an elevator with the PM before the doors could close, and in the brief course of ascending three floors had told him her name, background and present duties; and Pookie, sensual, overflowing, radiant, magnetic: her interest in people seemed wholly genuine and selfless. He was beginning to think that he wanted them both, at the same time, and somewhere as hot and shimmering white against royal blue as the island of Phraxos. All that water. There was a reason why he was spending so much time reading and writing about water. Water is sustaining. It can kill. It makes a barrier daring us to cross. Warm enough, salty enough, it becomes a womb in which one can float, thoughtless, like a foetus.

Emma handed the book back. "I read this doorstop. Sexist male fantasy bullshit. Trust me. This guy wouldn't know a real woman if she fell on him."

On a sunny Saturday after a week of drizzle, they all went to the house that one of the interns, Gilles, was renting for the summer. It was a small cottage on the Quebec side of the river and it had once been owned by Jack Pickersgill. Adam borrowed the family car, drove across the Macdonald-Cartier Bridge, got lost, asked three people for directions, got three different answers, and arrived forty-five minutes late.

A charcoal barbeque smouldered at the side of the house, and nearby a picnic table was set for lunch. Everyone was crammed into two rooms, a tiny kitchen and a front parlour taken up by Gilles' ten-speed, a large armoire that partially blocked the view of the river, an antique sofa upholstered in red velvet, and teetering buttes of books piled on the floor.

They were all talking at once, gesturing with beer bottles and free hands. Not wishing to appear clannish by moving immediately through to the other room, where the English-speakers had gathered, Adam stayed near the kitchen door and listened. He understood more than he expected he would. The gist was that Don Feeney, the PM's former Principal Secretary, was running for Parliament in a by-election in the riding of Halifax Citadel, and the intern office was now a *de facto* campaign force.

Pookie came in from the other room, slipped her arm under Gilles' and gave him a nuzzling kiss under one ear. Smug bastard, thought Adam, you hardly acknowledge her presence. She was clearly gone on the boy, who didn't deserve her despite the evidence of breeding in his strong nose, sharp cheekbones and expensive clothes: pressed tan slacks, sky-blue shirt of Oxford broadcloth with a button-down collar open at the neck, and brown leather deck shoes. He had one hand thrust into a roomy pocket. He said something that sounded, after translation, like, "Pigs don't swim unless called upon to do so."

Pookie came over to say hello to Adam. "You've heard?"

"It explains Feeney, Manitoba. What's he going to do, give a speech there?"

"He's launching the campaign there, actually. As far as anyone knows, he has no connection to the town, wasn't born there, hasn't any family there. Not an impediment to the plan, apparently."

"So he'll get up on his hind legs in the Feeney Legion Hall and tell them all just how impoverished their lives would be without federal government programs."

"*Quelque-chose comme ça, oui.*"

"Are we all supposed to go?" He pictured the two of them canvassing together, stopping for a beer and a bowl of clam chowder on the waterfront, telling each other things they had never told anyone else.

"I'm not sure. Nobody's heard anything official yet. Just what Ben knows." Ben, still in high school, worked in the Labour Minister's office and had heard about Feeney's imminent announcement from one of the secretaries there.

"Don't you feel—I don't know—used? All that work you put into that survey. It seems sneaky."

"Duplicitous."

"Manipulative."

"Underhanded."

"*Heavy*-handed!"

"You really are naïve, aren't you, Adam. I knew I wasn't conducting a census."

"You didn't tell them who you really were."

"This is politics. What did you think we were doing here, candy-striping?"

"No, I didn't think that. It's just...I thought the PMO would be involved in..."

"Matters of state, diplomacy, drafting high-minded legislation."

"Yes."

"My dear green-gilled boy. You can't do any of that if you're not in power, and you stay in power by holding onto more seats than your opponents."

Why Halifax? It was timely, she said. The incumbent was retiring for health reasons and the by-election would be held in time for the winner to be inducted at the beginning of the fall session of the House. And it was a safe seat.

"A shoo-in," she said. "A lot of new immigrants have moved into that riding recently. They see the Party name and they think "freedom." Right away they're embracing us. Think about it. For most of them, anything is better than what they left back home. They come here, they think, "I will become a new Canadian, I will exercise my franchise, I may even join this here political club, although, remembering who tends to get rounded up in the middle of the night, most of them forgo membership. They wave a flag on July 1st, pay their taxes on time, send as much of what's left as they can afford to their loved ones, and try their darnedest to get them over here to live. We've never known that desperation. We'll probably never know their urgency. We grew up stupid, Adam, stupid and complacent and happy."

He studied her face for a moment. Clearly he had misjudged her. She was more complicated and worldly than he had first thought.

Monday after work they attended a reception for the incoming Principal Secretary in a room off Confederation Hall in the Centre Block. It was a chance for everyone to meet Lorne and for the summer students to have a taste of the grander side of Wellington Street. Adam stood talking to Pookie, Eugène and Isaac, who wiped his brow with the cuff of his shirt every few minutes and repeated that the PM himself was supposed to make an appearance. "What do I say if he asks me a question?"

"Try your best, Isaac," said Pookie.

"But I don't know anything."

"It doesn't stop most MPs," she said.

Lorne spotted Pookie from across the room, came over and draped an arm around her shoulders, giving the far one a fatherly squeeze. She leaned into it, resting her head briefly against his chest. She was smiling in that hilarious way of hers, which to the uninitiated made her look as if she were on the verge of tears.

Lorne was in a dark, pinstriped three-piece suit. He had a natty sense of style, a step up the fashion ladder from academic tweed and intellectual distraction, but not quite displaying the PM's flair. Lorne Childs looked as if he would be as comfortable in a Bay Street boardroom as on the dais of an Ivy League lecture theatre.

He said hello and asked after Adam's father. "How do you like the work so far?"

"I'm enjoying it. I'm not sure about what we're doing, though."

"What we're doing."

"The PMO using its resources to put the person it wants into Parliament."

"This is a partisan office, Adam. We're not Canada Revenue."

"I know. It still doesn't seem right to me. I think Don Feeney should have to go the route every other candidate does."

"The PMO helps in the campaigns of many candidates in the party. I assumed you knew that." He looked as if Adam had suggested that the entire democratic system had collapsed. He began panning the room, looking for someone else to talk to.

Adam looked at the empty Champagne flute in his hand and couldn't remember draining it.

The PM, taller than Adam expected he would be, was making his way closer. Adam felt Lorne beside him stretching in anticipation. He thought about sweaty Isaac and his anxiety over not knowing what to say to the leader. Adam had already said something and it had been more than enough. Lorne probably had him pegged for an imbecile. His future on the Hill was now officially null. He imagined that Lorne had communicated Adam's pronouncement, either telepathically or via a sophisticated electronic device, to the PM. He was convinced that the PM was going to ask him the same question. "So, Adam Lerner, you don't think it's a good idea for the PMO to be a politically partisan body. You would prefer something like the Governor General's retinue, I take it, a household of servants in powdered wigs and velvet breeches, people whose ancestors stretching back many generations did precisely what their descendants are doing today. You would replace a cornerstone of our parliamentary system with something static and elitist. Am I reading you correctly on this? Can we even assume that you would allow the Prime Minister to remain a member of a political party or would you abolish that privilege as well?"

The great man was getting closer. To leave the reception now, before the leader did, would be the worst kind of insult, and yet that was exactly what Adam felt he had to do before he expired on the spot. The room felt airless, Death Valley hot. Pookie was whispering something in Lorne's bent ear. Isaac was talking to Emma. They seemed relaxed, even Isaac, who appeared resigned to his fate. The PM was talking in French to Eugène, Gilles and Jean-Marc, who had Che Guevara's dark looks and radical opinions. They laughed at something the PM had said. Adam looked at the exit. A large plainclothes RCMP officer in a dark blue suit was standing there, an earplug leading to a wire running under the collar of his jacket. Dark sunglasses in the chandelier-bright room. Deadly force. Would he even let him leave?

He caught Pookie's eye and gave her a brief finger-riffling wave so as not to draw the attention of the others. She smiled and returned the wave. He took a breath, held it, released it and walked out. The man at the door made no movement. Adam did not look back to see if the policeman was following him or whispering something urgent into his wrist.

Adam looked past Emma and saw metal wing and a section of sky. Cloud cover hid the ground.

She ordered a beer and after downing it in a few quick swallows wiped her mouth with the back of her hand. He was fascinated that she could still speak clearly after consuming the drink as if it had been a glass of water.

She was wearing the charcoal-coloured skirt and jacket she often wore to work. He glanced down. Her nipples were puckering the fabric of her top, an armless chemise he had noticed before. He didn't know silk from satin. He wanted it to be silk because he thought the sound of the word suited her, wanted her to remove the jacket so that he might see her bare arms again against the mauve singlet, her pale freckled shoulders and neck, the shape of her small breasts.

She returned her tray to its upright position and locked it into place against the back of the seat in front of her, tucked her plastic beer cup into the webbing that held the airline's in-flight magazine, a brochure for Oak Island and the emergency procedures pamphlet, and moved the armrest so that it was hidden flush between the backs of their two seats. Unbuckling her seatbelt she skooched closer. She slipped her arm under his the way Pookie had done with Gilles that day in Jack Pickersgill's cottage, and rested her head on Adam's shoulder. At first he thought that she had fallen asleep, but then she slipped her left hand across and undid the middle button of his shirt. Her hand slid in. They sat like that until the attendant leaned in to check to see that their belts were fastened. They were going to feel some turbulence on their descent into Halifax, said the captain.

Adam opened his mouth to say something. She put her fingers to his lips. She shook her head slightly and smiled as if to say, 'You didn't think you were going to be in control, did you?'

The approach was bumpy, the landing hard but steady. She dug her nails into the back of his hand. When he looked over she was gazing placidly out at the tarmac. The sky was low and dark. Fine droplets of rain played across the window. They put their watches ahead an hour. The time was now, the temperature five degrees cooler than it had been in Ottawa. Anything was possible here. Despite his *faux pas* in the Confederation Room, they had still asked him to work on the campaign.

They waited for the covered walkway to swing into place and the door of the plane to open. After he said that it was his first time in Nova Scotia, she told him that she had lived in Mahone Bay for two years when she was a little girl. Her parents ran a restaurant that didn't do well enough to sustain them, and they moved back to Guelph, Ontario. Those years were still vivid for her, the white churches with their high steeples, the brightly coloured monochromatic houses, the brackish scent of the tide.

She said that she wanted to be a little girl again. She was afraid of dying, convinced she was going to kick off at an early age.

"Look at this life line," she said, showing him her palm. "Look how it's all broken up."

"Yes, but it continues, don't you see? It picks up good and strong farther on. All it means is that you're going to change direction a couple of times."

She looked relieved but also flustered, even annoyed, as if he had stolen something from her moment of drama.

The last two off the plane, they caught up with the rest of the group around the baggage conveyance. He could still feel her hand against the skin of his chest. It had been light and heavy at the same time, dry and still but seeming in motion, heavy because he had been so intent on it. He wished he was more muscular and had more hair there. He thought he might be in love with her. What else could it be? She had staked a claim. All questions of who they were, what they were doing, how legitimate their cause, fell away. He looked around at their colleagues intent on the stream of luggage. None of them could claim independence from the office, the Party machinery, now, could they, so what did it matter?

It was like that mysterious car in the BSC parking lot. Something had happened there, something out of his control. He had taken a few steps toward it, instinctive steps, thinking that this was what one did, one made a show if not an actual effort to help. He had told someone about it, someone in a position of authority. That was the right thing, wasn't it? When he had returned, the car was no longer there. It no longer touched him. He no longer had to think about it.

The airport shuttle was a small rattling old bus with seats enough for about twenty-five people. They handed their luggage to the driver, who loaded it into a compartment at the rear. It cost twelve dollars a person one-way, twenty to return. Gilles complained that the PMO was becoming cheap. He thought they should be riding in a fleet of airport limousines or in taxis at the very least. Jean-Marc and Eugène said some things in French that sounded as if they were mocking him. Despite the appearance of insufferable arrogance, the boy seemed to be the genuine article. His rich tastes were not, as far as Adam could tell, evidence of affectation covering deeper insecurity. Adam appreciated the boy's unapologetic expressions of *noblesse oblige*. He still didn't like him being with Pookie, but in his mind that was a separate thing.

The highway took them past dismal terrain covered by exposed rock and stunted fir. Someone had propped an inflatable sea monster on a pole in a lake near the road. They came into Dartmouth, wended through streets of low-rent apartment buildings and crossed over a bridge spanning the harbour, a brawny, bustling, breathtaking expanse rimmed by glass towers, tall smokestacks, naval dry docks, with a second bridge off to their right. Adam tried to take it all in at once and felt the weird desire to get off the bus, climb onto the long arching support cable and jump.

Emma and Pookie were sitting together two seats ahead of him and across the aisle. He couldn't hear what they were saying. He didn't care. Yes, he knew he did. He wanted to know what they were saying and whether or not it was about him. Worse would be to know that they weren't talking about him. He wanted them both, neither more than the other but not at the same time. He was bedevilled by the thought of being with one and thinking about the other. How can one both have a desire and dread it? He wondered what he was doing there, so far from the familiar, in a pursuit he cared so little about. He had an open plane ticket home, courtesy of the PMO. At the first sign of trouble—but what was trouble, anyway, in this regard? The candidate floundering didn't qualify as trouble, since Adam held no emotional stake in the success or failure of Don Feeney's bid. Adam did what was expected and took direction well. What, then, might this nebulous Trouble be, what form would it take?

The bus pulled up on the street in front of the Lord Nelson Hotel, a handsome red brick building newly renovated with an inviting entrance and lobby. Isaac and Adam were given a room together, as were Pookie and Emma, Eugène and Jean-Marc, and Gilles and a newcomer named Oliver Schwartz, who came from Winnipeg. The front desk treated them with a reserved deference, leading Adam to wonder whether every guest was welcomed so, and whether they were perceived, given their affiliation and purpose, as invaders or liberators.

The next day, a Monday morning, Adam and Eugène were assigned to stay at campaign headquarters, which was also

Don's room, a large two-room suite in the hotel, to make cold calls introducing the candidate to those who did not know who he was or, if they did, trying to persuade them of his suitability for office. Every third or fourth person who answered hung up immediately. Some cursed before doing so.

Monica handed him a note on PMO memo paper. It said, "Mrs. E.M. Fallingbrooke. Important contact. Waiting for your call."

The woman who answered waited for Adam to complete his introduction before saying that she needed someone to take her to the shopping centre. Her grandson usually drove her there on Mondays so that she could have her hair done, but the man was away on a camping vacation with his second wife and her children by a previous marriage. Difficult teenagers; surely Adam knew just what she meant by that. She and her husband used to camp in a tent at Kejimkujik Park, but those days were long past. The closest thing to wilderness camping she did now was the occasional weekend retreat down to White Point Beach when the heat became unbearable, which hadn't been all that often in the past few years, despite what those Cassandra meteorologists said. She was a widow. How soon could he get there?

He asked her where she lived and she said, indignantly, "South on the peninsula," as if to live anywhere else in the city were inconceivable. He located the area on his map. It was not far away. He had to plug his other ear to block the sound of Eugène speaking loudly in English in the adjoining room in a voice so insistent and grammatically creative that Adam felt he could dissolve into giggles at any moment. The old dear on the phone was describing the horde of outrageously rude people she had seen on television eating grubs and throwing metal folding chairs at each other.

The room felt stale and muggy-hot despite the noisy air conditioner chugging under the window. He was supposed to stay and work the phone, but he had to take a break sometime, didn't he? Monica had left to supervise the canvassers. She would not have directed him to call Mrs. Fallingbrooke had she not thought it important. Perhaps the old kook was a big Party supporter. The sun was shining. An inviting expanse of green enclosed by a black-metal, spike-topped fence, a city-block's worth of lush Victorian garden, beckoned from across the road.

She was still talking. She had been a diplomat's wife. Once, aboard a vessel cruising the Black Sea, she seduced a Soviet spy and convinced him to divulge state secrets while her husband slept three cabins away. Adam was sure that if this conversation were being monitored, he would have been cut off by now and urged to move on to more profitable game. If she really were a staunch Party booster, her vote would be assured, wouldn't it?

Her house was an all-consuming project now, with eaves troughs to be cleaned, roof tiles to be replaced, shake siding to be scraped and painted. Her son wanted her to sell the house and move into the condominium across the street from her. Her house was leaning to the north quite noticeably. He would see that when he came, she said. None of the three floors was level. Her great-grandchildren had tried lining up an intricate domino pattern in her kitchen, to their lamentable frustration. If she moved she would lose her lovely little garden. She supposed she could grow plants in containers on a balcony, but it wouldn't be the same. Perhaps she could have a southern exposure instead of a western one as she had now. The condo tower was round, like a fairy-tale turret. Had Adam ever heard of such a thing?

He waited for her to take a breath and asked if she would consider taking a sign.

"Pardon?"

"A sign. To put on your lawn."

"You're not going to put pesticides down."

"No, of course not."

"But what would it say?"

"It would say, "Don Feeney Gets It Done.""

"Gets what done?"

"Well, any job he's given."

"I should hope so. That's the least he should do, wouldn't you think, young man?"

"He wants to be your representative in Ottawa."

"Does he now? Isn't that considerate of him. Tell him I know all about Ottawa. Tell him I don't trust the lot of them. I could tell you some things about Ottawa that would make your hair fall out."

She told him her address, which he wrote on the same piece of paper Monica had handed him. He ran his finger over the embossed red letterhead.

"Should I bring a sign?"

"The street is quite well marked. You're not coming from Clayton Park, are you? I tried to give directions to LB once and he became terribly lost." Adam gave the name of the hotel. "Oh dear. I suppose proximity counts for something. Quite direct, then: South Park to South, South to Wellington. If you miss it you can circle round and pick it up again off Inglis. I prefer to approach from the east off Inglis so that I'm making a right-hand turn. Cecil used to make endless fun of me for driving so far out of my way. That's the route I like and I'm too old to change now. I myself do not drive anymore, you understand."

He didn't tell her that he would be walking. He decided to bring a window sign and another for the lawn. On each, against the Party colours and above the slogan, was Don's smiling, handsome, craggy face, his full head of silver-grey hair cropped just this side of military severe. The visit would be a welcome diversion. He crept out without Eugène noticing.

Just as she had described it, the house faced west but leaned north. Across the street was the round apartment tower and beside it a white building that was as tall as the condominium but without balconies. A sign beside the door identified it as a student-family housing cooperative. A play structure stood empty beside it. On the other side, between it and the round condo, was a parking lot, and beyond that a grassy berm and what looked to be an elementary school in the distance.

"Please," a man's voice. Adam could not tell where it was coming from. "Please. If you please. Up here. I find myself to be in a bind."

He scanned the front of the white building floor by floor until he was looking up at a small brown face peering over the edge of the roof a dozen stories up.

"I seem to be locked out. Can you make your way up here, please, and let me back in?" It was the voice of someone educated in England or in an English colonial school. "Simply go inside the front door and buzz the office. I would be most grateful to you should you make the manager aware of my predicament."

Adam passed through the outer door and found the button for the office.

"Yes?" an impatient, adult-female voice.

"I don't live here, but there's a man on the roof and he can't get down."

"Who is it?"

"I don't know his name. I was walking by. He called out to me."

"I meant who are you."

"My name is Adam Lerner."

"What apartment number?"

"I said I don't live here."

"There's no soliciting."

"I'm not selling anything. I'm just letting you know about the guy on the roof. I think he's from Africa."

"We are all from Africa originally."

"Can you let me in or go up and check on him yourself? I think he's in trouble."

"Just a minute."

She appeared on the other side of the glass door.

"Let's see some ID."

Adam took out his PMO card and held it up so that she could read it through the glass of the inner door. The card had his photo and the words, "Temporary Permit" printed diagonally across it in green ink.

"Holy shit. I mean, come in." She unlocked the door and held it open.

"Thanks." He went to the elevator and pushed the "Up" button.

"Really sorry, eh. If I'd known—I mean, I'm sorry if I— have you, like, seen him or anything?"

"As I said, he called down to me." Was it her purpose in life not to listen to what anyone told her?

"No, I mean, you know. God, he's so..."

"Oh. Right." *He's taller than you think. I was at an event with him not long ago. Couldn't be bothered talking to the man. Another engagement I had to get to, don't you know.*

"You have? What's he like? Do you think you could get me his autograph if I gave you the address?" Without waiting for his answer she dashed into the office, which was nearby, and came out with two identical business cards that gave her name and position under the co-op's letterhead. "Gail Sykes, Office Coordinator." Adam signed the back of one, returned it to her, and pocketed the other.

"What's this?" she said with a sniff, squinting at his scrawl.

"Didn't you...?

"One for him, one for her."

He patted his pocket. "As soon as I get back to Ottawa, I promise."

"God, I can't hardly believe it." The elevator, which had come and gone once already, opened. "Take it all the way to the top. That'll bring you to the roof."

"Thanks so much, uh," fishing again for her card.

"Gail."

"Gail."

"There are stairs, too, once you're there."

"I'll look for them."

"Are you like a spy or something?"

"Sort of."

"What does he do with his—?" The door closed and the elevator began to climb.

On the roof a wooden picnic table sat beside a large metal shed that he figured housed the elevator's drive mechanism.

He was alone. Remembering that he had not tested the door before letting it close behind him, he tried the handle. The door opened easily.

Adam walked over to the eastern edge of the roof and put his fingers through the links of the steel fence. The harbour spread out before him in the middle distance: George's Island, a tall, obstructive building with the green letters, "ALIANT" near the top, the container terminal near the tip of the peninsula, an oil refinery on the Dartmouth side. How odd to be up here, he thought. How right it felt. He was beginning to forget why he had come to this city, when he heard a deep reverberant laugh coming up from street level. Looking down he saw the same man who had tricked him onto the roof.

"Enjoying the panorama, my man?"

"As a matter of fact, I am."

"Don Feeney Gets It Done. Do he indeed!"

Adam was puzzled until he saw that the man was holding a lawn sign by its wooden shaft, and he remembered that he had left both it and the window sign meant for Mrs. Fallingbrooke in the entrance to the co-op.

"What do he get done, mon? He hairdo?" Another rumbling James Earl Jones laugh, one so strong it could have moved boulders.

"Do you mind leaving that there, please?"

Riding the elevator down, Adam scolded himself for his anxiety. The election signs were inconsequential and had probably cost the Party a pittance. "You don't care, remember?" But saying this he saw that he did care.

When he got outside, the man and Adam's signs had vanished, and where he had been standing was now a sign proclaiming the virtue of voting for the local socialist candidate,

Lexington Bramwell Bliss, the kind of name you gave a lap dog or a treasured teddy bear. Aside from the silly pretensions suggested by the name, the situation had now deteriorated into theft, and regardless of his waning emotional commitment to the Party and the PMO, Adam felt duty-bound to retrieve their property.

Looking across at the leaning house, his destination, he saw a figure briefly part the curtains drawn across the large front window on the ground floor. An elderly woman, he could make out, before the drapes closed again. He wondered if she could tell who he was. Calling on her now, without an election sign to leave, might well be futile. She didn't seem the sort who changed her mind, and she had certainly expressed no love for Don Feeney, the Party and politicians in general.

The curtain parted again and this time a dark-skinned face peered out: his rooftop joker.

The front door opened and out came the man, holding a clipboard and a lawn sign, a duplicate of the one that had sprouted in front of the co-op residence. Everything was suddenly clear. Adam crossed the street.

"Mr. Bliss, I presume?"

"I'll be with you shortly, young sir," he said, driving the sharp end of the stake forcefully into the beating heart of Mrs. Fallingbrooke's crabgrass. He adjusted the tilt of the sign to match that of the house.

"Nice touch."

"It be the touches that nudge we starward."

"What were you doing up there, if you don't mind me asking?"

"'My' asking. Where you acquire you mother tongue, fool?" said Lexington Bramwell Bliss, now more Mr. T than Oxonian.

"You saw me coming with my signs."

"Sign, sign, everywhere a sign!"

"You can't just—"

"What you say? Can't just? Can't what? Yes I surely just can. And did. Ha!"

Adam looked past the man, whose tight-fitting white suit and red silk tie made him look theatrical and not at all like the typical candidate from his leftist party. Left-leaning party, left-leaning house. Bliss himself stood canted parallel to the angle of the newly planted sign.

The homeowner came out to stand, humpbacked, on her top step. She wore a simple black dress and a string of pearls with matching earrings. She looked to be ninety-nine and three quarter years old.

"As soon as I rang off from talking to you, I called LB, thinking, 'Oh, let's make this interesting, shall we?' Well?"

"Pardon?"

"You're coming in. It's your turn to persuade me."

"I thought all you wanted was someone to drive you to the grocery store."

"LB is coming back to do just that after he has completed his work on this street. Aren't you, LB?"

"That I am, my empress, that I most surely am!"

"I'm sorry, thank you for the invitation, but really. You got your laugh at my expense. What's the use?"

"Usefulness is a highly overrated quality. We quickly outlive our usefulness. Style trumps substance in all but the rarest case worth mentioning these days, and certainly always in the political arena. Isn't that right, LB?"

Bliss laughed heartily in agreement as he rang the next doorbell.

"I have to get back to the phones."

"Phones, drones. Waste of time, your intrusive cold call. Or are you targeting the potentially vulnerable, lonely widows like me with too much money and not enough sense? What they can do these days with a SIN, a postal code and GIS software. Don't look so surprised; I keep abreast. As for electioneering, now your push call, that's a tool of a different temper. The self-proclaimed independent survey. The subtly skewed question set. 'Given that the incumbent has been generally incompetent, how would you rate his chances in this election? Given Party X's colossal botch of the offshore oil and gas deal—oh, I forget, that was your party, wasn't it? Silly me."

She looked and sounded so delighted that Adam would not have been surprised if she and not Bliss were the candidate. It struck him then just how ill prepared he had been in joining the team, making calls, telling people about Feeney without knowing anything about his opponents.

All right, he thought, everything seems to be pointing inside this Leaning House of Pisa. Let's see what we have.

What he found was a room with walls painted a lemony wash and hung with paintings all of the same style, white on white, textured, arrogantly colourless. Thick dabs of oil paint applied with a trowel, it seemed, gave each work of art turbulence and depth. Looking closer he saw that the surfaces were particleboard, their angled wood chips adding to the appearance of frozen movement, to the patchy skin, the surface of a frothy sea caught and held. He noticed little else, not the texture of the chair she bade him sit upon, not the colour or pattern of the drapes, not the flooring, which he knew was more or less level but which could have been sponge toffee or slate, so intent was he on these slabs of ice and snow that seemed to pulsate and throw inexplicable dancing shadows.

"I'm sorry, but I cannot allow this to continue. You are simply too young."

Was she was referring protectively to something subliminal in the artwork, an image of Eros or terror or hard cynical adult reality that he had not lived long enough to see? He stopped staring and turned to her.

"I won't ask how you became enmeshed with that mob. Suffice it to say that you are here now, that it is never too late, and that LB certainly could use the help."

Still thinking that she was referring to the paintings, Adam shook his head. He wondered if this LB she referred to was the artist, having forgotten momentarily about the trickster candidate.

"I don't..."

"That's right. That's why you're here! My stars, think about it. What would the world be like if we all sleepwalked through our vigorous years?"

Not following, Adam reverted to received wisdom. "Don Feeney..."

"You can't work for them, you never did. Believe me. You think you do. You think that because they let you pick up the telephone and say the name of the office, it makes you important and what you're doing legitimate. I don't care how handsome that man is, how many times he jumps out of an airplane, how many movies he has acted in. He could be Mahatma Gandhi and I would say the same thing: he's the government and the government has no right co-opting the young. Don't you think it's time you made up your own mind?"

He didn't know what to say. He felt a rogue smile invade each side of his face.

"Don't just sit there like a naughty monkey. Tell me I'm wrong."

"You're wrong."

"No I'm not and you know it. When my husband and I were your age we were card-carrying members of the Communist Party. You couldn't be a freethinking, conscientious, sentient being and not be. Why? Because the young know. They know intuitively that greed ravishes and destroys all that is good. But as we age we grow cowardly and acquisitive, and our armoured shells grow thick. We stop caring about beauty and searching for truth."

Adam felt hurt and indignant because he thought she knew just how little he did care about what he was doing for the PMO. Was he that transparent? All that work he had done already and for no pay! And when it came time to go knocking on doors on the Hill, who would take a second glance at his resumé?

She saw his eyes stray again to the artwork.

"My husband painted them whenever we would be posted to some hot country. India, Sri Lanka, Egypt. He'd have Beaver Lumber ship the boards from home. Said that creating Arctic storms helped him stay cool. There are hundreds more, many of them stacked in the attic. I've given some away. Would you care for one? They're quite worthless, I would think, there being so many. You might get the National Gallery interested, if they deemed it different enough from those of his they have in their permanent collection. They've been pestering me for years to let them come and see what Cecil was doing when he wasn't promoting our national interests abroad."

"I don't even like politics."

"My dear boy, that's because you think politics is something that happens beyond the reach of people like you and me. Tell me your name." He did. "Adam. Adam What?" He told her. "Lerner, a name suggestive of opportunity, privilege. Of course you would gain access to the marble halls of power with such a name. Do you know what LB's name was before he changed it? Shadrach Achebe Kundule. Try getting past the velvet tourist rope with a name like that. Try getting elected. Concessions must be made. Certain adjustments. Nevertheless, Adam Lerner, what if I were to tell you that you, an individual citizen working alone, have the ability to bring down a government?"

He pictured toppled statuary, armed troops storming a legislature, women dressed in black holding keening vigil outside locked gates, the photographs of their husbands and sons curling in the wet oppressive heat.

"I'm trying to get people to vote for my candidate, that's all. It's what I signed on to do, I guess. It's like a game. We're on one side, they're on the other. It doesn't really mean anything."

She bristled, straightening as best she could in her chair. "If you say anything so thoughtlessly barbaric in my presence again, young man, I will have you thrown out. Take it back. I demand you take those insipid words back and swallow them. Do it immediately!"

"I take it back. I'm sorry."

"Good. We understand each other. I'm somewhat fatigued now. Our interview is concluded. Come tomorrow morning at ten sharp and LB will have your orders."

After returning from his strange encounter with Mrs. Fallingbrooke and LB, Adam spent a slow, unproductive afternoon on the phone, much to the delight of Eugène, who was keeping a tally of their respective positive responses. Monica, Don and the canvassing teams came back in the dreamy, hot, distracting time when they had to shut the curtains against the sinking sun, and all they could think about was supper. They went out, a sibling gaggle now comfortable enough with each other to tease and roughhouse on the sidewalks or pretend to listen while daydreaming or to hang back in intimate pairs to talk in a way they didn't when they were talking about politics. The city opened to them, spilling onto wooden patios that narrowed the summer streets, which were humid after brief rain. Florescent Halifax waved to them, unexpectedly, like the girl or boy you thought hated you in school calling to invite you to a party.

They went into a dark bar-and-grill on a street that ran parallel to the waterfront. A man was reading from manuscript pages into a microphone when they trooped in. He gripped the microphone stand with his free hand. He was slim, with grey hair cropped close to the skull, a white collarless shirt and black jeans. A delicate golden leaf dangled from one ear. He wore rimless round-lens glasses and his face was rough with a two-day mat of white and grey bristle.

The waiters kept moving while he read his story. Plates and glasses clacked together in the nearby kitchen. Adam heard the whoosh of a gas flame turned high. People at a table tucked into a nook beside the reader's little stage kept talking. Perched atop a tall stool, his feet tucked between the rungs, the spotlight cutting him off from his audience, beads of sweat decorating his forehead, the man read as if he didn't hear them.

The interns settled at two round tables. No one wanted to be that close to the speaker, but this was what was available.

They ordered pizza and draft-beer in jugs and smiled at each other as if to say, "Now we'll uncover the real you, the genuine me." In Ottawa they had been cordial colleagues, easy with the by-the-way, thought-you-should-know rhythms of the office. Those bands of habit now severed, their surroundings unfamiliar, they felt as giddy as children on a midnight orchard raid.

In the story, a man lived his whole life with his mother. Approaching fifty and unemployable, he was a sad, lonely, marginal sort, overweight though not bad looking. A sensitive loner, he became anxious in crowds to the point where he could no longer function outside his home.

He and his mother lived frugally on her pension and that of his father, who had died when the boy was a teen. His mother had taken out a second mortgage when she thought that she might turn her large Victorian house into a bed-and-breakfast inn. Stronger then, she had had the energy to dream such a dream and act on it, purchasing the necessary linens and towels, outfitting each guest room with a bath, upgrading the kitchen to code, buying expensive china and copper cookware.

He had never seen his mother happier than during the preparatory stages leading to the launching of her business. The last position she had held before retiring had been that of an event planner for the large manufacturing company she had worked for since graduating from high school. She had moved up from the assembly line to the head office, where she worked first as a secretary and then as the executive assistant to the vice president in charge of research and development. She had loved most of all the eight years she worked as an events coordinator, planning conferences, retreats and dinners, and now she had a chance to relive that happy time with the company but as her own boss. She knew that on his own her son was a defenceless lamb, though he was honest and obedient and cheerful when closely supervised. And so she dreamed not only her own dream of being a fine and gentle hostess, but a dream for her son, one in which he learned how to run the house as a business. She never spoke her dream aloud to him for fear of upsetting him and setting him against her project. Perhaps she should have told him. Perhaps it would have been better to tell him what she was planning. Then the Fates might have been kinder.

As it turned out, said the writer in a voice that was lulling and magnetic and unsettling, two days before the B&B was due to open, having passed its safety and health inspections, a thick brown oily sulphurous crud topped with a rust-coloured bloom of mould began to bubble up through the soil to pool on the front and back lawns, seeping into the basement, killing their flowers, shrubs and trees. The company, the same that had employed the mother, was found to be responsible for the contamination, which originated at one of its tailing ponds. Mother and son fell into each other's arms. He wept because she did, but he was also relieved, because he had been able to guess what she had been planning for him, and the thought of having to learn the business had been making him secretly sick. But that sickness was replaced by another and they could no longer live safely in the house. The company paid a few thousand dollars compensation, although nothing, no insurance policy, compensation, miraculous cleanser or prayer could reverse the damage.

They moved into a tent in a thickly wooded ravine. The son, who thought they were on a camping trip, did not realize until too late that he and his mother were destitute, subsisting on community and church welfare. Declining rapidly in health, unable to get warm, her appetite and her will having ebbed away, the mother died with the advent of winter.

The writer ended his reading there. They sat quietly, occupied with eating the last of the pizza, after contributing to a polite ripple of applause. Isaac said that after hearing the story he could no longer complain about anything. Eugène asked to have the last part explained: What had happened to the house? What was the substance on the grass? Pookie gave him a synopsis. They discussed the message of the story. Was nothing positive to be taken away? What happened to the son? Would he have to go into a home for those who couldn't take care of themselves? He didn't seem completely helpless. Perhaps necessity would bring out his instinct for survival. Jean-Marc invited the author to have a drink with them and explain what he was getting at in his "history." Was this not a perfect illustration of Marx's theory of capital?

"I wasn't trying to get at anything. That's the way it played out in my head."

"So bleak," said Emma. "Are all your stories this depressing?"

The writer leaned over to one side, dipped his hand into a leather satchel sitting on the floor, and straightened holding a thin paperback book. "What's your name?" When she told him, he wrote something in the front of the book and handed it to her. "Here. Find out for yourself."

"How much is it?" She opened her purse. "You have to let me pay you."

He refused. They were students, even if they were from "Uppity Canada" and working for the "Pernicious Mendicant's Office," even if they were "in league with Satan." They laughed.

"What happens to the son?" said Isaac.

"I don't know yet. I haven't finished writing it."

At Emma's invitation the writer tagged along when they filed out. The group moved like a spastic centipede down the hill to a pub closer to the water. Here a band was playing Gaelic music and the atmosphere was louder and more festive. The large front windows of the establishment had been removed, giving it a carnival-tent feeling.

Emma and the writer sat for a long time smoking at the bar. He leaned his ear down close to hear what she was saying. As Adam watched from across the room, he grew jealous of the man. Emma rested her hand on his forearm as she listened. He was telling her things Adam would never know. He would never be that old, that experienced, that attractive. Emma looked as worldly as the writer, the same age. Adam despised him and his little volume of stories, longed to be someone who had accomplished such a thing. That man knew who he was. Everything about him spoke identity. The years had done their sculpting, abrading, honing and polishing. Here were weary eyes, the exposed cheekbones of wisdom, the deep timbre of an immortal.

She picked her purse off the bar, got off her stool and walked toward the rear of the bar, where there were signs for the washrooms and telephone. Isaac was telling Adam something about the town where he had grown up, something about a lake monster. The band finished its set with a mournful ballad. Gilles and Pookie returned from where they had been dancing slowly in front of the stage. Adam thought he heard Jean-Marc say to Eugène that they—the interns from Quebec— were no better than wartime collaborators. Eugène shook his head and began whistling the tune to "My Way." They pooled their money for two more jugs of beer. When Adam looked at the bar again, the writer was gone. Emma didn't emerge from the washroom. Adam let a glassful of draft slip down his throat, inside and out, the froth overflowing. Someone yelled, "Shet the feck up, yuh friggin' frogs. Cornwallis shoulda finished the job and sunk all them ships yer ancestors was on before they got out of the Bay of Fundy," and Gilles gave the owner of the insult the finger and a haughty up-yours look. They finished their drinks and agreed it was time to go.

"Another place or home?" said Isaac.

"Home? Home? Is *Maman* calling for you?" said Jean-Marc.

Onward it was, then. Adam felt displaced as if he could float out onto the sidewalk. He had a sense of listening to himself say something without hearing what it was. The recorded music being played was the most beautiful, the best, the most rousing, the music voted most likely to make him cry with joy. Never had he wanted a night to continue endlessly the way he wanted this one to. As they walked along a different street sloping to the harbour, it became imperative that Adam vault over a parking meter. He howled like a wolf, took two or three skips as an approach run, placed his hands on top of the meter, and felt his body lift. The lights of the city shone bright. The winking stars in their curiosity intensified. Weightless he rose. Nothing, it seemed, tethered him to the compromised and fickle earth.

He was holding a gold-coloured box. It felt light beneath his mitten-clad hands, which were numbing with the cold. He was one in an army of children waiting to begin a parade, waiting for a number of important people to arrive: the Prime Minister; Robert Lavallée, who was now Secretary of State in charge of Christmas; the camera team that would film the ceremony of a thousand school children placing brightly-coloured gift boxes at the base of a gigantic blue spruce, viewed live on the evening news. He didn't think about what gift he might be carrying; he was too concerned with staying in line, keeping up with the person ahead of him and abreast of Emma, his partner: two by two they advanced, a boy and a girl, five hundred pairs of Christmas brides and grooms representing the next century of fertility and progress.

She began to cry softly about halfway along the parade route, which began in front of the East Block and wound snake-like across the snow-covered lawn below the Peace Tower. They had not said a word to each other, their eyes meeting only the once when a frantic woman who kept muttering, "There aren't enough boys," brought them together. Emma was wearing a modest wool pea coat, navy blue, ending at her knees. She had on dark tights and a pair of thin white vinyl boots. When he asked her what was wrong, she stifled her muffled sobs.

"My toes hurt."

"Too tight?" he asked, looking down at her go-go boots.

"No, cold." She began to cry again. "They're going to freeze."

She began to speak very quickly, her voice climbing until it became a high-pitched squeak. She had watched a program about explorers in Antarctica. All their toes had gone black and had to be cut off. This was going to happen to her, she just knew it. She wanted to go home, right away. Her mother was going to wait until the ceremony was all over and then drive her home, but she couldn't wait that long. She couldn't go any farther.

She looked behind her and Adam turned also. Behind them were as many sacrificial pairs as there were ahead. From the outset the line had not moved smoothly, jerking ahead in sections like a Slinky toy. They stopped, and she began to cry louder and to stamp her feet. "I can't feel them, they're turning into ice." He looked around for an adult. The line began to move again. She stood bent over her gift box, which she hugged tightly to her front, her head bowed, her twin pigtails dangling like bell cords on either side of the shiny gold paper. He kept moving with the line, which behind him split down the middle to go around her, and soon he could no longer see her as she passed haltingly through the bowels of the snake.

He caught a glimpse of her when the line doubled back on itself and headed toward the Perpetual Flame. She was sitting on the ground, her boots barely noticeable where they stood upright on the snow beside her, and another boy was rubbing her feet. Adam craned his neck to look at them as long as he could until it was impossible to do so and keep moving forward. He came, finally, to the base of the Christmas tree and placed his gift where the spotter, a young man in a parka, told him to, his fur-rimmed face looking composed but hinting at annoyance. Of all the things he could have thought at that moment, it was that Emma had not brought her gift forward to be placed with the others, and that the omission would surely be noted, if not on earth then in the spiritual realm where the larger power of Christmas and national pride resided. Even when he overheard a boy ahead of him in line say to his partner, "There's nothing inside. Go ahead, shake it. It's just for TV," the absence of her wrapped box under the tree continued to bother him. A piece out of the larger symbol was missing without her contribution. It was as if someone had set out to build a stylized maple leaf, in patio stones, say, or plastic milk crates, and had forgotten the triangle that sits on top.

Isaac was shaking him awake. Adam groaned and wormed under the sheets, hiding his head under the pillow. Isaac insisted, reminding him of the breakfast meeting. He slid out of bed and put on the same clothes he had been wearing the night before. They shuffled queasily down the hall to join the rest of the interns gathered in the headquarters suite.

Groggy, sheepish, green, they grazed where they stood around a long table where food had been laid: coffee in large thermal urns, fresh fruit, muffins, bagels, scrambled eggs, toast, bacon, sausages, buttermilk pancakes, the hot food kept warm in metal chafing trays heated by spirit burners. Only Pookie was animated, teasing Gilles with affectionate jabs at his fatigue, ego and lack of appetite. He admitted that he functioned poorly before ten in the morning. All he could stomach was black coffee. Unlike the rest of them, Gilles did not look haphazard and slovenly, but he was simmering in a dark pout because he wanted to eat sitting down. "Anywhere," he said. Adam pictured a greasy, formica-topped diner booth squinting through dusty Venetian blinds at some ugly commercial strip of roadway.

He wondered why Pookie liked this boy and not Jean-Marc, for example, who was handsomer, or Eugène, who made up for his homeliness with an infectious brand of Franco-vaudevillian humour. But given the choice, he would have chosen Gilles, too, he conceded after consideration, for Jean-Marc always seemed angry and defensive, brooding over perceived slights, and Eugène could be annoying, acting as if he knew everything there was to know about you, his tone increasingly confidential and pitying. "Dear boy, *how* are you?" meaning, "What have you accomplished. Anything? Anything at all?"

Adam's head pounded. He had a goose egg above his left temple and abrasions on that side of his face and on both palms. He remembered jumping to his feet from where he lay sprawled on the sidewalk, brushing the front of his pants, laughing along with the others. He had not felt anything when he hit the sidewalk. After that, where they went next, what they did, how he got back to the hotel, was blank.

He was wretchedly awake, in pain and seriously nauseous by the time Don swaggered into the room. Feeney, as he liked to remind people, had made his first of many tens of millions of dollars before the age of twenty-one, a year younger than Adam was, selling billboard advertising. He was the antithesis of the PM, exuding all the flair of a brown plaid sofa in a dimly lit, fake-walnut-panelled basement den.

How much were they loving the food? They swallowed, sucking their teeth clean and smiling their best picnic-in-sunshine grins. They smiled with their eyes and nodded their heads like marionettes, all the while plotting their escape. Too late.

"Kids. Let me tell you. And I gotta say. How many days are we into this race? Mon? Where are you, hon? Two? Three. Whatever. Because, man. Excuse my vernacular. I mean, *mon dieu* it feels good to be here, to be doing this. How many days, the exact number, matters to me less than—hello, that's okay, come on in there, little lady," he said to Emma as she tried to slip undetected into the room. "We'll get our chronometers synchronized afore too much more of our precious time elapses. Right? Right. What I wanted to say, today of all days, was that this fight, it's gonna depend on three things, and if you remember nothing else, it's gonna be this. Are you with me? I said, ARE? YOU? WITH? ME?"

They let fly with limp exclamations of "sure thing" and "*oui, certainment*" and "absolutely."

"Let's try that again, gang," and they did, repeating their affirmation until it reached the sought-after volume and unison.

"Great. Super-great, team. We're of one mind on this."

As Don explained the immediately forgettable three things, Adam wished that the man were one of his own billboards. A billboard said all that it meant to say at a glance. The viewer did not have to stand listening to a scattered, incoherent motivational speaker trying excruciatingly to arrive at his point, a point, any point.

Every cell of Adam's too, too sullied flesh rebelled against this. And the three things are, gang? Blood pooled in his lower extremities. He felt the growing prickly sensation of limbs falling blissfully asleep.

Adam shook his foot. He wanted Don to stop talking more than he wanted to pee, an urgent desire, or feel his toes again, or get his eyes to focus. Just stop, please, desist with this rant that says nothing except, "Here we are," and "There" *Where?* "is the enemy," and "It's going to take every ounce *Aren't we a metric country now?* of effort *newtons or kilojoules?* on each and every *Redundancy, two-point deduction* one of you to get out there and take that hill *Analogy? A more symbolic Hill, perhaps?*"

Whipped contrary to their better natures into a manic froth, despite feeling terminal and dumb and inert, they responded fervently to his one-more-times and his I-can't-hear-yous until they were hoarse. When Don left the room to go to a television studio, Monica gave them their assignments for the day. Adam moved his feet, a step here, a step back, as if pushing a cinder block. He wasn't sure his breakfast was going to stay where it was supposed to.

Adam was paired with Oliver, the Winnipegger, to cover a neighbourhood at the north end of the peninsula, its wide base, between Quinpool Road and Jubilee. Even the street names had a sunny, saucy tang: Binney, Bliss, Spring Garden, Summer. Oliver, who was a little younger than Monica, was an agreeable sort. Bright, well read, self-deprecating, he had recently abandoned a Ph.D. in law and was "doing what was expedient" to get himself positioned in the Party for nomination in time for the next general election. He exhibited a brooding intellect that, he admitted, he let out on a short leash only when necessary. In politics, he said, the candidate must appear as smart as but no smarter than the voter.

"But there's no uniform IQ in the electorate."

"Correct. So it's a matter of...?"

"I don't know. Averages?"

"No, perception. How to appeal to the broadest range of people, that's the magic trick. Of the politicians who have been most successful in this country over the years, what would you say was their one attribute that assured them re-election time and again?"

"Ability to network."

"Nope."

"Communication with constituents."

"You would think so, wouldn't you."

"It can't be sex appeal. Look at Mackenzie King."

"The answer is unthreatening image. The ideal is a competent MP who doesn't keep the voter up at night."

"You've made a study of this. I'm surprised you went into law and not political science."

In Oliver's face was the embodiment of his own principle: dependability and civic duty obscuring a lively skeptical mind. The face required shaving twice daily. The forehead was high with a hairline retreating toward male pattern baldness. The eyes were a reader's, weak, the small ears ursine. A thick neck and broad shoulders made him look as if he had worked toting rolled carpet or sides of meat. Adam pictured him taking his coffee break in the lunchroom of a factory or an abattoir, his open textbook propped defensively between him and prying, teasing, suspicious, misreading eyes.

"You never practised law?"

"I always wanted to argue both sides of any given case. I was more interested in cooperative than adversarial jurisprudence. Aboriginal tribal councils, for example, emphasize redress over retribution. That was the thrust of my thesis: adapting native sentencing procedures to white justice. I didn't get very far with it, mainly because my supervisor didn't believe in it, and he was the only one in the department doing work even remotely related to my topic. His thing was the effect of community-service sentencing on recidivism."

Oliver wanted to tear down most of the prisons and replace them with halfway houses, leaving only the most violent offenders behind bars. Would he make that a crusade if he got elected?

"Eventually. You don't want to scare people off. This kind of thing takes years, decades. It gets done, when the electorate isn't paying attention, by representatives who, as I say, don't appear to be making waves. And it all has to fit into the corset of party discipline. So much power resides in Cabinet now."

Oliver's calculated, bloodless strategy left Adam feeling chilled. For all that he felt detached from the Feeney campaign, he was disturbed to think that legislative change could happen with so little disclosure.

They reached their assigned neighbourhood after an easy, fifteen-minute walk from the hotel, and agreed to split the area. Usually when he rang the bell or knocked on the door Adam got no answer, and so would leave a flyer in the mailbox: "Sorry we missed you! Your support is important to us. If you have any questions for Don or for the Prime Minister don't hesitate to call. Remember: Don Feeney Gets It Done." Twice he triggered loud barking, making him feel like a burglar. One man who came to the door swore that he would not vote for "that deadbeat" Don Feeney unless they paid him a million dollars, which was the amount he said Feeney had bilked him out of, back when they were both young salesmen with the same life insurance company and Feeney had tried to convince him to invest ten thousand dollars in a mining project. Something about Feeney was untrustworthy, he said, and so the man had let the opportunity pass. Adam asked why and how not giving Don ten thousand dollars to invest caused the man to lose a million.

"You're not listening, you see. If he had been trustworthy, and by that I am referring to the distance between his eyes, which is not wide, you have to admit, I would have given him the money and I would be on Easy Street today. You have heard of Consumption Sound, have you not?" Adam pretended he had. "Well, there you go. Enough said. Projected ore body in the billions and that's conservative. So don't expect a vote out of me, young fellow, not for a mandarin parachutist who would do such a despicable thing to a friend."

Several people were impressed to learn that Don had been the PM's principal secretary. A woman with a toddler riding her hip and another circling her bare leg said, "That's great, a man being a secretary. We should all be so secure in our sexuality." A man asked if Principal Secretary was anything like Secretary General. Another, running up the walk and into the front door from a car idling on the street, wanted the government to ensure broadband internet access everywhere in the country. "You're lucky to catch me this time of day. Phone's out of juice, can you believe it, and I have to check my messages. My wife wasn't here earlier, was she? She didn't happen to mention a certain delivery? She wasn't here. You said that already. I am a bad, bad, bad listener."

By noon Adam was feeling tired but good about the number of houses he had been to and the number of people who seemed receptive to his candidate. Most of the printed matter he had been carrying was now in other hands. He had eight requests for election signs. Even when they said they weren't going to vote for Feeney, they were friendly about it. "No hurt feelings, eh, buddy?"

He was thinking about these welcoming strangers as he walked toward the restaurant on Quinpool where he and Oliver had agreed to meet for lunch. A club sandwich and a tall strawberry milkshake floated in tandem just ahead of him.

"Are you not aware of the time, Adam Lerner?" came a startling voice. A black Cadillac with darkly tinted windows kept pace as he walked, stopping when he did at the sound. The head of Mrs. Fallingbrooke, framed in the open passenger window, awaited his answer. When he gave none, opening his mouth only to close it, she said, "I believe we had a ten o'clock."

"You weren't serious."

"About matters of national security I am always serious."

He could not see who was driving. She lowered her window farther and handed him a sealed business-size envelope with his name on it.

"Don't disappoint me again, Adam. You owe it to yourself and your country. Cecil and I, as you know, travelled the globe, and I can tell you unequivocally that we live in the finest nation in the world, bar none. You are temporarily misplaced and misguided in your efforts, not an uncommon failing in people your age. In your case, however, given your potential, your fondness for intrigue and your recent experience in a certain government parking lot, it is best that you be returned to the shining path of idealism. So." She murmured something indistinct to the driver of the car. "It's all set out and quite self-explanatory, as you will see when you open it and read your instructions. Until we meet again, I bid you adieu."

The window rose, obscuring her smiling face, and the car moved smoothly away. He looked at the envelope in his hand, which was beginning to tremble the way it might were it holding an activated grenade.

Quinpool Road west of Robie Street lacked shade, pretension and taste. As Adam walked, he passed a sex shop, a supermarket, several fast food outlets, a bank, a manicurist, a barbershop window reflecting the yellow of old issues of *National Geographic Magazine*, restaurants Thai, Indian, Chinese and Greek, a skateboarding store, a candy shop sharing a wall with a health-food store, another that sold dubious nutritional supplements to body builders, a pet store, an electronics store and a tarot-card psychic.

Oliver was talking to Emma in front of the place where he and Adam had agreed to meet, the sort of diner he had envisioned earlier at breakfast. He wondered why they were standing outside. She tucked some hair behind her ear and adjusted her purse strap on her shoulder. She looked like a sales rep in her skirted business suit, sienna orange with matching heels and lips, pale face, dark eyes.

What was she doing there? He had been rehearsing what he was going to say to Oliver. If Emma had been alone Adam might have drawn her into the restaurant and demanded that she treat him better. He would probably tell her about Mrs. Fallingbrooke's note. Why he couldn't make his excuses to Oliver while Emma was standing there made no sense, except that now she was part of this. What was this need to make her his confidante? Would she even want to be included? She had probably been going somewhere else when she saw Oliver. A quick hello-goodbye, see you back at the ranch, was all that need happen. Then Adam could give his regrets regarding lunch to Oliver, the old sad-sack, stuffed-shirt-in-training. With heart tripping and lungs in his throat, Adam would set off to find the address written on the old woman's stationery, which had in its letterhead a nude bathing under a waterfall.

Close enough now to see their expressions, he understood that this was no chance meeting. Oliver probably always looked this serious, but Emma, glancing at her watch and shifting her shoulder strap again, was grim and fidgety. Her hands were working at the clasp of her purse when she saw him. Relief and impatience combined in her face. The hands kept making furtive movements with the purse as she spoke.

She told him what she had told Oliver, which was that they had to cut their fieldwork short and return to the hotel. Something urgent had come up. There was going to be a press conference.

"Did you have a good time last night?"

"Didn't you hear what I said?"

"I asked an innocent question."

"We should be heading back," said Oliver.

"I'll meet you both there. I have something to do first. It won't take me—"

"Yes, I had a great time, as a matter of fact. Stewart is so talented. Do you want to know what we did? Oliver, hold up a sec."

"No, I really do not."

"Adam," she said, "you have to come back to the hotel now."

"I can get the details from you later."

"No, you can't."

"Why not?"

"You'll see when you get there."

"Now who's being cryptic?"

"If I tell you, will you come back with me? Now? No detours?"

"He's too old for you."

"Stop changing the subject!"

"Well, he is."

"It's none of your business."

"Excuse me for caring."

"Listen. Just shut it and listen for two seconds, please. One of the other candidates is making incriminating charges against Don."

"Who? What are they saying?"

"Bliss. He won't say what he's got on Don. All he'll say is that he's infiltrated the Feeney campaign, and that one of us is feeding him information. He has a name."

"One of us?"

From the way they looked down and away, Adam knew that he was that name.

Opening the old woman's note, reading the address to which he was supposed to report and the name, unfamiliar at first then shockingly remembered, of the person he was charged to meet, Adam recalled what the old woman had said before closing the car window and preventing inquiry. How had she known? He wondered how much of his private life was known only to him.

LB had released a name to the ravenous press. Adam could guess what level of anxiety now filled the room occupied by the Don Feeney election team. The PM was supposed to touch down in Halifax to lend support to the campaign before continuing to a meeting in Brussels. The timing could not have been worse. Of all of them, Adam was the one who would be hustled onto another plane and flown back to the capital city. Knowing this, he did something that would very much have pleased his nine-year-old, James Bond besotted self. When Oliver, Emma and he got back to the hotel, Adam slipped out of the elevator just as the doors were closing and ran outside.

He had a route in mind, a circuitous one that would, he hoped, throw anybody following him off the scent. He giggled at the thought. Whatever had formerly kept him in traces, harnessed to obligation and duty, was gone. He was staying ahead of out-and-out panic by half a step. Like a surfer with a monstrous roller crashing its curl behind him, he felt fuelled by the energy of the gathering mass at his back. That he had been identified as a spy before he could become one seemed oddly right. He could deny it publicly while hiding a twinge of regret. He could sneak back into his room, pack, take a taxi to the airport, and fly home before anyone would notice. Except that yes they would notice, because he was the name. The press would want a face to go with the name and they would find him back in Ottawa. Better, he reasoned, knowing nothing about what might be reasonable in this situation, to let the wave break on him here. He was, after all, a member of a team. He had allies.

His route took him across the street and through the Public Gardens, where he sat on a bench under a drooping elm for a few minutes to see if anyone had come after him. He exited at the far corner, crossed Summer Street, entered the Camp Hill Cemetery, walked through to Robie Street and into the neighbourhood where he and Oliver had gone door to door that morning, came east along Quinpool and crossed Robie again, this time at the Commons, an open grassy expanse.

Men in white shirts and trousers were playing cricket, a game Adam enjoyed thinking about despite not knowing the rules. He sat with his back to a large tree near the sidewalk on Robie and watched. If anyone were following, they would have caught him by now. He looked at his watch. He still had a few minutes before the time indicated on Mrs. Fallingbrooke's invitation: "Proceed to the Breadfruit Bistro on Agricola. Arrive at two o'clock sharp."

He didn't want to know the rules. He wanted only to sit there with the new-mown-grass smell in his nostrils, close his eyes and listen to the sounds of men from distant lands:

Pakistan, Barbados, South Africa, Nigeria. Their chatter, less jittery and tense than might be heard at a baseball game, was singsong, punctuated by laughter and mock argument.

"I am cognizant of that!"

"You are bending your elbow far too much."

"I am always, always, always, always cold."

"Consider the alternative, brother!"

"Too hot, you mean?"

"No, feeling nothing at all."

"Your feeble mind is always six feet under. Rise up, rise up and be thankful."

The bowler approached at a run, the ball struck dirt, and the bat displaced air (did Adam hear it or was it only a passing car?) before making cracking contact. Still he resisted opening his eyes. More voices rose. Footfall neared, receded. Which of the loners in the field was chasing down the ball? Which stood daydreaming of tea and shortbread?

He did not care to learn the rules and he was not yet curious enough to demand to learn how the old woman knew about the exhaust-filled car in the parking lot of the Bureau of Secure Communication. How LB knew Adam before Adam knew him, why Monica had handed him Mrs. Fallingbrooke's name in the first place—he let the unknowns pop and fizz in their own ineluctable medium, and listened to the game being played on this other Commons, this parliament of recent immigrants on the grass.

Before he opened his eyes, Adam felt the shadow on his face.

"Wake up, young fool, wake up while you still can!"

He looked up, past the white shins, the crotch, up the broad sandwich board of LB's chest, his neck, chin, grillwork smile and mirthful eyes. Behind him were others similarly dressed. The over was over. Why, he wondered, had he not noticed the candidate earlier? He must have been standing far out in the field.

"Have you not a rendezvous? Are you not past the appointed time?"

From behind LB came a cacophony of laughter.

"When was the last time you were ever on time for anything, Bliss?"

"He was three weeks late for his own birth!"

"Birth? What about his wedding?"

"Which one?"

"Wedding! He'll be twice that late times three for his own funeral!"

Adam roused, stood, brushed grass clippings off the seat of his pants. Where was the restaurant, did anybody know? How should he go to get to Agricola Street?

"No, not that way! Go this. So much faster."

"You're out of your mind. If he goes that way, who can say what end of trouble he'll get his same self into?"

Using a stick to draw lines in the dusty bowler's track, one of the players sketched the Commons, its boundary roads and interior paths. Everyone contributed to the editorial process, lines erased and redrawn like those of a gerrymandered electoral map, and soon a walking route was established. Adam thought about pulling out the city map he had in his pocket, but decided that taking it out now would only complicate matters.

"Aren't you coming, too?" he asked LB. For the first time Adam thought about him as an ally rather than an opponent.

"Me? No, no. This is one meeting you must take yourself, Mister Adam. As you can see, LB is swimming against the swift current of political commitment." More ironic laughter.

"As you can see, he is giving a press conference as we speak!"

"Mrs. Fallingbrooke won't be there?"

"In spirit. Now off you go. We're both late. The fate of the free world lies in our hands, my virtuoso fingers and your lily-white lunch hooks."

Adam set off along a paved path that roughly bisected the Commons on the diagonal. He headed northeast toward a large brown stone building that looked like an armoury. A man and his German shepherd crossed the path ahead of him. The dog had a piece of wood the size of a small fireplace log jammed sideways in its mouth. The man's jeans hung so low that it looked as if they would fall at any second. A kid on a bike with a loose chain guard clattered toward him and Adam had to step off the path to let him pass. The boy had such thick glasses that Adam wondered how he could see anything.

He reached the far corner of the Commons, found the street he wanted and headed for the intersection where the restaurant stood.

The only other customer was sitting with her back to the door, and so when Adam walked in he went past her, sat at a table in the middle of the room, and didn't look over at her until she said his name. He got up sheepishly and went over to her table.

"Almost didn't recognize you without your trench coat on," she said, extending her hand but not rising. They shook hands and he sat.

The interview seemed so long ago now. He had given up hoping to hear from her. She had cut her hair short and replaced the dark jacket and skirt with jeans and a light blue blouse under which he could see the scoop neck and one shoulder strap of a yellow athletic bra. An amber necklace and matching pendant earrings matched the room's décor, which was bright, monochromatic, the colourful equivalent of a page full of exclamation marks. A carnival array, with joyful rhythmic music in the air and singing in a language that lifted his heart even as he tried to connect Hannah Pachter of BSC with the woman he was looking at now.

"Hello," he said. "It's good to see you again."

A man in a soiled apron appeared from behind the cash register counter and came out to take their order. Hannah asked him what he recommended and he suggested a dish of grilled chicken, mango and yams with a side of salad greens and the restaurant's special dressing. She said it sounded yummy and ordered two plates of it.

"You'll love it," she said after the waiter, who looked also to be cook, dishwasher and proprietor, disappeared.

"How do you know? Have you been here before?"

"Do you trust me, Adam?"

"Why? Shouldn't I?"

"You must have questions you want to ask me."

"I sure do. Do they skin the chicken breasts, for one thing?"

"You have every reason to be hostile."

"Who's being hostile?"

"Okay, defensive, confused, disoriented."

"And he's on the ropes, ladies and gentlemen. Dazed, defenceless, confused. Does he even know what's happening to him? The referee begins the mandatory eight count as he rubs rosin off the contender's gloves."

"Let me put it simply. At the moment you are a wanted man."

Adam laughed and felt his face grow red at the sound. The waiter peeked out of the kitchen door and closed it when he saw that no one was hurt.

"The press wants to talk to you about the information you've been giving Mr. Bliss."

"But I haven't! He knows more about Don Feeney than I do."

"Doesn't matter. The story's out there now."

He shrugged, blinked, looked out the window. He just wanted to go home.

"What do you want from me?"

"The better question is what do you want from you? Three months ago you came to me looking for a job. Not just a job, a career."

"I found something else."

"You're a volunteer working on the election campaign of the PM's man. You're a dispensable functionary. Do you really think there's going to be a job for you there when this is all over?"

"It's already all over. They want me gone so they can do damage control. Why exactly—what's your connection to this? I thought you listened in on phone conversations and stuff."

Before she could answer, the waiter brought water glasses, finger bowls and a basket of flat bread and a salsa dip. Adam felt as if he had not eaten in days. He took two pita triangles and ate them quickly without adorning them.

"Here's what I can tell you: very soon Don Feeney will resign his candidacy. Someone will be found to replace him, someone blessed by both the Government and the Opposition. Are you wondering who that will be?"

"Not really."

"Of course you are. Think. Who could possibly step in to replace Don and please the Party, LB and Mrs. Fallingbrooke at the same time?"

"Humpty Dumpty."

"Your cooperation in this is imperative, Mr. Lerner," she said, her tone now disciplinary.

"I don't know. I don't care. Conrad Black. Wayne Gretzky. Shania Twain. Me."

"Yes."

"Yes what?"

"Yes you."

"You're out of your flipping gourd, lady."

The waiter brought their entrees, giving Hannah an excuse not to respond. She directed her attention to the underside of her chicken, which she lifted with her knife and fork as if she were performing the dissection of a fetal pig in a high-school biology lab. Adam waited, not touching his utensils. If she didn't look up in three seconds, he told himself, he was going to leave.

She sniffed and said, "Grape nuts, I think," and cut a morsel of meat. She looked at it on her fork. "I'm allergic to pine nuts. Not grape nuts, though."

The three seconds passed and still she hadn't looked up. He stood. "I'm out of here," he said. "How much...?" He took out his wallet, removed a ten-dollar bill and tucked it under the lip of his plate.

"What if I were to tell you...?" She raised her eyes to his. She seemed almost amused, but also earnest, a new expression for her normally inscrutable face.

"What?"

"I've got this. Keep your money."

"Tell me what?"

"Nothing. Don't worry about it. Have a pleasant flight."

"I'm not up to this. Really."

"Of course you're not. I understand."

"My father got me this job. He said it would be the perfect introduction, a foot in the door."

"An honourable route. You're not the first to have forgone a salary to gain valuable experience."

"Tell me what?" Adam picked up the money and sat. She had him and he knew it. Being held by her like this, the way she might a hand of cards, made him feel secure. It wasn't a difficult thing, this being told. It bypassed so much that was complicated. He might just as well have said, "Yes, I'm yours. Take me. Tell me what to do."

"We have intelligence that Mr. Bliss—Kundule, rather—is a member of a terrorist cell planning an attack on public buildings somewhere in the Northeast."

"So arrest him."

"He's more valuable to us out of captivity. We need to keep him close."

"How close?"

"Ideally? We'd love to see him installed in an office in the Centre Block. In a substantial way it would give him a false sense of security."

"If he gets elected that will happen, won't it?"

"True. But as an MP he might go dormant on us, might feel it too dangerous to try anything given the scrutiny he'd be under. We think he realizes this and that's the reason why he trumped up the story about you leaking Don's secrets to him. He wants to lose."

"Why doesn't he just step down, not run?"

"We're not sure about that. Could be pride. Could be loyalty to the old lady, who has a zealous belief in his ability to win. She doesn't know anything about his background. For her he's a cause, the socialist underdog, the new immigrant, the man of colour poised to rise and assume his position in the assembly of the powerful. She's quite drunk on the idea, in fact. We figure he doesn't want to let her down."

"I still don't understand..."

"If you run you'll win. Don't ask how. It will be a given. Challenge me on it afterward and I will disavow any knowledge of ever having met you. You've seen *Mission Impossible*."

This was surreal. He, a Member of Parliament?

"You'd be given everything you needed. A staff, of course, and—"

"LB would be part of it."

"Now you're catching on. Excellent, Adam, excellent."

Without apparently taking more than the smallest bites, she had consumed almost everything on her plate, while his meal remained largely untouched.

"I'll need some time to think about it."

"Of course. Take whatever time you need."

"I don't think I can go back to the hotel."

"No, you're right, you can't." She took a phone out of her purse. The device was a little larger than a makeup compact. "I'll get you a room at the casino hotel." She called someone she knew by name, made the reservation and put the phone away. "Your belongings will be transferred. Don't worry, no one will know where you are unless you want them to."

"How are you going to convince Don not to run? I mean, I thought this was his dream from when he was a little boy."

She looked at him, lowered her eyes, raised them, glanced out the window and turned her head back. "I really need a smoke. I don't suppose..."

"No. Sorry."

"Don Feeney is a Party stalwart. He has always done the right thing. He will do the right thing this time."

As Hannah Pachter had promised, Adam's clothes and luggage were transferred from the Lord Nelson ahead of his checking into the casino. He had a sauna and a swim in an attempt to relax, watched television, walked the length of the boardwalk and back, ate an early supper, which he charged to the room, and thought about what Hannah Pachter had said to him. Maybe she had been joking and he had missed catching her dry sense of humour. Perhaps he had been hallucinating. No, that couldn't be it, for then he would be hallucinating even now, and the sirloin he was chewing was as real as the chair he sat on. Did she even work where she said she did? Maybe she was part of an even more shadowy operation that functioned outside of the government. She had known who he was before interviewing him, had either known he was going to be working at the PMO or had arranged it herself. But how was that possible? That would mean that his father had been involved, and Adam could not picture Mr. Lerner being involved in anything shadier than a Sunday snooze in the backyard hammock. It must be that she had been watching Adam at every step. The suicide in the BSC parking lot—did she have something to do with that? Thinking about it was knotting his stomach. Some spy he made.

He went up to his room and was lying on the bed when the phone rang. It was his father. He had tried to get Adam at the Lord Nelson and they had transferred the call.

"They ran out of rooms, Dad. Some mix-up. How are things there?"

"We're OK. Your mother had one of her feelings and she wouldn't let go of it until I called you. Some crazy idea you're not well. Are you all right, boy? Do you need money? Clean underwear?"

Adam laughed, secretly thanking him for giving him this small outlet for his tension. He told him that he was having the time of his life. The campaign was chugging along like a freight train. Unstoppable. No worries.

They talked about the weather, the PGA tour, international news. By the time they said goodbye, his father seemed reassured that Adam was all right.

The air conditioner blew a cold wind, preventing sleep. A knock came at the door. When he opened it a beautiful girl in a shimmering golden evening gown was standing there. She said her name was Tracy, she worked for the hotel's hospitality staff, and she was inviting him downstairs to the tables. She smiled as she held up a package of betting chips encased in molded plastic. She looked so much like a Bond girl that he thought he was dreaming.

"I should get dressed," he said, figuring that if it were a dream he might not require clothes, and when she said that, yes, it might be a good idea to put on pants, he blushed.

"That is," she added, "if you want to go downstairs. We could always stay in."

"This is for real?"

"Yes, why wouldn't it be?"

"How old are you?"

"Old enough."

"I don't suppose you know who sent you."

"My boss. He's usually the one who tells me what to do."

'So, what next?' hung unspoken in the stale, chemical air coming in from the hallway. He got dressed, put the door key in his pocket and walked with unreal Tracy to the elevator.

"Just so you know," she said as they descended, "I don't... you know."

"Ah. Right."

He played some blackjack after watching a few hands, lost a third of the chips Tracy had given him, and moved to the roulette table. He asked her where she was from and what she liked most about working at the casino, which had a desperate, muggy, soiled atmosphere, so unlike the image portrayed in the movies. The players looked punchy, slumped, sleep deprived. Not a tuxedo in the room.

Tracy said she was from Stellarton, that all of her friends had stayed there or gone away to school, but that she hadn't liked high school all that much and couldn't wait to get away. Halifax was like a dream. She loved the port city. There was so much to do. The people weren't quite as nice as the folks back home, but they were generous, mostly, with tips and advice and the like, and she got to meet people from all over the world. She asked him what kind of business he was in.

"Busking."

"Really? What's your routine?"

"I get myself into sticky situations and try to get out of them."

"Oh. Cool. I once saw a guy put his whole body through a tennis racket."

"That must have been a strain."

She looked at him blankly. She was so beautiful, with impossibly clear skin and plump lips and monumental cheekbones, that he felt the strong desire to spirit her away from this den of fractured dreams, to bring her with him when he made his own escape.

"What do you like to drink?"

"Vodka Martini," he said, never having tasted one. "Shaken, not stirred."

"Coming right up!"

How much did she miss? She was like a supple container he imagined would expand to accommodate whatever was put into it. An old woman at a video lottery terminal put her forehead to the console and began to sob. A security guard led her out of the room.

"How would you like to work for me?" he said after winning a modest bet on red.

"You mean as part of your act?"

"In a way. I'm going to be a Member of Parliament and I need a staff."

"Would I have to move? I really like it here."

"Yes, you'd have to move to Ottawa," he said, labouring slightly over the name of the city. Another cocktail appeared, its olive eyeing him suspiciously.

"Don't you, like, have to win an election or something first? Or do you get picked?"

He assured her that getting elected was going to be the least of his problems.

"That's right," said a familiar voice coming from behind them. He turned to look over his shoulder. It was Emma. He missed placing his next bet, not that he had many chips left.

"What are you doing here?"

"Same as you. So, have you decided yet?"

"Yes, I'm putting it all on thirteen."

"About running in the by-election."

He looked at her straight on. He was reminded of their first exchange on Sparks Street, when she had told him that she was keeping an eye on him. "We don't quite have a bead on you yet." Well, she—they—had a "bead" on Adam Lerner now. He was in their crosshairs. She waved at somebody across the room. Adam looked over and saw the others, Gilles, Pookie, Isaac, Eugène, Jean-Marc, Oliver. What a remarkably average-looking group they made. Did they know as much as Emma did about his impending decision? And why him? He was the least political of them all. He had no idea how to run for office, what his staff would have to do. He liked gathering information, but didn't care what it was used for. They wanted someone they could manipulate, someone naïve, bland, visibly attractive but not arresting, someone who would go down smoothly with the electorate, someone they wouldn't have to think too much about. Well, he would see about that. He would show them. But when he tried to formulate that next thought, the "what" he would be showing them, he drew a blank.

Then he heard himself say, "Yes, I've decided. I'm going to do it," as if hearing someone else, and Emma grabbed his upper arm with both her hands. "You'll need a chief of staff, someone with an administrative background. I'd be perfect, Adam. I have all these ideas about reforming the electoral process and getting better representation. Just think about it. Keep me in mind. We'd be perfect together. You might need some media coaching. I don't know, I've never heard you speak in public, but I bet you're great. If you did need some pointers, though—those scrums can be deadly, you have to think in three-second sound bites. I did my first degree in communication. Oh, Adam, this is so right on. Hey, you guys!"

They were all crowding around now, congratulating him, giving him hugs and good-natured punches on the shoulder. Eugène promised to teach him to speak French in two weeks. No one aside from Emma tried to pitch him for a job in his parliamentary office, but the air was charged with anticipation. When he said that he hadn't won yet, they laughed. Of course he would win, they said. But why was Don pulling out? What reason would Feeney give the press? None of them seemed concerned.

The PM was supposed to arrive the next day. Adam had never talked to him before. Would he remember Adam walking out of the reception for Lorne? He would expect Adam to be coherent, intelligent, informed. Didn't he have to live in the community he would be representing?

"You'll take ownership of the property that's in Don's name," said Pookie. "I heard Monica talking about it. It's a trailer or a cottage or something. You have to pay a dollar for it. You do have a loonie left, don't you? Tell me you haven't lost it all."

Nomination meeting, residency rules, duties, parliamentary procedure, rules of order, the passage of bills, committee work, party discipline—he tried to remember everything he had studied in grade ten history, when the teacher had tried to get the class excited about Canadian politics. The teacher had pulled out a board game thinking that the competition would make it enjoyable, but they were at age fifteen about as interested in politics as they were in the administration of pension funds.

The group dispersed. He saw his hostess, Tracy, talking to a middle-aged man, and Adam longed for those first moments, innocent by comparison, when she and he had found simple things to talk about. She reminded him of a crush he'd had in high school. There had been a couple of serious infatuations and one long-term thing that had lasted for two years at university until she went back to be with someone she had never told him about, an old flame who flared up just when her passion for him was waning. Mostly, though, he had friends who were female. He liked their company. He liked being thought of as good company, a pal, someone not likely to complicate matters with sex or love or, heaven forbid, both. It worried him sometimes. Would he ever fall in love with a woman who would be equally in love with him, and would it be something that would last?

After everyone else had dispersed, Emma convinced him to come with her up to her room to work on his presentation. She said she had something Monica had asked her to prepare for him, some things to say in front of the cameras when it came time to announce his candidacy, which was going to be very soon, she said. Lorne wanted it to happen the next day if he was ready.

They left the gaming tables and went to her room and immediately she began pulling his shirt off over his head without unbuttoning it, yanking his pants and underwear down, making whimpering noises, little stifled screams.

A number of times he looked at her and thought that he loved her, almost said it, may have said it, he couldn't be sure, the inside and the outside of him being indistinguishable as they moved in unison. He felt that every image that flashed in his head was immediately translated into words and spoken aloud at the top of his voice, and that somehow she was speaking through him, with him, as a single voice. How could it be that joined like that to her he could so completely forget who she was and what her motivations were?

Later he thought, *Wasted*. This is what addicts meant when they said they were wasted. Had there been a fire alarm at that moment he would not have been able to answer its call, don his clothes, put one foot in front of the other, one thought in front of the next. She lay with one arm flung over his bare chest, her face nuzzling the soft flesh where the pectoral muscle formed the pit of his arm.

"This is my new favourite place," she said. "I'm not moving from here."

He began to drift asleep and felt her trying to rouse him. Waking and dreaming became a liquid suspension. He sat up with a start, confused, heart racing, the alcohol (how many had he had?) making him believe that he could speak Arabic if he tried, but that if he did, terrible things would happen.

Groggy, still drunk, depleted, sticky, ridiculous in the bathroom mirror, he caught sight of himself trying to gather his clothes.

"Can I see you in the morning?"

"It is the morning," she said.

"When did you move rooms? Why are you in this hotel, too?"

"Everybody moved. I don't know why. Nicer rooms, better service."

"I don't understand what's happening."

"Why does it matter?"

"It just does. This is all so bizarre. I feel like I've got no say in anything. How do I know…"

"How do you know what?"

"No, it's nothing."

"Tell me."

"How do I know … if I can even trust you? I mean, this, you and me, it all happened so fast."

"Maybe you better leave. Now. Please go." She opened her mouth and closed her eyes and for the longest time no sound emerged.

"Emma."

"Get out!"

He hesitated a moment on the other side of the door. He could hear her crying.

When he got to his room, the phone was ringing. He said, "Emma, look, I'm sorry but I really don't know what's happening," before his father cut in.

He apologized for calling again so late, but it occurred to him that Adam had more to say.

"No, Dad, I don't think so. Everything's good here." The room looked impersonal, alien.

I have an ally, he thought, the notion undoing what remained of his composure, and he began to weep as openly and as childishly as he had heard Emma cry.

"I'm sorry, Dad," he was finally able to say. "You must think I'm losing my mind."

"No, no, not at all, son. You're under some pressure there. We understand."

"I'll be home right after the vote. Only three days away."

How was he going to hold out until then? He thought about Emma, fought back the urge to return to her room. Then everything, even the feeling he had had while talking to his father, curdled in an instant. All he wanted was to be home, where he could sleep late, read unassigned books, throw sticks for the dog to fetch, go to movies and pubs, not read anything in the newspaper except for the arts section and the funnies. Get a job, maybe in advertising. Find an apartment. Try his hand at writing. Put as much distance as possible between him and this darkening brown dream. It *was* becoming more dreamlike the longer he sat watching the blur of the fogged-in dawn. It wasn't real. He owed no one a thing. It wasn't as if they had paid him money. He would arrive home to find that it had all been a fiction, surely. Would he finally be awake?

In the morning Adam went downstairs to get a newspaper and something to eat. The newspaper box was in front of the hotel, near the semi-circular drive where cars could pull up under the overhang and unload. A bus was idling there. He walked out and knocked on the door. When it opened he asked the driver where he was going.

"Halifax International. Moncton eventually."

"How much for a one-way?"

The fare was more cash than Adam had in his wallet, but the man said he would take a cheque. Adam got him to wait while he ran back inside for his things.

"Four minutes. If you're not back by then, all you'll see will be tail lights."

The bus driver was a big man with a puffy face into which his eyes were sunk like dark pebbles in putty, a toothbrush moustache, a gut that hauled his spine out of alignment, and an attitude toward his passengers that was undisguised contempt. When he spoke it was to announce place names as if they were items on a list of communicable diseases. No one was allowed to sit directly behind him, because in those two seats he stowed the jacket of his uniform and a leather satchel, no doubt containing top-secret bus-company documents. Not until all the other seats had been filled did he grudgingly remove his things from that seat and stow them in the overhead compartment.

A requirement of the job was to pick up and deliver parcels sent via the bus to the depot stops, usually a gas station or a convenience store, often the two combined, strung along the route, and when he did heave his considerable bulk out of his seat, out of the vehicle, across whatever breathtaking expanse lay between him and the depot, it looked like the last walk of a condemned man. It appeared to be so painful, his shuffling stride, his belly moving independent of the rest of him, his back apparently in dislocation as a result of the weight pulling it forward and down, that Adam stopped watching him.

In Truro a man got on and tried sitting in the seat behind the driver. Redirected he sat beside Adam. He said his name was Alexei. He had dark curly hair, a trimmed moustache that was fuller and more attractive than the bus driver's, oil-stained fingers and black plastic-rimmed glasses with one of the lenses cracked.

Alexei said he owned a truck and made a living moving things for people. Most of what he talked about had to do with mechanical matters: a motorcycle he had bought and was restoring and assembling; diesel trains; an annoying camera that beeped when the flash was primed but which failed to operate if the electronic sound component malfunctioned. He fixed it by removing the tiny circuit board that governed the beep. Adam could not place his accent. Perhaps French Swiss? A hint of Afrikaner?

Alexei restored old bicycles for people, more as a conservational, car-reducing measure than as a business. In fact he seemed committed to making as little money as possible. He described old passenger rail cars he had seen recently in the Annapolis Valley. They had been newly painted with gold lettering on purple. He called it their livery as if referring to a horse and rider decked out in their stable's silks. He spoke at length about automobiles of a certain vintage, but not just any old cars. He was interested above all in innovation. Renault, for example, had built a modular car a few years back in which the left back side panel, say, could fit the right front or any other quadrant, reducing the number of different components any factory or repair facility would have to stock. It frustrated him, as it would any thoughtful person concerned with efficiency and waste reduction, that so much of what we buy today— radios, CD players, toasters—can't be easily repaired. It would cost more, for example, to fix the music player Adam had in his bedroom than to scrap it and buy a new one. Where older appliances and the more expensive current models were made out of metal and had parts held together with screws, today's toaster was made of modular plastic parts fused and attached with rivets, since it was so much easier to design a production robot that put modules together with a simple rivet gun than to have one turning tiny screws into place. What was the true cost of the downward spiral that business had created by moving away from reparable appliances?

The result, Alexei answered himself, was that workers were paid less and less because they were doing less skilled work than had their predecessors, and so could not afford to buy the better made items, those assembled with screws. Thus was perpetuated a culture of diminishing value. Items broke sooner, had to be replaced sooner, went to landfills sooner, all because they couldn't be replaced economically. The trend toward managed obsolescence extended even to fruit. Apple growers in British Columbia, said Alexei, tried to get their produce to ripen all at once to maximize their sales to the US market. Consumers in California wanted their BC Delicious apple to look and taste a certain way, to be of a uniform size, and so the trees were sprayed all at once with a maturing hormone. Apple pickers sat around until the appointed day, when they would go madly to work, an army of them competing during a relatively short period of time to pick as many apples as they could. The trees themselves were pruned to grow in two dimensions, rather than three, to facilitate picking, and so tended to keel over in high winds.

Adam thought about what Alexei was saying and decided that if he were running for office he would make this the basis of his election platform. It would take a plank from Don Feeney's slogan: Adam Lerner Makes It Work. The thought made him smile. To think that whoever would be responsible for getting him elected would actually let him stand up and speak his own thoughts. Absurd! Still, what if, he mused, as the dull landscape lining Highway 102 flashed past, what if we as a country made it a priority to make everything work as well and as efficiently as possible? Cars that didn't break down, that had easily replaceable parts, that ran on fuel cells instead of gasoline? It seemed the current system hinged on nothing but greed. Those making business decisions wanted always to make more and more money by replacing workers with machines, using ever cheaper parts and processes, contracting out manufacturing to eager poor countries, polluting because the resultant fines were still cheaper than having to keep the waste products out of the environment.

Who were Adam's handlers? Were they representatives of corporate interests, some cadre of the powerful operating outside the law, the Russian Mafia, the *Opus Dei*, the Hell's Angels? Any of these seemed equally plausible.

The 102 changed names at the intersection with the highway that ran in one direction to Cape Breton and the other to New Brunswick. Alexei the shirtsleeve economist had fallen asleep. I'll hire him to be my ideas man, thought Adam, and I'll hire Tracy the casino hostess to be my communications director. He hoped that before the bus trip was over he might meet a dozen more people like them, and if they wanted a job he would install them in his parliamentary office or in offices of their own. Eugène, his old office mate, Adam figured was going to get elected on his own eventually. Isaac the deputy premier's son was too afraid of his father to have an original thought. Pookie and Gilles—who knew? Adam saw them opening a restaurant on Somerset or Queen West or Bourbon or Clinton Street. Probably Montréal. Anywhere less urbane and Gilles would shrivel up and blow away.

The bus stopped in Wentworth, Oxford, Springhill and Amherst, Nova Scotia and in Sackville, New Brunswick. In

Moncton Adam waited in the terminal for the bus going to Montréal and Ottawa. It didn't leave for another forty minutes. He went to the washroom and when he came out he saw Mrs. Fallingbrooke's Cadillac pull into the parking lot. He knew it was hers because there was LB getting out and opening the door, holding it as she emerged, incrementally like cooling pillow lava flowing up out of a depression.

His stomach began to climb. Sweat beads broke on his forehead. How could they have known? What, did he have a tracking device planted on him? In a few seconds they would see him. He had to get out of there. But to what end? If they knew he was here they could find him anywhere. Where could he possibly flee? It was no use, none at all. They were coming inside. Adam had overheard a bus passenger say she was transferring to the train in Moncton, that the station was close, just down and across the street from the bus depot. He had no diversionary tactics in his arsenal. What arsenal? He wanted to cry, a wholly different feeling from the night before on the phone with his father. This was making him crazy. Why couldn't they just leave him alone? He was no politician. The electorate would see that as soon as he stood up to speak. Nobody, inside the Party or out, knew who he was. Weren't you supposed to have some sort of presence, weren't you supposed to have people behind you? He wasn't even a card-carrying member. It was as if they had pulled his name randomly out of a hat. If this was the way the country was run, he wanted out. But there was no way out without being seen. So what if they saw him? They could follow him all the way home to Ottawa for all he cared; they couldn't stop him. He stood, picked up his suitcase, and walked out the door in the direction of the Montréal bus.

LB saw him and opened his big hand in greeting, the palm a lighter shade than the rest of the hand, like the soft, rubbed, oiled inside of a cherished bowl. He smiled as though it were the best surprise ever to be meeting Adam here. The old lady caught sight of him, too, out of the corner of one eye. She was still turning away from the car and toward the depot. The car door had yet to be shut and it was a considerable effort for her to lift her head and take in everything that demanded to be seen. LB stood with his hand under her elbow and together they were the epitome of colonial symbiosis, he in his huckster white suit and pimp-pink fedora, wrap-around shades, red kerchief at the neck, and she in her impractical black dress with the ever-present string of fat pearls, and a hat that looked like something picked up off a pew one Sunday after services, 1955. Were those flowers *and* feathers *and* birds all together on a single headdress? Who was expressing her tribal connections and who looked like a fusion of Tom Wolfe and Marvin Gaye? Together they were some cruel joker's idea of bad taste, quite a few shades of subtlety shy of enigmatic. Seeing them made Adam want to shout with mad glee or curl into a ball, the urges alternating like an electric current.

Why even stop to talk with them? He had to, he knew, because he had grown up in leafy, staid, suburban Ottawa and was just now discovering he had a mind of his own and a curiosity that couldn't be sated in the classroom. He had to because this was the most intriguing thing ever to happen, not just to him but to anyone he knew.

There was no avoiding them. He put down his suitcase and waited for them to reach the spot where he was standing. How had LB's press conference gone? Had he shown up on time, shown at all? Had Mrs. F. been there? All of a sudden he understood that it didn't matter if she was there or not. She was running the show. She was a gradually hardening shell encasing a brilliant manipulative mind. How else could she appear to be aligned with the fringe and still be pulling the strings that made the middle dance, strings that reached past the visible and were attached to people and processes and policies that worked beyond the reach of accountability. She was Kurtz. She was Margaret Thatcher free of the stricture of Parliament. She was Charlotte Whitton, Indira Ghandi, Elizabeth I. What did she stand for? What would he be required to do under her auspices?

"Adam. Explain yourself," she said, Miss Havisham, Lady Catherine de Bourgh, Miss Jean Brodie.

"I'm going home."

"Yes, your departure was noted." He didn't need to know more. One of the hotel bellhops was probably a cricket buddy of LB's. Maybe the bus driver had pressed a secret button. Adam's theory of a homing device somewhere on his person, perhaps as something he had eaten, was not out of the question. "I would like you to come back with us."

"No thank you. I've had enough of this."

"Adam, ultimately I can't make you do anything. What Hannah said to you in the restaurant, she should not have said those things."

"She said that you," turning to LB, "were—are a terrorist."

LB's face broke into a series of ever increasing smiles punctuated by laughter that built to a crescendo.

"Oh," said Mrs. Fallingbrooke when LB had finally run out of hilarity, "she really should not have said that."

Who was Hannah Pachter? What was going on?

Hannah, explained the old woman, was her grandniece. She did work at the BSC, but as a technician. The day Adam had come for his interview, the man who was supposed to ask the questions had tried to kill himself in his car. He had not been a well man. His name was Jack Blaylock and he had been rescued before he could be successful in his suicide. Adam's alertness that day had apparently saved the poor man's life. Blaylock and Hannah had been a couple for a number of years until Hannah told him that she wanted to end the relationship.

The day of Adam's interview, Hannah, who wanted to be a full-fledged communications security officer but lacked the training, happened to be in Blaylock's office waiting to talk to him—they had had a particularly awful fight on the phone the night before—when Adam was escorted in. Hannah, not knowing where Blaylock was, and perhaps assuming that the man hadn't come to work that day, decided to conduct the interview herself.

"She shouldn't have done it. She knows that. But she was the one who saw something in you, Adam." She had no authority to hire him and could not even make a record of the interview. She gave him her phone number at work in case Adam called about the status of his application. She knew that he would eventually give up. But when he let it slip one day, in one of his last calls to Hannah, that he had taken the position at the PMO for the summer, she phoned Mrs. Fallingbrooke. She said, "I think I may have your Roy Romanow, Aunt."

"I have my connections with the Party, as you well know. The rest—well, you know as well as anyone. Hannah spoke with you at my behest. Again, I apologize. She had no right to say what she did.

"I'm not a monster, Adam, and I'm not some old Black Widow weaving intricate threads of intrigue. We just don't want you to go."

"Don isn't stepping down?"

"Not that we know of."

"You don't want me to stand in his place?"

"An unfortunate rumour started by Hannah and spread to your young colleagues. Romance at short notice is my niece's forte, to steal a favourite line from Saki."

"So what do you want from me?"

"Help LB get elected."

"You want me to switch camps."

"It's what we've wanted all along."

"LB never did hold that press conference, did you, LB? The reporters had been assembled, rumours were building like thunder clouds—oh, sex scandals involving Don and you young interns, national security secrets leaked, revelations of a past criminal record, kidnappings, planned revolutions with LB at the helm—but he let them stew in their own innuendo, didn't you, LB? As for my grandniece, I sent Hannah Pachter packing, advised her never to meddle in political affairs again, told her to stick to what she did best, which is finding information for people. Lucky for LB, Hannah's inflammatory depiction of him went no further than her chat with you. I could tan that girl's fanny, I truly could."

They drove back to Halifax together, LB at the helm, the old lady intermittently asking Adam questions, recounting long stories from her past, and nodding off. Where, of all places he had been, would he prefer to die? He had to think about that one because he had not travelled widely: Florida on a family vacation, England when he was four, British Columbia on a school trip, Lake Placid to ski.

"Iceland," he decided. "I'm soaking in a hot spring. It's winter, there's snow all around and the sun is shining. It disappears behind a cloud for a while. I wait for it to return, and when it does, when I have to close my eyes against its brightness, the warmth soaking into the skin of my face, people around me speaking a language I don't understand, I drift away. Then."

He looked over at Mrs. Fallingbrooke, who had fallen asleep again. Why exactly was he returning to Halifax? He pondered the answer to that, too. Not because they had asked and not because he felt any more fervently about LB's party and campaign than he did about Don Feeney's. It had been something Mrs. Fallingbrooke had said about people his age, about not being co-opted by authority. Always push through the obfuscating barrier, she told him, ask the difficult question, lead with the glass chin of his idealism. But what if the government was right, what if it did know best? How to tell? He had been the dutiful son, doing the right thing, for too long. It was time to do the wrong thing, the questionable act, the dance only he knew the steps to.

He stayed with Mrs. Fallingbrooke in her left-leaning house for the few days that remained in the campaign. She received phone calls from Don, Lorne and Monica, each expressing the measured, diplomatically worded, angry but still smiling message—the doyenne did, after all, contribute large sums to the Party despite what they would characterize as her recent misalignment—that if Adam Lerner did not return to Ottawa immediately he would face severe consequences.

"Don't let the blustering bulls and hissing snakes intimidate you. You are entirely within your rights as a free citizen to change your mind and do whatever your heart instructs. After all, what, really, do you know? You know that the town of Feeney, Manitoba, is due for an overhaul of its sewer system and you know whom to call if you need information about the federal remote sensing installation at Crystal Crescent Beach, Halifax County."

"I do?"

"You had lunch with her. You don't think she came to Nova Scotia just to talk to you, do you?"

"Ah. Well. Okay."

"And you know that Don Feeney has all the resources of the Prime Minister's Office mustered behind his campaign. Is that fair? No it is not. Partisanship rarely admits the governance of fair play into its realm. Will he make himself available to the good citizens who will bear him to Parliament? Think again. That's all you know, Adam Lerner, except for what's in your heart."

He had, against his instinct to flee, returned to the port city, where for generations they had been dumping their waste untreated into the harbour, and where now many were making pitiful moan and outraged squeak against the construction of a sewage-treatment plant in the vicinity of their rose gardens. Something about this fractious, halt-step, reeling march toward environmental responsibility Adam found attractive, and as he went door to door, again, to many of the same doors as before, he talked about what he guessed LB would do as their representative. He couldn't say for certain, because LB did not make his thoughts or his promises or his inklings known to Adam, his only campaign worker, let alone to the voting public. The only thing remotely connected to the election that LB talked about was the means of transportation he planned to use for his triumphant entrance into the nation's capital. He was split between paddling a dugout war-canoe up the Rideau Canal and floating in a hot-air balloon across the Ottawa River from the Quebec side. What LB would do, Adam said when asked, given that he would not be sitting in the governing block of seats unless all polling was wildly incorrect, was lobby strongly for more federal funding for the harbour cleanup.

One resident reminded him that the feds had already anted-up millions for just that purpose. "Already spent," said the man as he wheeled his green organic-compost container away from the curb and back down his driveway. "Walk with me," he said with a snicker, and Adam laughed. "Spent on snow removal or some such or other. Things don't change. Never will, until you make people put on wet-suits and take a nice refreshing dip in their very own municipal toilet bowl."

"We'll make it a priority."

The householder looked at him. "That I'd love to see."

"I mean the cleanup."

"Right. Right on. Go for it, bye! You got my vote."

"We do?"

"What do you think?"

"I don't know."

"There you are, then. Your known unknown." The man laughed and went inside his house.

Perplexed that someone could be so playfully evasive about such a serious issue, Adam was happy nevertheless. For the first time he was enjoying his labour. He was making it up as he went. When he wasn't sure about the answer to a question, he returned to the literature disseminated by LB's national party: withdrawal from NATO, universal daycare, revocation of NAFTA, resurrected passenger-rail travel, higher taxes on fossil fuels, incentives to convince people to use their cars less often. Reactions ranged from incomprehension to giddy disbelief, with equal parts hearty support and unapologetic apathy filling a plump middle ground.

"So let me get this straight. If I switch to an electric car, I'll still be able to drive it to work? Okay, that's fine. There's just one little thing, eh? Where do I get ahold of the $80,000 to buy one of them enviro-saving babies? You're blowing smoke out your bunghole, buddy. You're eating cloud pie."

It didn't faze him when people reacted this way. Maybe it should have. He smiled, made a note, thanked the constituent for his or her time, and moved on to the next address.

At one house Adam rang at the front door. No one answered, but he could see through the glass that the family was gathered at the breakfast table in the kitchen, at the rear of the house. He walked around to a side door that led directly off the kitchen, and knocked.

A woman answered.

"Hello," he said, "I notice you're eating breakfast."

She said, "No thanks" and began to shut the door.

Quickly before it closed, he said, "Are you sure the food you're eating is safe?"

The door halted, opened slightly. "What did you say?"

"Trans fats?" She invited him to step inside.

She had read the newspaper report, too. She was worried. Everything she bought, it seemed, had the artificial fats in them: breakfast food, cookies, potato chips.

"If my candidate is elected, he will work tirelessly to ensure that trans fats are eliminated from processed food everywhere in this country."

"Well," she said, "that's something to think about."

"Did you know," said Adam, now holding the attention of the entire family, father in shirt and tie, coffee cup poised, cooling, in mid-air, three little girls looking at him as if he were all the members of their favourite boy-band, "that for every calorie of food we eat, we burn ten calories of petroleum?" How far was going too far?

"I have to go to work," said one of the girls, who looked to be about ten. "I mean school."

A younger sister laughed. "You said work! Where's your briefcase? You said work! Ha, ha, ha!"

The third daughter joined in and the parents told them to be quiet, to finish their cereal and get ready for school, which was not regular school, the youngest clarified, but day camp. They called it school because they spent most of the day inside their regular school building, learning how to design robots using a computer and then assembling the automatons and testing them. "I'm going to be a robot when I grow up," she said without irony. She was seven and made her 'bots out of programmable Lego components.

The family was stalled in that inertial stage immediately preceding egress. Adam felt like an intruder. "I'll be on my way."

The father got up and left, his daughters trailing behind him to the bathroom, leaving the mother intently reading the ingredients listed on the side of the breakfast cereal box. An aged hound limped arthritically into the room and stood beside the woman, leaning against her for support.

"Good bye and thank you for your time. I'll let myself out."

She gave no response. When his hand was on the handle of the screened door, she said, "Do you have a card?"

All he had was LB's election pamphlet, which she held with the hand not holding the cereal box. She flipped the pamphlet absent-mindedly against her thigh.

"I was thinking," she continued, "maybe I would... volunteer?"

The campaign phone-number, he pointed out, Mrs. Fallingbrooke's, was printed on the pamphlet. "You can reach me there. I mean, us. Reach us there."

"Who's *us*?"

"The Party."

"To whom I am speaking?"

"Pardon?"

"Nothing. Lily Tomlin. An old routine," she said.

"Ah." He knew he would never see her again. Why, then, did he not want to leave? She fanned her face with the pamphlet. Where was the rest of the family? She looked down then up, directly into his eyes. It was the heat. It was being so many days in unfamiliar territory. It was the seduction of the election race. She was an attractive woman, older, not that much older than he was. Her husband was just down the hall. Her legs were bare, her feet in open-toed shoes. Strapless. She would do anything, answer phones.

Lick envelopes.

"I can reach you at this number?" she asked.

"You should come to my country," said LB as they stood on the grand wide porch of a large house in the city's south end. When LB rang the doorbell it made a musical chiming that resounded throughout the house. "You will see the plague orphans and then you will know. Your head and your heart will fill the same place, perhaps for the first time in your life."

Adam tried to picture his head and his heart cohabiting somewhere in the middle of his body. Man with head poking out from chest, pulsating with the rhythm of drumbeat heart. Maybe a mind so intimately positioned, sea-surge of pumping blood flooding, would better function, better feel, better know the fundamental truths.

In LB's country as many as six hundred people were dying every day of malaria and AIDS. He rang the bell again. "Think upon that, Adam of the silver spoon."

"Stop calling me that."

"A matter of relativity, my son, a relative matter. My father was a goatherd. To him you are one of the white gods, as alien as if you had fallen to earth in a burning chariot. This," he said, gesturing to indicate the wide portico, its neo-classical arches, mullioned windows, slate roof, pink-marble facing, "is a palace."

No one was answering. "We should go, don't you think?"

"Yes, it will be my first official junket at the taxpayers' expense. You'll accompany me as my events coordinator."

"I meant we should move to the next address." Was he incapable of being understood?

LB rang again, a prolonged chime followed by a series of quick angry pulses. "A house like this is never empty," he said. "How could it be? An entire village from my country could live here." He shook his head and grinned, a mixture of incredulity and childlike faith.

After the echo of the last ring had ended, they heard the precise click of hard heels and saw a figure approach. It was distorted through the facets of the narrow mullioned windows on either side of the massive wooden door, which reminded Adam of the door of an English manor or an Austrian chalet, where Blofeld brings the captive 007 and teases him with beautiful untouchables, an improbable harem, before locking him in an ingeniously life-threatening space, one involving rising waters, sharks, shrinking walls, thick constrictors, venomous spiders, electricity of lethal voltage, suffocating foam.

A primly dressed woman of middle age opened the door. She wore an apron but not one Adam associated with a servant's habit. This one was too feminine and personal for such livery, he thought, remembering Alexei's term for passenger-rail cars. It was flounced and spotted with the remnants of past culinary experiences. Something about the woman's face as she looked up at them indicated that these had been triumphs rather than defeats.

"Yes?"

"Madam, how extraordinary to meet you!" said LB, who introduced himself and Adam, his colleague, "a man of vast political acumen," and stated the purpose of the call.

"Oh, I'm not political."

"Do you buy food?" said Adam.

"What kind of a question is that, do I buy food?"

LB jumped in. "Do you drive a car, buy gasoline, give blood, rent videos, vote in elections, take hot baths, produce garbage, convince your husband—"

"I'm not married."

"Effusive apologies, madam."

"He died four years ago."

"Extreme condolences."

"What exactly...?"

"My point, dear lady, is that you are no hermit subsisting in the desert. Your presence in society is in itself a political act."

"I can give you ten dollars. That's all I have. Then will you go away?"

"Dear madam, exquisite lady—"

"Stop calling me that. Make him stop calling me that. I'm just the same as—we weren't always—my husband was smart with money and he was lucky. You won't make me feel guilty about that."

Adam held up one of LB's pamphlets. "We're only asking for your vote."

"Oh, yes, you're that—I mean, you're not the one from away, the prime minister's man."

"No, LB—Mr. Bliss here—would like to represent you in Parliament."

"Like?" the candidate interjected. "That's a small weak word. Fellow citizen, I would most vociferously represent your interests in the great legislature, your interests alone."

"How can that be, my interests alone?"

"I will think only of you, for your confidence is every vote of confidence, your remarkable face every face I see."

"Is he for real?"

"Sometimes too real," said Adam.

She smiled. "I almost didn't answer the door. I was about to make bread."

"We could come back another time," said Adam.

"I should really close the door. You're just after my money."

Adam touched LB lightly on the elbow to signal that they should move off, but the candidate was moving forward as the woman stepped back to close the door.

"Yes! Your money. Exactly what we are after. Let us prevaricate not a moment longer. Madam, rich lady, bread maker, you live comfortably."

She nodded. "But hardly extravagantly."

"And yet..."

"Yes?" she said, taking the hook, letting it set.

"And yet...I can see that you feel no small burden of guilt about your estate."

"I do not. How presumptuous."

"Oh, but yes you do," insisted LB.

"You're...you're just...wrong! My husband worked himself to death to get where—to get here, and how dare you...?"

"How dare I what, madam?"

"Please go away or I will call the police."

"And they will surely rush to your rescue. After all, look at this scene: a black man on your doorstep, a large, threatening, murderous, *political* black man. Frightening! Horrific!"

"I didn't say that."

"You were thinking it."

"Please go, please, please just go away."

"That it were as easy as that. I can leave your sight, Lady Privilege, but you know I will never leave your thoughts after you close that door. Which, I notice, is still open."

Adam had stepped onto a lower stair and now rose level with his candidate again. He felt he should pull LB away before she began to cry or scream or call for help, but he was also fascinated in that way in which one cannot pull one's gaze away from a scene of carnage or humiliation. She had not shut the door. She looked frightened. To replace the physical barrier between herself and the two men, Adam imagined, would be an even more frightening prospect, for then she would be alone again, and the thing unseen is always to be feared more than the fearful thing in view.

"Your money can do much good," said LB. "You see that, don't you, you see its potential. You have been feeling guilty about it for quite some time."

"No."

"You have."

"No."

"Admit it."

"No."

"What is your name?"

"Laura."

"Admit it, Laura."

"No."

"Yes."

She began to tremble, her whole body, as if an earthquake were concentrated beneath her alone. It lasted a few seconds and then she was able to speak. "All right. Yes. Okay. Yes. I said it. I have all this money and if I gave it all away it would benefit some who needed it, but then I'd have nothing, and if I gave away part of it, there would still be...you know."

"'And the poor we will always have with us'?"

"Well," she said, "yes. It's true, isn't it?"

"No matter what we do, no matter how much we try to change things..."

"You're making me confused. I don't know what I should think."

"What if I were to tell you—"

"No, please don't say anything else. Please go."

Adam intervened, thanking her apologetically and indicating the contact number on the handout. "If you need a lift to the polls or anything. You know. Questions. Just call."

"You can make a difference, Lady Laura!"

"LB, come on, that's it, we're gone. Sorry to have bothered you, ma'am."

The pair walked away. They were due to meet the party's provincial co-ordinator, who was canvassing with the national leader on LB's behalf in a nearby neighbourhood. Then they had a radio phone-in show at noon, a newspaper interview at one, a visit to a senior's facility in the north end at two-thirty, tea at the Dalhousie University faculty club at four. A TV spot on the news at half-past seven. It tired Adam out just thinking about it.

"You shouldn't have brow-beat her like that. It's no different from harassment."

"Young Adam, young Adam, young Adam, one day you will be with a woman and you will understand what I am saying to you."

"I've been with a woman."

"Have you really? Then you know that "close" is a defeat, a failure. That woman wanted me to push her, she needed me to be pushing her, she was not going to get there on her own."

"Get where? We were invading her privacy, making her uncomfortable."

"Precisely. We were bringing her to that state of abandonment that is also a place of enlightenment. She needed our help. She kept her door open, you noticed. I charge you with a task: you will call and invite her for luncheon. I will meet her at one o'clock. Choose an expensive restaurant, conspicuous."

"You think she's going to have lunch with you."

"I know so."

"How?"

"How do I know anything? How did I know you would return to work with us? How do I know I will make my entrance to Ottawa from a helicopter landing in front of the Peace Tower?"

"I thought you were set on a parasail?"

"Unpredictable. Winds change."

Adam called Hannah Pachter, who, back in Ottawa, was distant in tone but cooperative, and by cross-referencing street address, car license number and the woman's first name, she found Laura Bowen's unlisted phone number. It was soon enough after the visit that Laura remembered him when he phoned her, and he was amazed when she agreed to have lunch with LB. They chose an expensive new restaurant that had just opened on Spring Garden Road.

The next evening, Adam was still shaking his head when he got back to Mrs. Fallingbrooke's. He couldn't say which had surprised him more, LB's behaviour during the all-candidate's meeting or Laura Bowen's acceptance of a lunch date with the man.

Each candidate—Don, LB, a university student from Saint Mary's running as an independent, and a member of the Green Party—spoke for ten minutes and then took questions from the audience. LB chose instead of a speech to sing a song in his native tongue, one that had many in the audience on their feet, swaying, laughing, clapping in time to its infectious rhythm, until the moderator of the debate pounded her gavel and called the proceedings back to order. When it came time to field questions, LB scurried off the stage and was the first in line at one of the microphones set up in the aisles.

"Mr. Bliss, you are not allowed to ask questions, you are here to answer them," said the humourless chair, a retired high school principal whose tone indicated that she had been transported in these surroundings, this old high-school auditorium, back to 1969 and the controversy over hair length and dress code. Adam imagined her saying, "The blue-jean dungaree is, was and ever shall be a garment reserved for incarcerated felons."

LB argued that he had a right to ask himself a question.

"Ask yourself a question?"

"Thank you, Madam Chairperson, Your Excellency. Very well, Mr. Lexington Bramwell Bliss, is it true that you have come to this country for the sole purpose of subverting democracy, hypnotizing our young people with your overtly sexual music, your marijuana cigarettes and your lustful body movements, stealing from the haves and giving to the have-nots, turning all weapons into shopping carts, reinstating the welfare state, making the Senate an elected body the sole purpose of which will be to intercept the intrusions of telemarketers, renaming Ottawa "Trou d'Eau," banning the term "blacklist" and replacing it with "white-wicket," and learning how to skate on thin ice?"

They watched as he ran up the aisle, leapt onto the stage, resumed his seat, pulled the table mike closer to him, and answered, "No, no, yes, yes, yes, yes, maybe, definitely and probably."

All was shouting and hooting and gavel-pounding and hilarious pandemonium for a good four minutes until the event appeared to exhaust its fuel and people began filing out, still chuckling, some wiping their eyes with the backs of their hands. Adam had been sitting beside Mrs. Fallingbrooke, who sat with the quiet, proper elegance of someone listening to a sermon, who appeared to be taking it all in, analyzing it, storing it for future use, but who could just as easily have been daydreaming about a shipboard intrigue in the China Sea. Not even LB's antics altered her demeanour.

At one point Adam caught Pookie's eye. She was sitting with her group, his old PMO buddies, on the opposite side of the auditorium. She and Gilles waved back. The others looked Adam's way and turned back to the stage, as if to acknowledge him now were a treasonous act. Emma refused to look at him.

When they got home we found that Monica had left a message on Mrs. Fallingbrooke's machine, asking if he would please return his PMO identification necklace at his "earliest convenience," a phrase she invested with all the weight of a diplomatic communiqué charged with the highest level of concern for the health of future relations between sovereign nations. Adam would keep the necklace, he decided, as a memento.

LB had lunch with Laura Bowen and she gave him a cheque for $50,000 for his campaign. It didn't matter to her that the election was only a day away.

On voting day LB was nowhere to be found. He called a week later from Cape Town to find out how he had done. He was more curious than anything else. He was back home and was going to use the money to build an AIDS hospice.

"What if you had won?"

"Then you would sit in my place. I would appoint you," said LB, who sounded as if he were speaking from the next room.

"I don't think that's allowed."

"Why the blazes not? It should be. I can't be in two places at once. How is my empress?"

Adam told him that Mrs. Fallingbrooke had taken the loss quite hard. LB lost by fewer than two hundred votes. The only consolation was that Don Feeney had not won either. The victor was the first-year political-science student, the independent candidate. His win was a remarkable feat given that most of the city's student population was still scattered, working at summer jobs across the country.

Mrs. Fallingbrooke recovered from the defeat after a night's sleep and a strong cup of percolated coffee. She bought Adam a first-class plane ticket home, since he had had to relinquish the unused portion of his refundable ticket after leaving the Feeney campaign. She told him to do something he had never done before.

"Go west, work in a lumber camp, wash dishes at the Banff Springs Hotel, prospect for gold in the Yukon. Then you should come home and get a job in the city. Not in government and not in politics. Ideas. Publishing. You would make a good editor, Adam."

"How do you know that? You haven't seen me edit or even write anything."

"Trust me. I know. The qualities of a good editor and publisher are ones primarily of character: the ability to judge, to see the value beneath an imperfect exterior, to take a chance, gamble, cross the floor even if by doing so you lose something dear. You crossed the floor, Adam Lerner. You followed your instinct."

"Is he really going to build that clinic?"

"Yes, I do believe he is."

"Then it all worked out."

"Dear boy, I must draw your attention to your annoying penchant for stating the obvious. Please divest yourself of that habit before you undertake your next adventure. I insist."

He promised that it would be the first thing about himself that he would change.

"One final matter."

"Yes?" he said.

"When it is the nadir of winter, and snow and ice are all around you like a hard white coffin, promise me you will have put some money aside—you must earn it, I'm not going to give it to you—to spend a week in the sun. It doesn't matter where: Martinique, Paros, the Galapagos. Go and be warm so that you may return with a full and magnanimous heart. Because, you know, this—what we tried to do here—it's not finished."

Yes, he promised her, he would begin to save his pennies for just that necessary extravagance.

Famous Last Meals

IT WAS CHANDRA'S IDEA that we should call our dinner parties, "Famous Last Meals," each a re-enactment of the final meal of a famous person who had died before the age of thirty. Three friends, acquaintances or family of the soon-to-be deceased would complete the table. I suggested Famous Last Suppers, but Max, a devout Catholic, vetoed it. Beth added that Christ was thirty-three when he died and that no women had been present when he urged his disciples to perform their rite of metaphorical cannibalism.

"Mary Magdalene was there," said Chandra. "Look at the figure sitting to Christ's right in da Vinci's painting."

"That was John the Evangelist," said Max. "He had the face of a girl. Besides, if Mary had been there, the food would have been better."

"She was there and it wasn't to cook," said Chandra with a wink.

Chandra could imbue the driest fact with the urgency of warm, moist, smooth, flushed skin. Knowing that knowledge is sensual she extracted it from obscure niches the way a pickpocket can lift cash out from under a tight garter.

We were discussing, over dessert, the subject of our next month's dinner. When Beth, who had not yet had a chance to play the doomed personage, suggested she be Isadora Duncan,

Chandra pointed out that the dancer had been almost fifty at the time of her death.

"Who made this before-thirty rule?" said Max. "I say we throw it out."

The age restriction did limit our pool of choices. When we first formulated the concept, we had wanted to be able to identify easily with the subjects and also to flirt with mortality. Thirty is the gateway to adulthood. Once past that milepost, we have to leave the nursery forever and accept time's icy breath on the backs of our necks.

I had one foot or perhaps a toe still in the nursery the year I met the reincarnation of Isadora Duncan. I was twenty-three, a recently graduated B.A. with no prospects to speak of. I had spent the summer painting houses. Two houses, to be exact. To the many job queries I sent out, over the course of a fallow fall and winter living once again at home, I got few responses and just one interview, with a business-reporting firm in Toronto. My lack of knowledge of the world of business was to my naively optimistic mind no impediment. To make a good first impression I bought a navy blue blazer with a faux nautical crest on the pocket, grey flannel trousers with wide cuffs, and a new pair of Italian shoes, black, pointy-toed and half a size too small, the salesman having convinced me that the supple leather would quickly stretch with use.

On the phone the woman who scheduled the interviews had said, "Expected salary. Ballpark."

I guessed a figure.

"Excuse me?"

"Is it too low?"

"You are aware, aren't you, of the kind of work we do?"

I wasn't, even after looking through the company's prospectus for that year. "You rate businesses. You write reports and the like."

"Why don't we try again," she said.

"You predict market trends? You're a consumer watchdog?"

"What do think would be a reasonable starting salary, given your..." I heard the rustling of paper, then her dismissive sniff, "...qualifications?"

I lowered the number by what I thought was a considerable amount. She made a different nasal sound, repeated the time and place of the interview, which she must by then have been thinking about as potential entertainment for her and her colleagues, and abruptly closed the connection.

I took an early train from Kingston and, never having taken the subway, decided to walk north along Yonge from Union Station to Carlton Street and east along Carlton past Maple Leaf Gardens. By the time I got to the company's office, the backs of my heels were bleeding into my decidedly not supple new shoes and I was walking with an abbreviated and pigeon-toed stride, trying to keep the pressure off my heels by not letting them touch the ground. Barely on time for the interview, I immediately asked to be directed to the washroom.

"Are you all right?" asked one of three men assembled to conduct the meeting.

"Oh yes, fine. Absolutely. I'll be right back."

In the washroom I took off the shoes and gingerly peeled my blood-caked socks away from raw blistered skin. I rinsed the socks in the sink, wrung them out and slipped them on over makeshift bandages made of folded paper toweling. The shoes, when I tried to put them back on, had apparently shrunk. I was not getting them back on without suffering a procrustean adjustment, and so, careful to remove my resumé first, I jammed the shoes into my thin, zippered, leatherette portfolio.

She came through the door so confidently that I was sure I was in the wrong washroom. No, I thought, eyeing the porcelain fixtures on the wall, those were definitely for stand-up types like me. She was about my age and dressed in a well-fitting, summer-weight, light-blue suit with the top made to resemble a Nehru jacket and the skirt short enough, ending mid-thigh, to be covered by the jacket when viewed from behind. Her red hair, almost orange in the soft light coming from recessed pots in the ceiling, reached to the small of her back. In heels she was about an inch taller than I. Her long legs were bare and tanned, with the sculpted calf muscles of a runner or a cyclist.

She smiled and looked down at the wet spot my socks were leaving on the tile floor. I opened my mouth to let her know that I was a visitor, that I was there for a job interview, that I was a Libran, a lapsed Anglican, a romantic, a humanist, a believer in Northrop Frye's literary universe and Joseph Campbell's connective threads of myth, and that I was open minded about most things including the changing roles of men and women and certainly the right of a woman to do whatever she wanted and go wherever she pleased. Custom and law would simply have to catch up. I stood there, a perfect mute.

She moved smartly to the nearest stall, opened the door and removed a few squares of toilet paper from the roll. Then she went to the first urinal in the line, hiked up her skirt, removed her underwear in a deft motion that left me doubting my eyes, turned, straddled the receptacle, leaned forward while thrusting her hips backwards, and relieved herself, all the while looking directly at me as if to say, 'I bet you've never seen anything like this and probably won't again, not for a long time. But hey, stay tuned.'

I was heading for the door when she said, "Where do you think you're going?"

The same sense of impotent propriety that had made me avert my eyes kept me standing there.

"You can turn around now." I hesitated before I did turn, wondering if she was going to be standing there naked. She had smoothed down her skirt and was running a brush through her hair while looking in the mirror. "I was going to do that whether you were here or not."

"That's fine," I replied, thinking that she must not value her job very much. What if I had been someone who worked there? What if, instead of me, her boss had been there?

Two weeks later, after we had become friends and she had begun to unravel every assumption I had ever held about life, thought, social intercourse and love, I did ask her those questions.

"I needed to experience it, that's all," she replied. We were sitting on the grass in Allan Gardens, eating lunch. She was a member of a small new dance company called Red Bugatti. It was research, she said. "If the CEO had been there and called Security on me, well, I was prepared for that, too. Anything can happen. Anything will happen. Be open, Colin. That's all a person can do." The new dance she and her colleagues were learning required several of the women to adopt male personae and postures. I didn't tell her that hers had been the least male posture I could imagine.

My interview, predictably, did not go well. By the time I had returned to the meeting room, I had forgotten about my sore heels and was oblivious to the fact that I was standing in sock feet, pant cuffs wet and dragging on the floor. All I could think about was Jane, what she had done in the men's room and what she said after we introduced ourselves.

"We should eat lunch," she said. It was all of nine-thirty in the morning.

I told her my reason for being there.

"That's fine, I'll wait for you."

"Where...what office do you...?"

"Don't worry, I'll find you. That's one less thing you have to worry about."

"One thing fewer."

"Oh, I see," she said, putting her hand on my shoulder for balance as she slipped off first one shoe then the other, "a grammarian. One thing fewer. This is going to be fun." She kept her hand where it was, then moved it to brush the hair near my ear. I remember shivering. We were standing eye-to-eye now.

"What is?"

"Your transformation."

Isadora Duncan's two children, Patrick, three, and Deirdre, five years old, along with their governess, a Scotswoman named Annie Sim, drowned fourteen years before Duncan herself was killed. The three were trapped in a car that rolled backwards into the Seine. Jane told me this while we drove together in a borrowed car across the Saint Lawrence River on our way to her father's summer place outside of Waterbury, Vermont. The driver, Paul Morverand, had brought Isadora's children to luncheon, at an Italian restaurant in Paris, with their mother and Patrick's father, Paris Singer. Afterwards,

Isadora returned to her studio in Versailles to rehearse. Jane could hardly keep her hands on the wheel as she told the story.

"Imagine. To have that wound the rest of your life. It must never have closed over. And to have had the privilege of owning that grief and sublimating it and directing it in her work."

"You talk as if you envy her."

"Oh, but I do! How could anyone not?"

I looked down at the water as we crossed the bridge at Cornwall, Ontario, and felt an overwhelming vertigo. I was on the verge of telling her to stop to let me out when she continued the story.

On the way home from the restaurant, the car in which Deirdre and Patrick were riding stalled beside the river. When Morverand got out to crank the motor, he realized that he had left the vehicle sitting in reverse gear. I felt an immediate affinity for the man, who had made such a careless, momentous blunder, a mistake that on a level stretch of road would have been inconsequential. Anyone might have done it. Perhaps the slope was not even noticeable. Why had he not engaged the hand brake? I needed more details. Had they just crossed a bridge and were they headed up the embankment on the other side? Had they been following a road that hugged the shore?

We reached the American side of the bridge. We had been four hours in the car and had stopped only once, outside of Belleville, and so pulled into a large gas station and restaurant complex. I looked across the roof of the car at her as she stretched. She clasped her hands behind her back and, keeping her arms straight, bent forward so that her interlaced fingers pointing skyward were all of her that remained visible.

Although I failed to get the job with the business-reporting firm, one of the interviewers, sensing that I was not at my best that day, took pity on me. He was the most senior of the three men and wore a better-tailored version of my hopelessly conservative ensemble. He escorted me out, rode the elevator with me to the lobby, and as he shook my hand goodbye gave me the card of a small publisher located three blocks north. "Use my name," he said. "They owe me a favour or two."

I thanked him. As the man turned and walked back to the elevator, Jane emerged from where she had been sitting in a chair behind a large fern. Still barefoot, shoes in hand, she asked me how the interview had gone.

"I think it went pretty well. We put on dresses and watched porn. Then we tried out some different bidets."

"We'll go back up and I'll explain everything to them. I'll demand they give you another chance." I almost believed she could work that miracle. I told her about the kindly old gentleman and the lead he'd given me. "More up my particular alley."

She repeated that she was starving. She knew of an organic restaurant not far from there. "Take those off," she said, pointing at my socks. She grabbed them, yanked the shoes out of my portfolio and threw them all into the first trash bin we came to. A few doors down the street she pulled me into a shoe store, where she bought us each a pair of sandals. "Isadora never wore shoes," she declared.

In the restaurant she took hold of my feet one at a time under the table. "These are the most important part of a dancer's body. Cramp the toes, allow the arch to fall, fail to keep all the joints, ligaments and tendons in tone, and your entire instrument seizes up." As she massaged, she told me what each pressure point on the sole governed. "This is connected to your liver. Feel that? It's helping drain the toxins away."

"I don't really..." I bit my lip. Gradually I relaxed. She took some hand cream from her purse and rubbed it into the raw blistered area at the backs of my heels. I closed my eyes. She talked about movement the way an evangelist speaks rhapsodically about prayer. "You're so tight. You hold too much in," she said, pressing suddenly on a spot on the ball of my left foot. A tongue of pain flicked at the base of my skull and I cried out. "See how locked you are?" she said.

Our food arrived, and while we ate she showed me how to stretch my neck and shoulders. Going rag doll, as she called it, I let my head hang loosely so that my chin dropped towards my chest. Jane reassured the waitress that I was not having a stroke. I brought my shoulders to my ears, released them and thought about her stunt in the washroom. What sort of person had to experience everything? If I held out my hand, would she nuzzle or bite it? Our food disappeared. I didn't want to leave. She talked about dance, how it felt to exhaust herself in rehearsal, lose her identity in the role, learn each movement and sequence, not as something stored in the mind but as a memory held in each cell of each muscle of her body.

The day before she died, Isadora Duncan reportedly saw a girl who reminded her of her daughter. "I cannot live in a world where there are beautiful blue-eyed, golden-haired children," she told her friend Mary Desti. When I reported the details relating to the death of Isadora Duncan's children, Beth immediately wanted our next Last Meal to be that fateful lunch in 1913. It had been April, the city unfolding in soft floral splendour.

"Did you know that Mary Desti was the mother of Preston Sturges, the 1940s comic filmmaker? *The Great McGinty*,

Christmas in July, *The Lady Eve*. He helped keep America's mind off the war. One of the first to make the transition from writer to director, and for a while, until booze and his restaurant, The Players, diverted his attention away from the screen, the highest paid person in Hollywood. Did you also know that the word 'restaurant' originally meant a purgative?"

We looked at Chandra with a mix of incredulity and hilarity on our faces, for we knew that she was never wrong and that her sense of comic timing was never left to chance. "Restoratif. All the rage during the reign of *le Roi Soleil* and successors, right up to the nineteenth century. People sometimes had three and four enemas a day." As she had meant to do, she had punctured our paralytic unease: the last meal of an adult, especially that of a dying or condemned person, is difficult enough to contemplate, and we were finally steeled to the unsettling though strangely erotic reality of these poignant scenes; the last meal of two innocents who would die so soon after a joyful though brief sojourn in the company of their parents, was so utterly not right, so unalterably bleak, as to negate any sense of the social gusto sought by our quartet. This was too far in the wrong direction away from thirty. This did not remind us of our mortality. It didn't make us thankful for each day we had lived blissfully beyond the age of five. It made us lose our appetite for the entire conceit.

"Then," said Max, ever the restorer of order, "let us re-enact *le dernier répas de la Belle Duncan*, as we first planned."

"She and Mary had a light meal together at a restaurant near their hotel in Nice," said Chandra. "Just the two of them. Then they returned to the hotel to wait for Benoît Falchetto, the race driver, to deliver Isadora's new vehicle, probably an

Amilcar. People think it was a Bugatti, but that might have been just the nickname she'd given it in the showroom."

"This is silly," said Beth. "She's too old, her children were too young, there were only two at her last meal. We're none of us, except for Colin, all that wild for French cuisine. Let's start over and pick someone whose last meal we can enjoy."

I almost said something then about our taking undue enjoyment from the suffering and ultimate demise of others. What were we really gaining by this? Rarely were these meals—those of the doomed—anything to stir the imagination or the palate, and often we embellished generously upon the entrees Chandra found for us to cook. We had to. Usually the subject was so ill that he or she could no longer eat. Often the food was irredeemably bland. Nevertheless, I voted for a re-enactment of the Duncan case, mainly because I saw how dearly Beth had her mind set on it.

I was trying hard then to be accommodating. We were seeing a marriage counsellor, a woman highly regarded and sought after for her sensitivity, compassion, tact, intelligence and common sense. She saw, for example, that I was a typical fixer, someone who strove immediately for a solution to a problem. Beth, on the other hand, needed to talk at length about how any given difficulty made her feel, and her need to do so was not necessarily, as I had erroneously perceived it to be so, an attempt to rub my guilty snout in the particular dirt of the moment.

"Beth is not blaming you for the way she feels. She is not punishing you when she asks you to please sit beside her and listen, just listen. This is merely, but let me add, crucially, her way of talking through to health."

One day we watched a TV profile of Jane—she had become Jacoba Wyndham by then—who declared that Isadora was not only her muse but that she was the present-day embodiment of the iconic modern dancer. "Do you mean you believe you're the reincarnation of Isadora Duncan?" said the interviewer, his low, hypnotic voice betraying his skepticism. "Yes," she replied, "I do."

My memories of Jane came flooding back, after years of successfully keeping them buried. Yes, Isadora reincarnate, *sans doute*. Duncan was the perfect subject for our Last Meal series of intimate dinners, for was she not physically and emotionally forever an Under-Thirty? Who was I to stomp on Beth's choice? She wanted Isadora? Hell, I decided, for the sake of our happiness, she would bloody well get Isadora. The one nagging question was how to get Isadora without Jacoba tagging along, too.

Beth wanted children. I was pretty sure I didn't. We talked about it, becoming beached on shoals of impasse, not necessarily stalemates, but points beyond which I refused to venture any farther into that theoretical territory without a strong drink, a long sleep, a forty-minute trudge in the snow, or all three in succession. The Jane I knew adored children. Who knows if Jacoba did? Her dance, *Demolition Nursery* would suggest otherwise. Isadora died to a large extent the day her children drowned, and, in retrospect, I found much of what Jane used to say, about being jealous of Isadora's wound and wishing she had a similar grief to swaddle and feed and mainline into her performances, an elephantine load of crap.

A knee injury sidelined Jane the summer we met, and she was forced to drop out of the company. The equivalent would be a writer no longer able to fashion sentences or a scholar no longer able to remember what she had read two minutes ago. Jane spiralled quickly downward after leaving Red Bugatti. She got prescriptions for antidepressants but never followed their regimens for more than a week at a time, complaining that the drugs left her unable to feel anything except the sharp pain in her knee. She had a series of operations on the joint, each of which "fixed the one problem but fucked up the perfectly good part beside it," to quote the patient.

I wondered if this was the incipient Jacoba Wyndham finding her voice from somewhere deep inside the miasma of her pain. The nadir of her dive came when she got herself admitted, against her will and because of an incident in an elementary school where she was the visiting artist that day, to custodial psychiatric care. Allegedly she stripped and danced naked atop the desks of a classroom full of Grade 5 children before cowering, muttering gibberish, beneath the teacher's desk. I went to visit her in the locked ward and found her perched on the inside sill of her cell's high window, a remarkable feat attesting to her still extraordinary balance, given that the sill was barely five centimeters wide. I asked her repeatedly to come down and talk to me. I left forty minutes later without having been able to engage her in eye contact and without hearing her say a word beyond a low cooing sound that was somewhere between a purr and a gargle. If her knee was bothering her as she crouched so precariously on that ledge and looked out, fingers jammed into the metal mesh obscuring the colourless sky, she did not give any indication of pain.

I didn't understand why she couldn't pull herself out of this hole. I'd seen her confront, with the same fearlessness, policemen, bank managers, beggars and aloof passers-by, seducing them all with charm and guileless optimism. Where was my bright warrior now? How dare she give up and hide?

You've probably figured out by now that I wouldn't have felt so indignant and abandoned and hopeless over Jane's breakdown if I hadn't been in love with her. We fell in together the day we met, allied from the moment we thumped up the stairs to the three tiny rooms comprising Wolf Moon Press.

"Don't look too needy," she said. "Sniff around a bit. Let them see your condescension. Make them realize how blessed they are going to be to hire you."

The publisher, Myron Saukville, a distracted man in shirt-sleeves, worn brown corduroy trousers and carpet slippers, frowned when I handed him his own business card.

"The man who referred me to you, his name, it's there," I said, turning the card over in Saukville's hand. He read the handwriting and furrowed his brow even more.

"Ah, his marker. The Black Spot."

"I'm sorry?"

"I don't suppose you have any publishing experience."

"I'm a pretty good proofreader." I was not.

Saukville said that his second editorial director in a month had quit on him, leaving him alone to fill a contract for three thousand copies of a mail-order catalogue for a company that sold replicas of American Civil War miscellany: uniforms, tents, camp desks, canteens, tools, rifles, pistols, knives, swords and the like. The catalogue, yet to be designed, was due to the printer in less than three weeks.

He looked through the pages of my CV for a second and a half, mumbled something about my probably being able to figure it out. "It's not difficult work. I can't pay..."

"That's all right," I began to say.

"He's not working for free. That's a line we don't cross."

At "we" Saukville raised his eyebrows and peered at Jane over the top of his glasses. "You've come with your agent, I see. Much. I can't pay much. Minimum wage to start. Maybe after this catalogue job we'll see where we're at."

"I'll take it. I won't let you down. I'm an exceptionally quick study. You'll see." With Jane there I felt fearless.

I began working twenty-five hours a week for Wolf Moon Press. Myron Saukville proved to be sharper, kinder and more interesting than I'd assumed the man was. A book of poetry the press had published had won a major prize in Italy. Saukville was a champion of new Canadian poetry. The commercial contracts—catalogues, brochures, flyers, family histories, vanity projects—almost paid for the chapbooks and hundred-page short-story collections he published. Rather than peer over my shoulder all the time, he let me make mistakes on the job and correct them. To a point. If it was going to cost money he couldn't recoup, Saukville intervened, cutting me off from disaster, showing best how something should be done, whether it was a matter of laying out text and graphics together on a page, working with colour reproductions, handling phone calls from creditors or deciding which bills to pay and which to transfer to the bottom of the pile.

Poor doomed Deirdre's father was Gordon Craig, the brilliant, uncompromising theatrical designer. Patrick's father was Paris Singer, heir to the sewing machine fortune. Nine years after her children drowned, Isadora met Sergei Esenin, the poet laureate of the Russian Revolution. He was twenty-seven, she, forty-four. He was an alcoholic egotist prone to depression and delusions. Against her beliefs—she considered matrimony a woman's prison—they got married to avoid being hassled when they travelled to America, where anti-communist paranoia was fervid. They were still detained, interrogated and threatened with expulsion when they disembarked at Ellis Island. By October 1923, after travelling together in Europe and America—Esenin particularly despised New York—their relationship was finished. They never divorced. In December 1925, after signing himself into an alcohol-abuse clinic, he left suddenly and checked into Leningrad's Hotel d'Angleterre. In the same room where he and Isadora had stayed, he burned all his manuscripts, opened a gash in his wrist, dipped the nib of his pen into the blood and wrote a farewell poem that ended, "In this life, dying is nothing new, / But living, of course, isn't novel either." Then he hanged himself from the water pipes.

"I am so unhappy," Isadora wrote to a friend. "I often think of following his example, but in a different way. I would prefer the sea."

When Jane told me this story we were on the Toronto ferry, returning to Harbourfront from Centre Island. It was the Sunday of the Canada Day long-weekend and the boat was crowded with people who looked as if they had enjoyed too much of a good thing. Faces around us on the upper deck, where we sat looking back at the islands, were sunburnt, drowsy, boozy, happy. A man was teaching a young boy a complex clapping game. Two teenaged girls dressed identically in shorts and halter-tops tossed breadcrumbs to a squadron of hovering gulls. The vessel, sitting heavy and square, ploughed ahead through the chop, surprising us with the occasional plunge into a deep trough.

"Why are you with me?" I asked her. "I'm nothing like the people you admire or work with."

"I told you the first day. You're the ideal candidate for reconstitution."

"What if I don't want to change?"

"Of course you do. You have a poet's soul. You were born to live a large life."

"I don't feel it. You want me to be Isadora's crazy Russian."

"Not crazy. Too sane. He saw too clearly. He saw what a futile chicken-run this life is."

"It's not. You don't know what you're saying." But I was unsure, also. The sunny, brave, out-there Jane I'd known for the past few weeks wouldn't make such an existentially bleak statement, would she? We'd spent every free moment together. She'd found me a bachelor apartment in the same building where she shared rent with two other dancers. Vacated for the summer by an actor performing at the Shaw Festival Theatre, the tiny sublet had a kitchenette, a Murphy bed, two old leather armchairs from the lobby of a defunct hotel, a toilet and a shower stall. Every week I changed the roach traps. I bought a small electric fan to use during the hot nights, and when that wasn't enough I squeezed out the window and onto the fire escape. Jane's apartment sat two floors above mine and on the other side of the hallway. One night, while I sat on the fire escape and drank beer from the bottle, she joined me from above.

"I was going to surprise you," she said.

"You must have come over the roof."

"Do you know you have a disagreeable penchant for stating the obvious?"

"No, but hum a few bars and I'll wing it. And it's *penchant*."

She grabbed my nose and squeezed. "Try it now, priggyboy. Pon-shaw, pon-shaw!"

I wriggled free and she helped herself to a long swig of my beer. She was wearing almost nothing, a camisole and the briefest imitation of the boxer shorts I had on. I told her that if she hadn't shown up in the next ten minutes I was going to make my way up to her window.

"Oh, were you now, my bare-chested gallant? My Cyra-nose."

We sat on the steps of the fire escape all night. Though I went inside and got us another two bottles of beer, she insisted on drinking from the one I was holding. She would wait for me to begin taking a drink before grabbing my wrist, halting the bottle a breath away from my open mouth. "I adore that look on your face, Colin, so noble, so intelligent."

"I thought you didn't put poison in your instrument."

"I don't," she said. "Beer is an essential food group."

"Food group, is it? Fascinating."

"That's correct. It contains all the necessary nutritive yeasty fluids."

"All. Yeasty. Fluids. Check. Continue."

"Yes, all emulsions of that kind, naturally occurring and artificial. Man-made or should I say woman-made? Well, hello there. Is this Aquarius ascendant?"

I excused myself and passed as quickly as I could without injury through the window. Nothing in the bathroom, not cold water, not the smell of the toilet or the chlorine cleanser, not even the most disagreeable thought, could alleviate my sudden tumescence. When I came out of the bathroom, she was sitting on the edge of the bed.

"How do you know you won't wake up inside the wall every morning?"

"I don't. That's the thrill of a fold-down."

"With two people there would be less chance of that. I would think. Did I say that correctly? Less?"

"A-plus. Yes, more weight is always desirable."

"Am I a desirable weight, Colin?" She said it in such a tentative quiet mouse voice that I almost looked around to see if someone else was speaking.

I had never wanted anyone or anything more. I told her so.

"I thought as much."

"Jane."

"Shhh. Don't. Just get over here." I wanted her to add something like, "before I lose my nerve" or, "please" or, "if that's what you want, too," something to make her that smallest bit less confident and me an equal measure more so.

Chandra and Max Nazreen had two children. Beth and I didn't babysit them, not because it would have been a chore—they were delightful children and Beth loved to get her hands on the baby whenever she saw him—but because we were afraid that providing such a service, stepping up in a pinch, might compromise the friendship. We would, of course, have refused compensation, leaving the door open to the suggestion that we were being taken advantage of, although none of us in the foursome was a strict accountant in that way. We were always bestowing gifts on each other, of food, new dishes we had discovered, great finds of wine, fresh flowers, travel trinkets, toys for the children, toys for the adults. It was a good balance of intimacy and respect for privacy. We were not like those four-cornered friendships that topple because one-half of the square becomes a parenting unit.

One reason for this gyroscopic sense of balance was that Chandra, the emotional center of our tidy square, expertly compartmentalized. When she was with Beth and me, with or without Max, her concerns were always adult. She refused to be one of those mothers whose brains become single-issue receivers and transmitters of all things infantile. To draw again upon the image of the nursery, Chandra was in adulthood still very much like a child, jealously guarding her free time when she wasn't lecturing or supervising graduate students. Max, an insurance underwriter of African art and artefacts, specialized in being out of town. Chandra taught four days out of five, barricading the fifth, whatever weekday was free that term, as her personal day. For a time she devoted it to horseback riding until a fall ruptured a disc in her lower spine.

Usually we would meet on Friday at lunchtime. The trysts were exciting at first, always delightful, respectful, adult, carefully wrapped in a mantle of performance, never dissolving into acrimonious pleading or character assassination. We didn't throw things. We didn't talk about Beth or Max. We made no reference to her children or anything remotely personal, unless it had to do with our research or the courses we taught or Famous Last Meals.

Once, when the approaching re-enactment was going to have a Hollywood theme, with Max attempting his best Rebel Without a Clue as the actor James Dean, she asked me if I thought other women found Max attractive. He was more Sal Mineo than Jimmy Dean in appearance and manner, but he was a superb mimic, and without his glasses he could, conceivably, in the right light, be said to have been handsome. I told her so.

"Handsome and attractive are not always the same thing," she said as she brushed her hair in the mirror. We were sated. I was still in bed, unmotivated to return home to my considerable dung heap of marking: post-colonial critiques of *Heart of Darkness*. Inexplicably, or perhaps not, the thought of having to grade those essays reminded me of the first time I saw Jane Burden dance.

The venue was a crumbling community hall, a First-World-War-era building meant to have been temporary but so sturdy it remained standing after newer structures around it were razed. It's there today and has had many incarnations: army drill and recruitment hall, homeless shelter, health clinic, government office, storage facility, youth drop-in centre, daycare, new-age temple, even a repertory movie house for a spell. The paint on the high arching ceiling was unfurling, plaster dropping in chunks, the radiators clanked loudly in winter when the boiler was working, and in residence were generations of rodents so used to people that they were said to occupy empty chairs during performances. Poets came here to stand on the low risers at one end of the long space and read from their precious pages. The acoustics were good. Theatrical productions, if they were not ambitious, could be carried out there. The space seemed best suited to rallies and massed suppers. A benevolent society still serves a meal to the indigent there on Sunday afternoons.

The first time I watched Red Bugatti perform, it was a hot day, one buried like shrapnel in the sweaty flesh of similarly unrelieved days and nights that stretched ahead and behind for weeks. The temperature rarely dropped below thirty degrees Celsius the entire summer, and the humidity stayed jammed near one hundred percent or as close as it could get without it causing rain, indoors and out. The rare rainy day brought little relief, contributing to a spike in the humidity without a corresponding dip in the mercury. A fan in the high ceiling sucked the thick air up and away from the audience. The wooden folding chairs we, an audience of nïne, sat upon looked to be the same vintage as the building, but they were sound though thinly padded. The hall's dim lighting was augmented by stands of theatrical lighting set up above and to either side of the stage and along the wide central aisle, where much of the performance took place.

I took a seat on the left side of the center aisle as one faced the "stage," and about halfway back. Red Bugatti was performing a piece that can only be described as industrial techno-grunge, a posture already a decade out of style in the music-video world but which, because it dressed the gyrations of the street in the weeds of art (Johannes Pittfield Paul, the company's choreographer had taken master classes with Peggy Baker, Danny Coleman and Sylvaine Delacroix), was supported by funds from all three levels of government.

Jane was unrecognizable and in her role unintelligible. I knew by then just how flexible she was. Without warning she could kick a leg up over her head and lean its full length vertically against a wall, stretching there as if doing the splits on the floor. The few times she came into my bed that summer she used her considerable suppleness to felicitous effect. Having this intimate knowledge of her body's ability to bend well beyond what most of us think of as its natural limits, I was nevertheless unprepared for the crabbed, torture-chamber-inspired, arthritic pose she was forced to hold, moving only when moved—rolled is the more precise term—by another performer. I didn't know who or what she was supposed to be portraying. Neither was the story of the dance ever more than fleetingly evident. Story is too bourgeois a term to be applied to the aesthetic that night. Even to admit responsibility to the audience, to fulfill the tacit communicative contract, reaching past the fourth wall to bridge the span between conception and execution, to translate, to be understood—this bunch wasn't stooping to any of that.

At one point Jane, clad only in a kind of loose cloth diaper, her breasts and shoulders smeared with veins of blue paint, was rolled by a male dancer down the center aisle. She came to a stop against an empty chair two rows ahead of mine and moved her head just enough to clamp her mouth onto its leg. A computer governed by a random program was generating the "music," and whenever it squealed with deliberate feedback Jane let out a corresponding loud moan, all the while keeping tight hold on the chair. If the seat still exists, her teeth marks are there. Her legs, flung back behind her head and crossed in a half-lotus posture, her shoulders positioned in front of the backs of her thighs, created the sense of two separate sets of body parts put together terribly wrong, by an inebriate or a Dr. Frankenstein with a demented sense of humour. I tried to watch the performance and ignore Jane. I was unsuccessful in both.

Later I would recall brief snatches of imagery from the rest of the dance: a woman simulating giving birth as she crouched on a chair being held aloft by two men; a couple, male and female, slapping each other rhythmically on the face, endlessly, each whack coming hard with the same palm against the same reddening cheek; a group of three forming a closed hoop that rolled around the perimeter of the hall continually until the performance ended. As with Jane's character, each dancer produced startling sounds that came like the emanations of a madhouse and had no discernible connection to either the movements of the artists or the theme suggested by the title of the piece.

Afterwards she asked what I had thought of the performance. "I was enthralled."

"You were?"

"Definitely."

"I detect a tone."

"No, no tone. I believe I am tone-free."

"It left you feeling uncomfortable, I can tell."

"Yes, but you opened my eyes."

"Really?"

"Really, yes."

"To what?"

"Well, to a new way of perceiving, for one thing."

"New way of perceiving what? I'm curious." This could not end well.

"Pain," I said after too long a pause. "A new way of perceiving human pain and suffering in all its various guises." She was expressionless. Say something, I thought. Nod your head. "Yes," I blundered on, "how often do we pass by our fellow humans oblivious to their pain? The frozen mask, the hunch of the shoulders, the cramp of an uneven stride, the stiffness of an arm that won't swing. These are all the indications we have. But your dance. Your dance made me..."

"...feel others' pain." Even after saying this she was revealing nothing.

Certain now that I had expressed a colossal misread of the dance's meaning and had been blind to the themes of connection and healing implied by the title, I began to think I should admit that I had neither enjoyed the dance nor understood it.

"Jane," I began, abducted by the urge to confess, "what I mean to say is..."

"You're incredible, Colin, you really are."

"You're right." She had seen through me. What did I know about the artistic value of her performance and that of her equally highly trained peers? Who was I but a narrow-minded, thinly educated, introverted lout who knew more about psychiatry than I did about interpretive movement? She could see this. She had flushed me out.

"I have to tell you, I was prepared for you not to like it—it is a difficult piece, making so many extraordinary demands on dancer and spectator both—and I guess I was braced for the possibility that you might not get it completely, but—"

"Jane, I know, and I'm so sorry."

"You're sorry? About what? I was going to say—"

"Oh. Then I shouldn't have interrupted. Go on."

"But why are you sorry?"

"I'm not."

"You just said you were."

I had run out of ground cover. "I was starting to say that I'm sorry I didn't—"

"But don't you see? You did!"

"I did?"

"Yes. You expressed it beautifully. I wish I had recorded Johanne's words during rehearsal so that I could play them to you now. What you said, you know, about pain being at the core of all miscommunication, it's, I kid you not, almost his exact words. It was like you were listening in on us. You weren't, were you?"

Too stunned and relieved to reply, I jigged my eyebrows a couple of times and grinned with incredulous lips, keeping my teeth hidden. A toothy smile would have given me away. I must have gotten it, then. I couldn't have made it up. All that was secondary. She had been impressed by my assessment. For the first time with her I felt other than a make-work project, a man-in-embryo for a girl to incubate, hatch, nurture and educate. For the first time when I looked at her I didn't feel defensive, my wary eye no longer on the lookout for the expected projectile thrown at me from the wings.

Jacoba Wyndham is better known in Europe than at home. In Germany she is renowned for her punishing performances that can go on for two hours without pause. Audiences there appreciate her uncompromising commitment to her art. Dance purists here in North America dismiss what she does as agonized masochism, even those who remember (or would learn about if they took the time to read beyond her website) the car accident that destroyed her knee. Even the least knowledgeable among us, armed with this telling information, would understand the extent to which she had to change her style to accommodate the injury. She takes her brace off only on stage. The pain is omnipresent.

Critics have called her an original and a fraud, sometimes in the same review. They have never known what to make of her. She refuses to go away, even after such a brutal failure as *Demolition Nursery*. How to describe the effect of that dance? Imagine yourself on a train, not a North American commuter train, an Amtrak or a Via Rail, those cattle cars reminiscent of a Greyhound bus, but the compartment of a European train, the kind with seating for four and access to a common corridor. The train has pulled away from the station and you let out the breath you've been holding, because it appears you have the compartment to yourself. You prop your feet on the seat opposite. Just when you think it's safe to close your eyes, let go of the difficult world, pick your nose or slip a hand down your pants, in comes a woman who has the close-cropped head and bearing of a Marine Corps drill instructor and the clothes of a bag lady, but who moves with the tread and balance of a cat. Instead of taking the seat across from or beside you, she straddles your lap and begins to kiss you with garlic-laced breath. She plucks your eyebrows one by one, criticizes your kissing for being too stiff. She replaces your secretive hand with hers. Her fingernails are ragged and dirty.

In the car on the way home from the hospital, Jane said she wished she'd been hurt in the accident before the performance I watched in the old drill hall. Then she'd really have known what it was she was supposed to have been feeling, as a crab or human pretzel or whatever she was supposed to be, rolled about the floor. I doubted a torn-up knee would have improved her role in that bizarre show. She certainly wouldn't have been able to fold herself into a lewd beach ball. But she was serious. She was the kind of person who would have taken a ball-peen hammer to the joint. To prepare. To get it right.

I had my first inkling of this when I drove with her to her father's house in Vermont. It was the weekend after the performance. As she told me more about Sergei Esenin, I tried to gauge just how far she would go for the sake of art and, nearer my own concerns, what she might expect of me, as a friend, lover and confidant.

The house was composed of two connected log cabins that had been transported across the border from Quebec and reconstructed on the property, making a roomy but still intimate L-shaped space. One of the cabins was two-storied, and the three bedrooms were situated on its upper floor. The large fireplace, kitchen and living room area were in the smaller cabin, which, because its open space concentrated warmth, sustenance and the comfort of two long, deep, blanket-draped sofas, was the place where people tended to congregate. On the ground floor of the larger cabin Jane's father had a study with a sofa bed. Down the hall were a mudroom with laundry machines, a second toilet and a storage room.

Jane's brother Tighe was there that weekend with his girl-friend, Francesca. Tighe was about three years older than his sister, and he and Francesca acted like a married couple. I liked Francesca immediately. Short (she preferred, "compact") with a pretty face, kinky black hair, full hips, round breasts and the faintest hint of a moustache, she had refined the art of nagging into a form of entertainment. She never stopped smiling while she nipped at Tighe's heels. He was built like a pro wrestler, though lacking the proto-human rolls of flesh at the back of the neck, the bullet-shaped shaved head or the long, ape-man tresses. He was so big I wondered if he took steroids. Tighe had a placid nature, however, suggesting that he had achieved his extraordinary muscle mass as a result of exercise, diet and inherited genes. Nothing Francesca said to him ever made him drop his big open grin.

They worked at the same club in Montréal, she as a wait-ress and he as a bouncer. They spoke English with a hint of a French accent. We saw them for supper two of the days, for brunch on the day before we were supposed to drive back to Toronto, and the rest of the time Tighe and Francesca spent riding their four-wheeled all-terrain vehicles along an old rail-road bed.

We did all go swimming together on Saturday afternoon at a nearby quarry. Jane wore a bikini that kept threatening to fall off. "I used to be fat," she explained, adjusting a shoul-der strap. "Fatter." She was as thin as a noodle. She had to hold everything together with her hands whenever she jumped off the edge into the water, a thirty-foot plunge from the top, where we'd spread our towels. Tighe grinned approval for her bravery.

He and Jane had a quiet rapport. They were well past the awkward years of mutual sibling exasperation. Something in the understated, quasi-secretive nature of their exchanges—they often looked away when speaking to each other, as if keeping one ear open for distant signals—spoke of a history of solidarity and mutual dependence.

Their mother lived in rural Connecticut with her second husband, a man she had met in rehab. Their father was away on business somewhere unidentified and would not be joining them that weekend. He worked in Montréal as a planner or architect—he could well have been an engineer; it didn't register with me at the time. Jane said that her father came in and out of their lives, as if he were a distant uncle. The summerhouse had interested him up to the point at which the construction had been completed. Now he was looking for lakefront property in Quebec's Eastern Townships and had his mind set on a house built of straw bales and wattle. Tighe, when he referred to his father, spoke with a dismissive tone: the "old man," the "scatterbrain." "He" had forgotten to stock the beer fridge. "He" had neglected to put gasoline in the ATVs. Again. Jane intervened, reminding her brother that neither had Tighe done any of these chores, and reminding him further of the various maintenance tasks that had to be completed around the property. I had the feeling she wasn't so much defending her father as closing family ranks, keeping private matters private. I was more than a friend, she made that clear from the way she hugged and kissed me in front of the other two, but I wasn't all the way "there" yet. Certain doors remained closed.

I got on easily with Tighe. We found subjects of common interest to talk about, and I never felt from him the disapproving scrutiny of the protective older brother. One of his interests, I was surprised to learn, was stagecraft, Tighe moonlighting as a set builder. Theatrical illusion fascinated him. He loved making something flat appear three-dimensional and fully functioning in a movie. He talked about the art of distressing new objects with paint, dirt and grease to make them appear old. The designer only got in the way. Yes, the vision was necessary, the initiating idea, but a director needed creative, resourceful people who could work with their hands, work with what was in front of them to make something out of nothing. An entire house erected in a morning and torn down before sunset, that was the kind of thing Tighe was talking about, a whole dining room you can pack up and put in a suitcase.

"You should hear them when him and his friends get together," said Francesca, who had wormed her way onto his lap. It was well after supper and we were sitting outside in Adirondack chairs on a sheltered, flagstone patio off the kitchen. "Talk about your hyper-bowl." She and Tighe wrestled playfully for a few seconds, subsided into cuddling, and appeared to fall asleep.

I wondered about the antecedents of this interest in theatrics, in brother and sister. As far as I know, neither of their parents had acted, sung or danced except during family gatherings. Perhaps the talent and compulsion had skipped a generation. Or maybe it had more to do with something that had happened to them when they were growing up. An outside influence? A child never stops trying to get his parents' attention. I asked Jane. Was their approval an easy thing to get?

"No, it wasn't. I heard about it when I didn't achieve to their expectations."

"And when you did?"

"Did what?"

"Achieve."

"Not a word."

"You're kidding."

"No, I'm not. When I got anything less than a perfect mark, my father zeroed in on the one- or two- or five-percent deficit. He would make me sit with him and go over the mistake and re-do the problem until I got it right. To him this was the only real opportunity for learning."

"And for you?"

"In a word: torture. All I could think about and feel was his disapproval, his disappointment."

"Does it still seem that way? Are you able to see through his eyes now?"

"On a cold, intellectual level, maybe. It still hurts."

"He loved you. He wanted the best for you."

"What is this? You some kind of operative? Has he got you working for him now, Colin?"

"I can't believe that his only wish was to punish you. What about your mother?"

"What about her?"

Did she take the same approach? Did she dwell, as their father did, upon the absence rather than the substance?

"Why are you so interested in this?"

Stars filled the black dome. When I tilted my head back it felt as if I could open my mouth and swallow a pail full of them. Light-headed, I said, "It helps me to get to know you."

Tighe and Francesca roused, excused themselves and went up to bed, she leading the way. He held her hand and looked like a slouching bear. Once inside she giggled and then screamed his name in mock outrage. Hearing them on the stairs made me feel jaunty and playful, too. I considered this weekend a turning point in my life. Yes, I was living and working in Canada's largest, richest city. Yes, I was having what I considered a serious relationship with a beautiful uncompromising artist, someone principled, with a locked private side but an intense interest in me. And yet, until this trip away together, I hadn't felt completely on my own. I hadn't really thought I might never go home to live with my parents again. The new me, set-free, flying-up-to-the-stars, giddy with potential, was talking now. I could do anything, say anything, and so I asked again: How did her mother react when Jane failed to live up to her expectations?

When she looked away into the distance the way she had with Tighe, I thought we were going to share a similar inner-circle connection. She leaned forward and up until she was perched on the edge of her chair, let her feet fall heavily to the ground and stood. Still she avoided looking at me. I was afraid she was going to go into the house without saying anything. What should I do then? Should I follow her inside, through the first cabin, up the narrow staircase and into bed with her as I had done the first two nights? Should I wait for a sign? Or should I feel my way to the third bedroom and sleep there? I had no previous experience of this kind on which to base a decision.

That I had pushed too far with my questioning was achingly evident; she didn't need to say anything about that. How do two suddenly separated people find their way back to each other, how do they traverse the yawning space? The continents move steadily, incrementally apart, we don't even notice the drift, and it's easier to let them take us with them than to throw a line backwards to the place we were a minute ago, to the one moving the other way on solid ground.

"Please let's not talk about this anymore," she said. "Not tonight, not tomorrow, not ever."

"You mean talk about her."

"Don't be a prick."

"Excuse me?"

"You're an ever-correcting prig. Were you aware of that, Colin? You push and push and push."

"I only—"

"Shut up. Don't say anything else. This is who you are. You are never going to be anything else, I realize that now."

She went inside, letting the kitchen door slap closed behind her. I sat for another hour, maybe longer. The dew fell cold on my bare legs. The eastern horizon began to lighten. Nothing I could think of could put this back together. Older, with a few more scars on my psyche, I might have tiptoed up to her bedroom, gently stroked her hair, whispered my apologies softly in her ear. I often think about what might have happened, where I would be today, if I had done just that. But I was newly hatched. The shards of shell weren't going back together, the fluff was drying and the fledgling ego was growing at alarming speed. I couldn't get beyond the idea that I was right and she was over-reacting, and Jane, I wanted to say, what about leaning into the teeth of the gale? What about hitching up your skirt in front of a stranger and taking a piss all over his blue suede shoes?

I was tired. She would forget about this by morning. Such was my hope as I made my way, not upstairs but through to Mr. Burden's office and its foldout couch.

I woke late, close to noon. Tighe and Francesca had gone off on their ATVs. At least I assumed they had, because the vehicles were gone. I showered, made a cup of instant coffee and sat at the kitchen table. The day's heat was already penetrating the thick walls of the house. I heard a car approaching from a distance down the gravel road leading to the property. It pulled into the driveway and stopped close to the house. The back door swung open and slapped shut. A man with a grey crew cut and Jane's angular cheekbones and sunken eyes stared at me.

"Who in God's name are you? Where's Tighe?"

I told him my name and that I was a friend of Jane's. When Mr. Burden asked if I knew what had happened to her (not where she was, intriguingly), I replied that I didn't. "Isn't she asleep upstairs?"

"Come with me," he said. I followed him out to the car.

He drove for a long time before he spoke. "You really didn't hear the phone?"

"I'm sorry. I must have been sleeping pretty deeply."

He spoke his thoughts, wondering where his "lunk of a son" had been. "Out tearing around on that infernal noise-maker, no doubt, up at first light, scaring the wildlife into the next county. No wonder the duck hunting's the pits. What did you say your name was?" I told him. "Ah, her latest victim. She's told us all about you."

Who was "us" and what had Jane said? That she had said anything about me was encouraging. She must be fond of me, then, I thought. She thinks about me. She tells her family.

"And you really don't know where we're going?"

"Not a clue."

"When she said, 'Will you go back to the house, please, Dad, and get him?' I assumed she was talking about Tighe."

"Maybe she was."

"Do you know where I was when they called me?"

"Jellystone National Park?"

"Funny. You're a laugh riot, you are. You should work up a little routine, take it on up to the Poconos. No, my young friend, I was on the top floor of a very tall building in Manhattan. As luck would have it, the man I was meeting there keeps a helicopter on the roof. I'm going to have to tell you what they said to me on the phone, aren't I?"

"Not if you don't want to." A passing sign welcomed us to Burlington.

"You know, I think she really did want me to bring her brother instead."

"Did something happen to Jane?"

"How did you ever keep up in school, boy? 'Did something happen to Jane.' Priceless. Do you see that green sign with the big "H" on it up ahead? Well, you keep you eyes peeled for the next one, because there are going to be a series of them, like a trail of breadcrumbs. Did something happen to Jane. Tell me you didn't have anything to do with this stunt."

"I assure you I have no idea what you're talking about."

Jane had been moved from Emergency upstairs into a ward. "You," she said when she saw me. Her father had indeed grabbed the wrong "him." One of her legs was in an elevated cast. She had a black eye, a swollen upper lip, and an abraded face. I asked her what had happened.

"Tighe sat on me."

"They're trying to find a cable long enough to haul your car out of that quarry, Jane. So let's forgo the wisecracks, shall we?"

"Don't lecture me, Father."

"You could've been killed. Let's be somewhat more forthcoming with essential details, please."

"You're only going to get mad at me."

"I'm already there. If I get any angrier I'll pass out. Have you any idea what it costs to rent a helicopter and pilot by the hour?"

"About a dollar?"

He turned to me. "You talk to her. Maybe you'll have better luck. I'm ready to leave her here."

"I wasn't trying to off myself, if that's what you were thinking about. Dad?"

"What?"

"Tell me that's not what you were thinking. At least give me that much credit."

"The car you were driving is sitting in a hundred and fifty feet of water. The road ends about a quarter mile away from the edge of the quarry. What am I supposed to be thinking? There was no ramp, so you obviously weren't trying to jump to the other side. Were you? I didn't think so. What does that leave, then? You thought it'd be keen-o-cool to plunge in a borrowed car to the bottom of a water-filled rock pit, you know, see what it might feel like. Life is obviously not supplying you with sufficient jolts per second."

"This is exactly what I mean," she said, making no attempt to bridge the gap between past arguments and this one. "Everything I do you run down. I could tell you what I was doing, but you'd say something sarcastic the way you always do."

"I want to know," I interjected.

"Operative. Stooge."

"Jane, I'm going down to the cafeteria. If by the time I've returned you have not told your boyfriend what happened to you out there, I promise you I will get back in my Hertz Sunbird and drive away, and you will have to convalesce in this very public ward, and when you are well enough to go home it will be your mother and not I who will come to wheel you out. I have never been more serious."

Unlike the night before, mention of Jane's mother elicited no discernible reaction in her.

"He is always never more serious."

"Did you hear what I said?"

"Yes, Father Dear."

I used to believe that coincidence was merely that, the product of random motion. Max chose James Dean for his starring pre-mortem role at dinner. The night she damaged her knee, Jane Burden said she was trying to recreate the car race scene in *Rebel Without a Cause*, the one in which Dean's character jumps out from behind the wheel before the car he is driving beetles over a cliff. Not so lucky his opponent. As far as I knew, Max had never seen Jacoba Wyndham in performance, and even if he had, I was familiar enough with her oeuvre to know that nowhere in it did she make even the most cryptic allusion to the film. If only her attempt at cinematic re-enactment had been as thrilling as what we get to experience in the movie.

After Mr. Burden left the hospital room, Jane made me swear on the lives of my unborn children that the story I would tell him was that his impetuous daughter, in recreating the famous "chicken" car duel scene from the movie, threw herself out of the car before it plunged into the quarry and sank. Hitting the ground at such a great speed, she broke her knee and sustained minor abrasions and lacerations to the face, head and hands. But above all I was to say that she came away from the experience knowing, really knowing, what it felt like to cheat death. "He'll believe it if it comes from you."

What had really happened, an amateur sleuth could have deduced. A chat with the attending doctor, the one who had put the cast on Jane's leg, would have revealed that the trauma to her knee came not from it striking the ground with great force but from a considerable weight having been applied to it. Given that the dirt road leading to the quarry ended at a locked steel gate four hundred meters away from the quarry, a barrier imposed to prevent the kind of stunt Jane wanted people to believe she had attempted, was it probable that the car was even down there under the water? Deep ditches lined each side of the road. Even if she had been able to circumvent the gate without leaving an important part of the vehicle's undercarriage behind, large rocks strewn about near the old mining pit made speed and a straight-line approach unlikely.

"You mean the car's not down there? Where is it?" I asked.

"Probably in some chop shop in Albany by now."

"Somebody stole it?"

"Not exactly."

She insisted that she had indeed set out, early in the morning before Tighe, Francesca and I were awake, to recreate the film scene in question. Her reason for doing so didn't become clear until much later, when I was able to connect her anger from the night before with a much older wound. As described, the gate was impassable. She backed up and when she directed the car at a sharp angle into the left-hand ditch, the front left wheel sank into the loam. She tried to free the car by spinning the wheels forward and back, only to cause it to sink further, up to the axles in the loose sand and gravel. She was ready to leave it there and walk back when a truck drew up behind her.

A man got out and said he had seen the lights of her car from back on the county road. He offered to help pull her car out, and before she could decline he was attaching a chain and hook from the front of his pickup to the back of her car. His breath smelled of liquor. She was afraid of what he was going to want in compensation. His oil-stained coveralls and grimy baseball cap suggested that he worked in a garage or on a farm. If she could get the man's car keys she might be able to outrun him and get away in his vehicle. Not very likely, she conceded. How to incapacitate him? He looked to be a hundred pounds heavier than she was. Short of clubbing him with a rock on the back of the head, she had no means of escape.

Meanwhile he eased his truck slowly backwards until the chain rose from the road. Jane's car began to move, but it was at such a pronounced angle that it was in danger of toppling onto its side. He asked her to get back into the car and put the key in the ignition so that she could shift into neutral gear and also straighten the front wheels. She did so, leaving the driver's door open. The car began to move with her in it, gradually tilting even more.

"Get out!" he shouted, easing forward, letting slack come into the chain, but both wheels on the driver's side were in the ditch now and the car was on its way over. There was no stopping it. She heard him shouting at her. She couldn't stay on the seat. She hadn't fastened the seatbelt. Climbing up toward the passenger-side door was impossible. Slowly, like something being dumped into a trash receptacle, she slid out.

She tried to scramble up the other side of the ditch before the car fell on her. The man was yelling something. Her feet slipped in the sand and she thought she felt a heavy hand holding her down, pinning her like an opposing wrestler waiting for the referee's ruling. At first, because her adrenaline was up and because she was working to extricate herself, her free leg braced against the doorframe and pushing as she lay on her side, she felt no pain. Then, as her pinned leg moved, she felt tearing and searing in her knee. She screamed.

The man came into sight. He said that he had secured the car with another chain so that it would not move any farther, but she could not picture what he was describing. He said, "Hold on, hold on, don't go anywhere," and she laughed at such a notion. It came out as a groan.

He returned with a car jack, felt around in the muck and began to dig out a depression with his fingers. It took forever. Finally, when she thought she was going to faint from the pain and couldn't be sure she hadn't lost consciousness for a minute or two, he got the jack into place under the car's frame and supported on a flat rock that he had wedged in there.

"I'm sorry this happened to you," he said as he fit the tire iron into the jack and began to crank. The jack opened, expanding on its internal teeth like a little person coming out of a crouch, and the car lifted enough for her to slip out. She was so pumped full of fright and energy that she tried putting weight on the leg and cried out again. She collapsed, striking the ground hard with her face.

The man picked her up and took her back to his truck. He took out a heavy blanket, folded it in half, put it on the ground and stretched her out on it lying on her back. "You sure are pretty," he said. "Don't try and get up."

When she woke she was lying on old pieces of carpeting in the back of the moving truck and was covered by the horse blanket. The sun in her eyes flickered like glinting low fingers slapping along a picket fence of live trees. She couldn't roll over. The knee screamed out at her again. She heard the back window of the cab slide open.

"Where are we going?"

"What?"

She repeated the question three times only to give up, having no louder voice. He was saying something to her. "Where's my car?" She didn't know whether she had thought the words or said them.

As if he had heard her he yelled, "I'm taking you to the ER. Your car is totalled. Sorry. Couldn't get her upright so I had to drag her on her side."

"You can have it."

"What's that?"

"I said," straining for greater volume, "you can have it."

"I didn't do nothing bad to you. When you were out."

Out where? she thought before realizing what he had meant. "Do you have any aspirin?"

"Pardon me?"

"Aspirin. Painkillers. Anything."

He passed a bottle out the window and she reached up to take it. The first mouthful came out too quickly and sloshed over her face. She raised her torso and supported herself on her elbows for the next gulp. It burned all the way down, its warmth spreading. The knee continued to throb, but from a distance now.

They were on a highway that had at least three lanes going in each direction. Cars passed them on the left and the right.

She sipped and slept, woke to find that the bottle had fallen over, losing what had been left of the liquor. Take me far, far, far, far, far, she thought. Away, away, away. It was like being carried by a fast-moving current. A hot spot in her stomach churned. Tall buildings flashed by. Signs with exits, names of streets. She heard horns, sirens, car radios, whining transmissions. When she turned her head to the side, all she had drunk poured out her mouth. She smelled her stomach acids and gasoline fumes, and saw small birds strung on an overhead wire. She closed her eyes.

She opened them when the tailgate dropped with a dull clang and hands slid her out in her cocoon onto a firm soft surface. Metal sidebars came up left and right, clicked in place. Someone wiped the vomit from around her mouth with a cloth. She heard the word, "vitals."

"What's your name, Miss?"

"Jane."

"Jane What?"

"Burden."

"Burton?"

"With a 'd.' D-e-n, as in heavy load."

"Do you know what happened to you, Jane Heavy Load?"

"More or less."

"Sir? Sir? Somebody tell him—no, you have to—hey! Hey! Stop him—I can't believe this—don't let him drive away before he talks to us. Do you know that guy?"

"Who?"

"The one who drove you here."

"No, I don't."

She thought about what he had said: "You sure are pretty. I'm sorry this happened to you. I didn't touch you. While you were out." Miss Jane, while you were out a strange man from a trailer park did not violate you in any way. But he did take the car you were driving. It's only fair, you have to agree. As payment. Of a sort. No, not for saving you, since he was as much a contributor to your injury as you were. This must be the cost of remaining...what? I was going to say, "healthy," but it may not be the best word to describe someone in your condition. Maybe this is the price women have to pay from time to time to ensure that they stay alive. Small price? Certainly, a pittance to pay for one's continued existence. Especially since it wasn't your car to begin with. The person you borrowed it from, understanding bloke, is he? She. Splendid. It did look to be something of a beater. You did her a favour in disposing of it, then. Say it went over the side and down to the bottom. Not even worth retrieving. Let oxidation do its work. Except that the authorities and their representatives tend to be sceptical types. Police officers and insurance investigators and that ilk, they like to see for themselves. Chances are they're going to send a diver or two down with powerful flashlights. Who can say what they'll find? Now, let's go over your story again, shall we.

I waited for the boom to fall. I didn't think it would be anything like a large heavy object falling out of nowhere to smite me for my stupidity. Our stupidity. Retribution of that sort would've been too biblical for the likes of Chandra and me. I was pretty sure Beth knew. Beth and Max were known to phone each other from the folds of their workday, just to say hello or ask a question, about Zulu head-dresses or cold remedies, the latter being her bailiwick. If Max didn't know, then he was more of a deserving cuckold than I assumed he was. Beth would make me pay, in high emotional currency and physical isolation, for What I Did. Beth would never say, "make love." Scots-Dutch hybrids like her are too earthy and straightforward for the likes of that. She liked honest, diligent, hard-consonant Anglo-Saxon words. She would say that Chandra and I had "fucked like two barn cats in heat." Fair enough. I wished she would just come out and whack me with it. It was the waiting that was murder.

I was never sure about Max, who had told me about his junkets to Thailand, his perverse gorging on the young. He even went so far as to tell me about the night he killed the girl he was having sex with. It wasn't his fault, he insisted. We were into our third snifter of cognac in the Cellar, a place to sit by the fire after work on a cold day and avoid going home.

He began by saying that Chandra was punishing him for something she'd learned. Normally she didn't get angry with him for merely being away for a week or ten days at a time, unless he forgot to return with a gift, which he rarely did. She wouldn't have found out about his latest side trip, from Johannesburg to Bangkok, had the airline not left a message for him on their home phone stating a change in his departure time. He tried to explain it away by saying that he had heard about an art dealer who had recently moved his operation from Pretoria to Thailand. Still dealing in the same artefacts as before, carved African masks, the dealer found he could move them in a far greater volume in Asia. It was wobbly, as lies go. Wondering why he didn't tell her that he had gone there to price Thai masks or some such thing, I reminded him that his wife, by dint of being a professor of English literature, was a student of depravity as well as of saintliness, and would most certainly have known why so many European and North American men suddenly had business in Thailand. Sometimes it seemed that Max truly did not know the woman he had married.

Apparently forgetting his wife's ire, he began in that intimate way men have of trying to impress their friends with tales of conquest. He lowered his voice, forcing me to lean closer.

"Their muscle control, it's like nothing you've ever felt, Colin."

"I'll have to take your word for it."

"You're coming with me, next time I go. I'm serious. It will make you believe in heaven. It's beyond comprehension."

"Aren't you afraid of bringing home something bad?"

"You're always dwelling on the negative. I do believe that wife of yours is rubbing her clinical pessimism into you. Speaking of which, have you convinced her to be somebody other than that crazy dancer? One day the bad karma of our little gastronomical skits is going to turn and bite us on our four asses. I picture poor Dr. Beth, robes entangled in the wheel spokes of her motorcycle."

"Sports car."

"Either way, dead."

Without pause Max recounted his most recent junket. He made a point of saying that the girl had been nineteen, the same age as his eldest niece. She was someone Max had been with before, and he asked for her by name. She spoke no English but enough French that they could communicate. She was on top, the most comfortable position for each of them given the difference in body weight. She weighed less than a hundred pounds.

The whore—so ancient a term for one so young—knelt astride Max, facing his feet as he lay on his back beneath her.

I pictured low light, a ceiling fan, bamboo walls, reed mats, a gecko frozen on the wall beside the doorframe.

"My God, the humidity, it is there like a third person in the room," said Max. "No, strike that. It is there like a planeload of British soccer fans returning from Spain after their team's defeat." He had been so slick with perspiration that he hardly felt the girl moving, that is until she tensed those famous muscles.

"I don't know how to explain it. I was anticipating it but she still surprised me. I suddenly have the worst charley horse I have ever experienced, in the thigh near the back of the knee. And man! I have to flex, you know? Or I'm going to fucking scream."

He lifted his leg straight up with a violent jerk, involuntarily, like someone with a jolt of adrenaline lifting a huge weight to extract someone trapped beneath it. The girl, who had been prone, still kneeling but now lying face-down flat on his legs, tickling his feet, playing with his toes, sucking on them, was launched sideways off the bed, a high, European-style frame with mattress and box spring, reserved for the foreign "businessmen." Her head struck the hard edge of a porcelain sink basin at the temple. She probably died immediately.

The police investigation consisted of Max being questioned briefly the next day in his hotel room. The dead girl had no bruises on her body to suggest that she had been in a struggle. It appeared that she had died just as he had described. The policeman said that he had every reason to believe that no charges would be laid.

"No reason to believe," said Max, as if clarifying a point.

"As I said, sir. Any further investigation would be merely a formality."

"Formality. Yes. Ah," said Max, nodding. He reached into his pocket and took out his wallet.

"They love Yankee greenbacks, Colin. Aussies, if you don't have those. First time I tried paying for something with Canadian money the man thought I was kidding. "Kiddie toy," the shop owner said. "Playtime money. Monopoly, yes?""

I didn't ask him how much the girl's death had cost him. "Did you go to see her parents?"

"No."

"Did you even think of it?"

"Of course I thought of it. What good would it have done? Her family probably sold her into the life. It's usually the case: they're farmers with too many hungry mouths to feed. To them a daughter is a liability at home. Sell her to the city. Get something substantial for her."

"Nobody should die that way."

"What way? It was an accident. It couldn't be helped, I told you."

"Really?"

"Yes, really."

"Do you hear yourself talking?"

"Don't. Don't tell me that if I hadn't gone there that she might still be alive, because that kind of cause-and-effect bunk, it's for the birds. Listen. If not me, it would have been someone else, some other circumstance, maybe one not so nice."

"Some other hairy dude with a leg spasm."

"No, some mean bastard with dark issues in his brain. Some venomous rat with a blade."

"This is all becoming so much clearer, Max."

"What is?"

"Your motivation for going there. You're not in it for the sex. It's the power. The danger. You like to picture yourself in the place of the venomous rat. You get off on it. Maybe you get a little rough from time to time." From the little Chandra had told me, Max was a placid, sensitive lover. "Cuddly," was the word she'd used.

"Outside," he commanded, standing, swaying slightly as he sought equilibrium. "You can't speak that way to me. I demand satisfaction."

"Sit down before you hurt yourself. You're pissed."

"Damn right I'm pissed. I'm going to teach you a lesson."

"Oh, you're going to refute my allegation, are you? You're going to prove what a pacifist you are by hitting me. That makes a whole lot of sense, Max."

"You come outside with me, Colin. Colon. Sphinctoid. You come and defend yourself while I proceed to kick your holier-than-thou ass."

He didn't wait for me to respond. I grabbed our coats off nearby hooks, paid the bill with cash, and followed him outside. It was snowing lightly. I put my coat on and held Max's out to him.

"I don't want that."

"Suit yourself."

"No, you suit yourself. Me, I choose shirtsleeves. Now, where shall this trouncing take place?" He peered with exaggerated intensity up and down the sidewalk, his chin raised. He was daring the sagging sky itself to stop him.

His phone rang in the pocket of his overcoat. He stood a few paces away, squinting down a narrow alley between the buildings. I took out the phone and said hello.

"Max? Who is this?"

"Colin."

"Colin? Where's Max? Are you two being bad?"

"We're outside the Cellar. He's looking for a place to fight me."

"Put him on, please."

I held the little device up in the air. "It's your wife."

"You talk to her. You're good at that."

"She would like a word."

"Tell her that we men have some business to attend to. Tell her that for once I choose not to share."

"He says for once he chooses—"

"I heard him. You tell him that I am here, waiting. Remind him that I have tickets, our regular seats at Place des Arts, and the symphony begins in thirty-nine—no, thirty-six minutes."

"The symphony," I informed him.

"Mahler," he groaned. "God help me." He grabbed his coat from me and shuffled in a circle trying to fill his sleeves.

"This isn't over," said Chandra.

"It isn't?"

"I'm talking about you explaining, at some later date and in exact detail, why my husband wanted to strike you with his bare knuckles in a public place."

"Yes," I said, "sure. Later."

"This isn't over," he said as he got into a cab. I pushed his head down the way the police do to protect the captive, and slipped the phone back into his coat pocket.

"Yes it is, you big bully. Just get home safely."

I closed the taxi door and heard him say my name.

"What?"

Tears dripped from both cheeks. He looked at me imploringly, unable to speak. The driver made an impatient noise in his throat. I made sure the hem of Max's overcoat wasn't hanging out before closing the car door and thumping twice on the roof.

About a dancer one must believe this above all else, that the physical laws governing the rest of us do not apply. Thus a leap hangs longer than gravity should allow; a fluid bend, the yew-bow give of it, is in each frame frozen in the eye contrary to its fleeting passage; and a body can pass unchanged through another, be at once repelled and attracted, and can change shape with the elusiveness of smoke. All this we can say about the artistry of Jacoba Wyndham without contradicting a different portrait of her, that of an ugly terrorist upon the stage, for she was that accomplished, that committed to her art, that she could subvert the beauty of her body's genius, make it submit to the most difficult of all aesthetics, one that threatened to exclude her audience and exile her to a far, unreachable place.

Unlike Isadora Duncan or Martha Graham, Jacoba does not draw upon mythology for her dances. To call her a mere contortionist, as have some lazy reviewers, is unfair. Similarly she is more than a shock artist, for she takes the time to prepare both the idea and the ground in which she means it to take root. The root in her case is a killing one, the relentless and indestructible tap that drills into the hardest substance, the least penetrable cant, the ruling spitefulness of our time. Think of Goethe writing about the mind of Hamlet: like a tree planted in a delicate container, eventually it must burst forth, shattering that which has tried to hold it.

When she was still Jane she cracked the husk encasing my mind. Her body combined with mine, setting alive every nerve, teaching it new ways to transmit sense and me to move without movement, to both reflect and be a larger mind, the boundary between our duality erased. Can it be that I had her to myself for so short a time, the eight or ten weeks of a blast-furnace summer in Toronto? How naïve of me to think that I had had her to myself. No one, not her parents, her brother, her fellow dancers in Red Bugatti or her teachers, had exclusive access to or sway over her, exclusive possession of her attention.

In one of her dances, choreographed in conjunction with the Danny Grossman Company to commemorate the thirtieth anniversary of *Les Ordres*, Jacoba illustrates that sense of her being entirely communal, owned by none, shared by all, alone and yet woven into society's cloth. On stage she is backlit, creating an aura around her as she stands in loose-fitting black clothes, a shirt and trousers resembling the Chinese Communist Party uniform. Her face lies obscured in shadow. The light moves with her. It is such a sophisticated piece of equipment that it can be programmed to anticipate her every movement, and yet she has decided to let the halogen spot miss its target now and then, to allow it to shoot out from behind her and smite the audience. It is so Jacoba, this bit of assault theatre. She is always blinding her audience, temporarily, in one way or another, until they have learned to see in a new way. The setting of the piece is unspecified, although it could be a city street. A sidewalk, hot air blowing up from a grate, stirring the folds of her clothes. Had her hair been longer—she cut it short, a severe crew, soon after her accident—it too would have danced in the subterranean wind. And during the entire performance she moves her feet not one step forward or back or to either side. She could be bolted to the floor. In case you are picturing the old Vaudeville gag, that Hope-and-Crosby bit of lame illusion, put it from you, please. What Jacoba did sent such sophomoric stunt-making back to its dim place of origin, namely to the land of the tired, the realm of imitation and artistic bankruptcy. For this is her complex conceit, so simple in execution, so difficult to carry out: she is standing as if bolted in place, a volcanic wind escaping from the rift beneath her, a light that is no sun or moon or any known lamp shining like a laser upon her back. She is as alone as one would be in a desert of infinite sand and yet around her, passing close by her, threatening to climb over her, through her, is the continual progress of bodies, all painted white, harshly so, stone-age, sinewy, angular, made to look emaciated. Their muscles are strings that threaten to snap. Their eyes peer out from deep black sockets. They dance like the flames of a heatless white fire, licking close, never touching, but exerting such a force upon her that she is buffeted in their wake.

I winced at times, so violently did she move. I expected her to be broken, purple welts raised on her skin. I expected her to be heaped on the stage when it was over, mere residue, aftermath, bone pile, something to be swept up and carted away. Oh, I know what you're thinking: how yesterday, how done, the notion that each of us is alone, that we inhabit concrete canyons that trap artificial light and sap energy, that too many of us live and work this way like ants climbing over each other, colliding, breathing each other's foul exhalations, deafened by sirens and screams and unholy prayers, even our dreams invaded so. Who can refute the axiom, now a cliché: we live lonely, soulless, disconnected, over-stimulated, undernourished lives. Woe and woe again unto us.

So do something about it already! Move to the countryside, get a hobby, commit good deeds. Get an air exchanger, earplugs, a vibrator. Take up yoga in a purified, buffered, softened room. Move deeper into the bliss. The ways are many, the techniques proven, for counteracting the destructive effects of modern life. But were it as simple as that. The point, gentle seeker, is that these words go only part way toward conveying the singular experience of that dance, and no synopsis or analysis, no intellectual pigeon-holing is ever going to come close.

Like her character in that performance to come, Jane could find no comfort or refuge in any one person. Being alone with someone robbed her of her ease. Whenever we made love, she had to have the window to the fire escape open so that she could hear the night sounds and, although she never admitted it, to have a ready exit. I wonder if I was the last person she was truly alone with. We were so young. We felt we were old souls, two immortals on our own in a great graphic novel, a kind of cut-out cartoon empire populated by poor, deluded, dull but endearing types who at least were trying to do something worthwhile. Above all else we paid tribute to endurance wherever we saw it: collateral damage from the high-tech sector, stunned babies in stiff new suits wandering from job interview to temp work to employment office; the independent butcher cleaning animal-rights obscenities off his display window; the obese young woman ferrying a rope-clutching line of sun-struck toddlers, all wailing, across a downtown intersection snarled by construction. We thought we were the first to discover the old adages: the journey trumps the destination; better to dive into a fast-food restaurant's dumpster than toil behind its corrupt counter; a single moment lived in the pursuit of art is better than a plodding lifetime spent in exhausted defeat. What I didn't know was that Jane was living her ideals whereas I was only pretending to. We both thought I was as passionately committed to our vision as she was, when really I was merely enamoured, not with art or justice or knowledge or enlightenment but with a person, a complicated soul. Her.

Beth and I were sitting in our favourite Turkish restaurant, sharing a plate of its Special Meze, when she asked me if I'd ever loved anyone more than I loved her. She had a knack for exploding little ordnances like this under my nose while I sat salivating in wait for my Beyti Kebab and Hunker Begendi. Although I had told her about Jane, I didn't feel comfortable revealing intimate details about that summer, and so would steer the discourse away from the personal, away from Jane and toward Jacoba. Beth was more knowledgeable about dance than I was, having studied ballet and jazz and a year of modern dance while she was growing up. She more than I could appreciate the physical demands of the art form. She was forever "taking her hat off" to people like Jacoba, a comic image because Beth in a hat resembled a piece of antique decoration, an accessory to furniture. She didn't have the head, hair or body shape for it. Nevertheless, her hat went off. "I could never do it," she said, and I concurred. Who could do what Jacoba Wyndham does? Who could endure the intense public scrutiny, the misunderstanding, the pain?

Somehow, despite my attempts at diversion, Beth knew that I had suffered a broken heart before meeting her. Sensing the engagement of her intuition, and having nothing to lose by telling the truth, still I panicked when she asked the question. No, I assured her, I'd never loved anyone more than her at that moment, and as I said it I felt guilty, like a child caught with something stolen in his possession, and indignant. How dare she make me answer such a question. I conveyed both of these sentiments in my response. Don't be angry with me, her eyes seemed to say, I'm only asking. Why so defensive? You're holding it right there in your hands, Colin. Shall we try this again?

"Really? I was sure you were going to say that dancer."

That dancer. Why do men continue to lie to their wives and lovers even after the truth has been exposed? It must be that women want something, if only a thin ply of words, between them and the battering male fist of reality. Do women want to be lied to? Not in the way men understand it. Beth may not have wanted to be lied to, she may not have wanted to know that I was lying to her, but she needed just as much not to hear the truth from me, especially at that point in our marriage.

A woman who has her mind set upon having a child but cannot is the saddest, the most pathetic, the purest in harrowing wretchedness, the most righteous, the noblest, and the most beautiful, tragic figure we in this jaded world can conceive. Beth wanted a baby, I didn't, she became upset by this to the extent that in her eyes our union was bankrupt, we received counselling, followed the expert advice, made gains along a proscribed path of recovery, she asked me a question that took the measure of my love for her, and while waiting to be served a meal of lamb and eggplant on a bed of warm rice on a cold winter day, while gentle instrumental music played in a sonorous melding of East and West, I reached across the table, my hand spanning the Hellespont to take hers in a false gesture of reassurance.

It wasn't a lie as hideous as the one Max told Chandra about the nature of his travels. It was hardly in the same ballpark as my not telling Beth about my affair with Chandra, whom I continued to love for her companionship, intelligence, resourcefulness and tact. Why then did it, little and white and innocuous, continue to eat at me?

The last of the Famous Last Meals was our re-enactment of the final repast of the children of Isadora Duncan, and despite the ages of the characters and a frisson of unease, the foreboding we as the characters should not have been feeling but did, we carried it off rather well. With Chandra's help, Beth improvised a dance solo to cap the meal and send the children on their way. A further loose interpretation of events came when Beth, transformed now in character from her usually melancholic, slightly nervous self to the overtly erotic, graceful, intoxicating bohemian, took Max's hand under the table and drew it up under her long skirt. It was wholly believable that Isadora should do such a thing. Had she not given birth to two children by two different fathers, marrying neither? Had she not danced along the edge of a live volcano's rim with the mercurial Russian poet? To live is to burn hot! To be is to embrace every urge. I looked over at Max, who as Paris Singer had an appropriately haughty, proprietary grin on his face.

I didn't learn about this historically unsupported bit of hanky-panky until later in the evening, when Beth came out of her bathroom, her hair towel-turbaned, face slathered with night cream, and told me what she'd done. She said it in such a matter-of-fact way that at first it didn't register. She could have been stating that she had signed a petition that day calling for the abolition of plastic grocery bags. She tended to state almost everything the same way, without much inflection, somewhat arrogantly, with an edge of defensiveness, arming herself, daring the listener to challenge.

"Oh, by the way, Max felt me up under the table during dinner. I wasn't wearing anything under my dress. He sniffed his finger afterward."

I sat on my side of the bed. "Why are you punishing me, Beth? What have I done to you?"

"Nothing. Not one thing. *Nada*."

"Tell me."

"It was a success, don't you think, the dinner? I'm still abuzz. I'm still her. I think I could fly if I tried. I think I will. Have you ever felt that light, Colin, that buoyant? Those poor, poor, poor babies. How could we pick that one of all possible days? Whatever were we thinking? I could skip across the surface of a deep river right now, I truly could."

I slipped in between the bedcover and the top sheet, which was still tucked in. I was turned away from her, my bedside light turned off. Usually I flipped the radio on to the quiet smoky voice of the jazz host, but this time I left it turned off. I wanted to give the impression that I'd fallen asleep. I thought about Max's hand moving up Beth's leg. That puerile, reprehensible, completely natural and understandable gesture of putting the tip of his finger to a nostril and inhaling. Elemental communication. Such small but effective revenge, intended or not, given his own transgressions, those open secrets, and yet why did knowing about it make me want to commit murder? I feigned sleep. She could tell by my breathing.

"A mother in love with her children is the happiest, freest, most fulfilled being on earth. That, minus the heaviness of heart that attends any parting, must be what she was feeling as she prepared to return to her studio that day. 'Drive safely, my darlings. I will see you this evening. Be good for Nurse. Sit still for the driver. Do what he says.' No, despite these obvious feelings, this is not the reason I am as light as ether," she said. "I will tell you. I am impossibly, madly, impetuously happy because I know there lived a woman who truly understood what great unending anguish I carry with me every day. Someone lived who suffered more than I do. I am a mere child in my petty pain compared to her. She was the Grand Duchess of Harrowing Loss. How can I possibly complain, how yearn, how mourn? She takes all my grief from me. She makes me insignificant and insubstantial."

Substantial enough to let another man grope you, I thought. I bristled, seethed, ignored the molten kernel of her meaning. How could I have been so dense, so self-involved, to have let the moment go by as I did? And yet I did.

After Jane was dismissed from psychiatric care, I heard she went to live in Prague. I kept in touch with Tighe, who went on to marry Francesca. Meanwhile I stayed on at Wolf Moon Press through the fall and winter and kept the little apartment after the actor let it go. Tighe said that Jane had had a number of different treatments for depression, including electroshock. Prague, we agreed, knowing almost nothing about the city, was a good place for her to have gone. We'd heard that the arts scene there was open and vibrant and experimental the way Paris was in the first two decades of the twentieth century. She'd spent a few weeks in Amsterdam before moving on to Prague, and Tighe hinted that the easy access to marijuana had also been a factor in Jane's move to Europe. None of the painkillers she'd been prescribed for her knee worked as well alone as it did in conjunction with good old pot. It made me think about the day we met, when she said she put no poison in her temple-pure body, her "instrument." We change, we grow scar tissue, we figure out how to get to the next square on the board.

I'd put some money aside. A car-buying guide the press published sold exceedingly well and Mr. Saukville paid me a generous bonus, one he couldn't afford but one I wasn't about to refuse. I had also reconnected with a friend from university, Max Nazreen, who revealed that he was recently married. He had taken over the family business after his father's death. Max had been to a Club Med on the island of Guadeloupe, and he convinced me to fly down the same week he and his wife were going to be there.

I'd been thinking about flying to Prague to see Jane. Since seeing her that time in the psychiatric ward, I was wary, afraid of what she had become or what in her had been revealed. It was cowardly of me, I was the first to admit. I should have gone to see her more often. I should have been the friend in deed that everyone tries to emulate. I was young, self-centered, tired, sick of the city and its volatile weather. I needed to get away from everything.

We arrived on separate flights. I spotted Max ahead of me in line while we waited to pass through Customs at the Basse-Terre airport. The woman beside him stood a head taller than he was. They were arguing, a low, controlled, barely audible tiff, the tension felt more than heard in the wet-wool mug enveloping us. Apparently, there being no more double-occupancy rooms vacant at the resort, Max and his wife had been told that they were being put in separate rooms, he with another man and she with a woman. "Unless some other arrangement can be found," said the official in bored French.

Max lit into the man in a torrent, of which I understood the gist: Max had assumed that since he had paid SO MUCH MONEY he and his wife would be spending their PRECIOUS time TOGETHER. It was unconscionable, insupportable. If the man in the crisply pressed white uniform did not THIS VERY INSTANT provide them with a room of their own…. He let the threat hang unspecified. The official looked mildly alerted to Max's urgency while continuing to hang onto both his ennui and his appreciation of the awkwardness feeding the situation its humour.

"*Écoutez, monsieur*, I cannot change the accommodation at this time. I do this for le Club as a courtesy to them and to you so that when you arrive off *l'autobus, voila*, it is all arranged and you do not waste a single moment of your precious time, as you so correctly point out. I am a very busy man, as you can see from the number of weary travellers standing behind you in wait to have their passports stamped." He looked directly at me as he said this, as if he expected me to speak in support of his position. "When you arrive at le Club I tell you this is what you must do. You must ask to have the changes made at that end, *n'est-ce pas*? It is understood?"

Chandra didn't think the accommodation mix-up was that big a problem. "We'll sort it out, Max, come on," she said, but he dug in stubbornly.

"No, I'm sorry, this is not on. This will not fly. Let me speak to your superior."

The supervisor worked in the city and could not be reached. "You are causing these good people behind you unnecessary delay, *monsieur. Venez. Sois raisonable*"

With Chandra's insistence, Max relented, but not before letting everyone within earshot know that he had travelled the globe and had never, even in the most straitened outposts of Africa or Southeast Asia, been treated so shabbily.

"Monsieur, je vous implore. Calmez-vous."

"Listen to yourself, Max. Come on. Tut-tut."

I stepped forward and said hello.

"There you are. Have you been here all this time? Can you believe this shemozzle?" Max introduced me to Chandra. We shook hands. She smiled and said hello but distractedly with one eye on her volatile husband.

I suggested that Max and I share a room, at least for now, and let Chandra, who was now looking at me with guarded hope, room with a woman travelling alone. As soon as we got to the beach resort, I promised, I would add my voice to theirs in pursuit of a more desirable arrangement.

We claimed our bags and climbed aboard the bus that shuttled twice daily between the resort compound and the airport. I sat in an empty seat behind them and they half turned to converse with me. It would be all right, I promised, not yet grasping that if another heterosexual couple did not willingly vacate their room and split to form two same-sex pairings, he with me and she with this as-yet unidentified woman, my promise was an empty one. That would leave me rooming with this stranger, who, unless she was a free spirit like Jane Burden, would probably balk at the notion. But then wouldn't she be there on her own and did that fact not carry a certain connotative weight? This was, after all, a resort devoted to hedonism. Were we not adult? Each room came with two double beds. Why could a man and a woman not share a room solely for the purpose of having a place to sleep? Because, Chandra informed me, a man is a man and a woman is vulnerable. Equality in such a situation has yet to be established, unless she is armed with pepper spray or a nice little gun.

We were treated to a more pleasant version of the reception we'd had at the airport, but the essential message remained the same: the resort as a rule did not put a man and a woman together in the same room if they were not married to each other. An unoccupied room was not available. Max and I would therefore have to do the gentlemanly thing and room together, as would Chandra and her mysterious roommate, who was due to arrive in a few hours. The management was truly sorry. If we four were to come to an unofficial agreement in the meantime, that was entirely up to us. For the record, however, this would have to be the way it stood.

Predictably Bethany Van Doren, the woman travelling alone, was not open to bunking with me, as pleasant a man as I appeared to be. Increasingly, however, we passed the daylight hours together, our companionship more the result of design and guilt than mutual regard. Baldly put, she and I got out of the way so that the newlyweds could have a room they could use for sex. No one said as much; we were too polite and reserved and Canadian for that. It simply worked out that after lunch Max and Chandra would disappear and Beth and I would know that the couple had gone to one of the two rooms. We never knew which one the Nazreens were using, which made us all the more reluctant to venture in that vicinity.

The surprising change was that after three days they stopped disappearing in the afternoons, preferring to stay out on the beach with Beth and me or to join us on the tennis court or take the daily bus excursion to the other side of the island. On one such outing we were led by an ebullient Frenchman who insisted we take off all our clothes and play a group game that entailed passing a rubber ball to a person of the opposite sex without using one's hands. He had a way of making us feel aged and un-hip if we didn't take part. Wine flowed in abundance. Beth and I drifted away from the group. From a palm-shaded bluff we watched Chandra and Max frolic like puppies in the surf.

On the fourth morning Beth wasn't at our usual spot on the beach. I wandered toward the point, a brief sand spit where the beach turned a corner and beyond which was a hidden strand where guests could sunbathe nude. We'd been told about this beach. I was curious but didn't know the protocol. Was it acceptable to walk among the unclad if you were dressed? How close was too close? At what point would I be expected to doff my shirt and swim trunks?

While I deliberated I spotted a couple face-to-face in the water, only their heads and shoulders visible. They were kissing, and the gentle swell was making them rise and fall in the same rhythm as the waves. Immediately I thought of Jane. I wished I'd followed her to Europe. I missed her body, missed the way she pushed me around with her challenges to all things complacent, missed her assaults against received wisdom. The ground was never solid beneath my feet when I was with her; instead it was like walking uphill in sand over dune after endless dune, lost but happily so, seeking a solace I couldn't put adequately into words.

The woman in the water threw back her head, opened her mouth wide, brought her hands up to her partner's head, grabbed fistfuls of hair, and cried out in a high pitch. The man answered with a triumphant groan. I was about to turn away when Beth stood up from where she had been lying on her front—she too must have been watching the couple in the water—and she waved, motioning me to come closer. She wore only a wide-brimmed straw hat. She had full hips, a firm stomach, well-toned arms, short, strong, shapely legs, and the most desirable breasts I'd ever seen outside of the pages of *Playboy*. Seeing her there I was struck dumb, immobile. To come closer and undress would be to reveal my arousal. Watching the couple in the water had made me feel intrusive, a voyeur; seeing Beth naked made me feel almost insane with mirthful desire. I wanted to run up to her, gather her in my arms, press my skin against hers, get in under that ridiculous hat with her and be safe. Safe, depleted and replenished at the same time. She was so different from Jane. Jane of the rubber limbs. Jane of no breasts, and nipples too sensitive to touch. Jane who made me turn away sometimes, her gaze could be so penetrating. Jane who nudged me ever closer to the immolating flame.

Many times I've played an imaginary dialogue over in my mind:

"What were you doing that morning you drove out to the quarry?"

"What do you think I was doing, Colin?"

"I haven't a clue, Jane. Tell me."

"Then that makes you clueless, doesn't it?"

She must have forgotten about the gate or thought she could circumvent it. I think she was trying to kill herself. I've often wondered how I would go about broaching the subject if I ever met her again. I think about her pre-emptive denial in the hospital room in Burlington, Vermont. Maybe she said it because her father was there. Had she been honest with me about anything? She spoke the truth about dance. That was one thing she couldn't make up.

It had something to do with her family. She saw Tighe and Francesca together and thought, "I'll never have that." Maybe that was it. Or, "If this is what awaits me, this vapid barnyard-animal devotion, then no thank you." Or, "This is for everything, Mum and Dad. This is for me never being good enough in your eyes. This is for making it clear that what I said and did were the least important matters in your world." Or, "This is a meaningless act. The instant I finally decide to do it, to actually carry it out, I will regret it. It will cease to have meaning. It will be the single most decisive, important, irreversible, meaningless act of my life. Nothing else will be as real."

Beth stood gesturing for me to join her. She was the most real, appropriate, joyfully uncomplicated figure imaginable in that bright, simple, pleasure-giving landscape. I took off my clothes. She smiled when she saw my erection, but paid no further attention to it, or didn't do so noticeably. She applied sunscreen to my back and got me to rub some on hers. Chandra and Max were asleep in her room, she said. The Nazreens had been up all night dancing and had knocked on the door early in the morning before she had gotten out of bed. They said they needed, just once, before they returned home, before this week in paradise ended, to sleep in each other's arms. "How could I refuse such a request?" she said. "I hope that when I get married I stay as in-love as they are."

A backgammon board was lying on the blanket beside her. She'd taught me how to play and I assumed we were going to have our accustomed three games, but when I opened it and began to distribute the stones she stopped me.

"The sun's getting strong," she said. It was no stronger than it had been on any of the previous days. I suggested we move back behind the line of palms and into their shade. She lowered her eyes and lifted them, slowly, deliberately. We dressed. She took my hand and we walked back to the main beach, up to the refreshment kiosk, through the main hall, and out to the accommodations, which were set back amid the undergrowth. The air smelled of mold and disinfectant and the perfume of tropical flowers. She had draped around her a length of floral print fabric, as if she had recently emerged from the shower. I couldn't see her face under her hat. Now that she was covered again I felt uneasy. We were moving in an irreversible direction. We paused under the shade of the main building's high roof.

"Are you sure about this?" I said.

"Are you?"

My knees began to quake as I opened the door to the room that Max and I were ostensibly sharing. There were no keys, no locks on the doors. We'd left our valuables for safekeeping at the main desk, exchanging money for beads worn around our necks. We'd embraced a pared-down existence from which the city, our workaday concerns, all our political battles were barred. Why then was I so nervous with this woman, alone with her in a room mid-morning in a climate that made clothing superfluous?

The hat fell, we kissed, her sarong dropped away, the entire day dropped away without our being aware of it until, late in the afternoon, Max came in to change his clothes, and we drew the bed sheet up. He apologized for interrupting us. He looked surprised but not unhappy. We told him, no, we were the ones who should be apologizing, and began to bustle about, gathering items of clothing, keeping our eyes averted.

When we looked up again he was gone. While we'd been fussing like two people caught unprepared for an important test, Max had managed to gather all his clothes, his toiletries, the damp towel from off the shower rod, and jam them all into his suitcase. He'd completed one-half of the exchange without our having been aware of it. I sensed something of heft shift in me then as if, lifting a piece of furniture, I felt a hidden counterweight roll from one side to the other.

Beth and I rode the bus into Basse-Terre. We were in that delicate state of togetherness in which lovers say little for long stretches and then begin speaking simultaneously, only to break off into laughter. I sat beside her, terrified that if I were to lose contact, my skin with hers, she might disappear. I was sure that either I was going to be sucked out one of the windows or she was going to rush to the front, demand that the driver stop to let her out, and slip into the dense undergrowth that threatened to swallow everything, the road, the bus and all tentative signs of humanity.

The children we encountered looked happy. They went about shirtless, often naked. Their little bellies stuck out like smooth taut gourds. What child who plays outside all day is not a filthy urchin? It didn't dawn on me then that they were probably eating dirt and with it ingesting germs and parasites, their gastrointestinal tracts seething with worms. Onward we rode in the shiny bus with its air-conditioning and its big Mercedes symbol like a peace sign on the grille. We waved at the children and little pink palms waved back, toothy smiles brilliant against dark skin. Weren't we the attentive anthropologists taking in a smattering of steel-shed culture on our way to the shopping district.

She was quiet as she looked out the window.

"What are you thinking?"

"Oh, nothing," she said, meaning, Oh, everything. Everything I have no control over. Every potential mine that threatens to explode under me if I make the wrong step. Every turn that ever took me into unfamiliar territory. I didn't know then, for example, that she hated to travel, that for her the pleasure was to be in one spot and to stay there, as still as possible, soaking in the pleasures. Her favourite expression was, "Beam me up, please." She hadn't even wanted to go to Basse-Terre, she told me after we'd flown home, I back to Toronto and she to Montréal.

She was working as a university fundraiser, had been so for a year since graduating from Concordia with a degree in biology, and had no trouble shifting her allegiance, immersing herself in McGill's history, its current achievements, and its barnacle-like hold on the dynamic city spread out below the mountain. Her strong message to me was, "You come here. You get on that train, buster, I love you. Move here, be with me, please, on my terms," which I'd assumed were the terms of a fierce independence, but which in fact were the defensive entrenchments and makeshift fortifications of a woman who feared change as much as she feared growing old.

Young Anglos bilingual enough to live and work in Montréal were moving back to the city, reversing somewhat the exodus of 1978 when René Lévesque and the Parti Québécois took power in the province. I enjoyed being in the city whenever I went there to visit Beth, every other weekend and every possible holiday. She was on her own, her parents dead, no siblings, a rich aunt in Scotland and some cousins there she'd lost touch with. She had also some Pennsylvania Dutch relations she'd never met.

We found a flat together off Saint-Denis south of Rachel. It had high ceilings, ornate moulding around the doors, and large, dusty, impractical windows we had to cover with plastic shrink-wrap in winter. Our dining-room table was a massive masculine piece in dark dry wood that Beth had inherited. It fit the room in size and style, crying out for an elegant centerpiece, linen tablecloths and napkins, silverware, and the eight other seated guests who would have completed the tableau. We were even then haunted by absent bodies. At least we didn't make that sad picture at mealtime of the wife and husband dining at opposite ends of a long table, too far removed from each other for easy conversation. We would hug one corner of the curved piece of thick, manorial furniture, and if we began the meal in separate seats, usually by dessert and coffee time she would have made her way onto my lap. Or I onto hers, playfully, gingerly. You couldn't say we were pining for company then; we were too myopic in love for that. How extraordinary is the ability of new love to block out all but the most insistent of external demands.

I was standing in line for coffee one day when I felt a tap on the shoulder. I turned around to look at the man who had apparently recognized me. Shorter than I and wearing an expensive dark wool overcoat, red scarf framing a suit and tie, sharply pressed trousers, Blundstones on his feet—I should have recognized Max immediately. It had been two years since Guadeloupe. We'd exchanged a Christmas card and some lengthy email messages, digital photos attached, in which we'd tried to keep alive the unreal splendour of our time in paradise. He was sporting a Van Dyke beard, stylish then. He looked delighted to see me. When I finally recognized him we hugged. He said he was in the city on business.

"Thinking of relocating here, in fact," he said. The cost of living was reasonable. Many of his clients were in Montréal. And now that he had bumped into me, well, "That's a sign from above, wouldn't you say?"

Max could make anyone he was talking with feel like the most important person in the world. He could be pointing out how immensely wrong-headed you were for thinking something, but he always did so in a way that embraced you affirmatively, locked a beam onto your attention, a bear hug of engagement. No one strayed from his attention.

Max and Chandra moved to Montréal eighteen months after our chance meeting in the café. His business was thriving. She joined me as an adjunct in the McGill English department. They bought a house in the country. He began to travel often.

One day he said, "You have to go there," meaning South Africa, "now that the whites have to take their place in the democracy instead of acting like arrogant tyrants." He could say such a thing with a straight face, betraying no hint of the connection between himself, whose people would have been labelled coloured and would have enjoyed a relatively better life than did the blacks, and the Afrikaners, who were watching their way of life burn, seemingly overnight. Max's people were Asian South Africans who had emigrated to North America in the 1960s, not because they deplored the way blacks were being treated but because the opportunities to make money, they thought, were greater in Canada and the U.S.

What puzzled me was that Max never seemed all that excited about the items he insured and about which he was a supposed expert: Kaffir robes, Zulu headdresses and spears, Damara drums, Bechuana thumb harps. Not once did we have a prolonged discussion, passionate or otherwise, about these items, what materials they were made of, how they were constructed, what they represented or were used for, how they were valued, not in resale but in cultural terms. Who made them? Was there a cottage industry? Did he have a little factory in Soweto? "You have to go there" meant—and I understood this too late to change the way things turned out—"you have to let yourself be jolted out of your North American complacency and relocated, transformed for a short time, long enough to experience a way of life that teeters on the lip of a yawning void." The food, the music—he was bringing back recordings of Ladysmith Black Mombasa and other black musicians years before Paul Simon discovered them—the way they smelled, which he admitted he found intensely erotic. The sound of gunfire in the night? The stench of burning rubber tires? Corpses came attached to those sensations, I wanted to remind him.

"I cheat death every time I have a virgin," Max said after one of our last Last Meals. "Think of it. We're supposed to be thumbing our noses at the Angel of Death every time we observe the final meal of someone famous who died young. But how does it make you feel, Colin? Are you rejuvenated?" I admitted that, no, all I felt was bloated and drunk. Chandra had been Joan of Arc that evening. We had attempted a medieval series of courses, and in honour of the future saint's means of expiration had added the fires of cayenne and jalapeno peppers to an otherwise bland fare. "My stomach is scorched," I moaned.

"And your cock is limp," said Max, laughing with an edge of cruelty. "You are no more the master of time than is a summer peach lying in a warm damp bed of grass. Face it, this is an elaborate excuse for us to meet to tell each other how great we look, how wonderful we are, how young and unwrinkled and stylish and urbane and..."

"I get it, Max."

"In Lesotho the girls call me Simba. I kid you not. Someday you're going to see for yourself, and you'll know, really know what it is to be a man at the peak of his virility. I mean, come on, face it. You can't have equality in bed, not if both partners are going to get where they want to go."

"Doesn't the word, 'partner,' suggest something equitable?"

"Fine. Not partners. Poor choice of word. A man takes a woman. He takes her. There is no other way to describe it. She must submit to his will, his urgent desire. Otherwise she is diminished."

"Not the best arrangement for longevity in the relationship, you have to admit."

"And I do, I do. Don't you see that I am speaking about two wholly different animals here, two separate entities? There is the marriage, for the creation of children and the consolidation of home, wealth, social standing, citizenship, community. And then there is that which a man must do in the world in order to be truly a man. He must go forth. He must conquer. He must spread his seed. Do not laugh!"

"You're so full of shit you're starting to grow saplings out your ears."

He continued to be outrageous, to drink while we did the dishes (I washed and dried, he sat and drank), to condemn me for being "whipped" and "milquetoast" and "Teddy Telemachus." Chandra and Beth, as was their custom, had remained seated at the dining room table and were sipping liqueur and speaking intimately in voices punctured by sudden screams of laughter. Jokes about Joan, Beth said later. Could the Maid of Orléans have been around all those soldiers and remained a virgin? Yes, they decided, if the soldiers had been French. Or English. Or in armour…. Or men!

"What," I asked her, "do you possibly gain from deriding men?"

"Hope," she replied.

"Hope? Hope for what?"

"Hope for a better world, you dumb cluck. Lighten up!"

Beth could say that kind of thing most days of the week without hurting my feelings, because her smile always led a playful advance party. If, on the other hand, Chandra ever said such a thing, and she did from time to time, not often though often enough to have made it memorable, it stung. With Chandra everything was serious. She was not necessarily always a serious person; she could be as silly and outrageous as Beth could, especially when they were a team, one feeding off the other's infectious hilarity. But for me, Chandra was someone to think about, deal with, be with, be apart from, in a serious way. It was the way I thought about Jane Burden. With Jane I always felt I hadn't been given the latest update to the script. Seriousness with her was usually a product of my intense concentration, my effort to catch up to and stay abreast of her, to understand the terms and the context, grasp the rules, if there were any to be learned. Jane was making it up as she went along, the form, the means of expression, the terms by which others would take part, the duration of events. The rules of engagement.

It wasn't the duration but the consequence of our time together that had felt unsatisfactory. It came to an end abruptly soon after her accident. She was released from the hospital in Burlington after a night of observation. Her father came to see that she be released properly and not sooner than she should. She broke down after a visit from the police, admitted that the car she'd been driving had not in fact sunk to the bottom of the water-filled quarry, but that the man who had driven her to the hospital had taken it. She gave a description of him to

the officer, and the man was picked up a few days later claim-
ing that Jane had given him the vehicle. She said she didn't
remember saying such a thing. She'd been in intense pain. The
man had given her liquor to drink. Who knows what she said
to him in her delirium? She knew that telling the truth at that
point was probably going to either nullify or severely reduce
the coverage provided by the owner's insurance. The car was
never recovered. The most plausible theory, corroborated by
the man, a petty criminal, was that the car was in pieces and
that those pieces were by then replacing lesser or worn or damaged parts in a dozen other vehicles. It was as just a situation
as one like this could be, given that the robbery had promot-
ed conservation and environmental protection: old cars were
being kept on the road and out of landfills longer. The friend
who had lent Jane her car got over her dismay when her insurance company paid enough for a large down payment on a
newer model. Except for the injury—Jane made jokes about
finding that chop shop and getting a new knee—everything
seemed to have turned out for the best.

Tighe and Francesca drove us back to Toronto, Jane and
I uncommunicative in the back seat despite our proximity.
She had to sit with her back to the door and the injured leg
stretched out straight across both seats and under my raised
knees. It should have been an intimate posture. I wanted to
touch her, but was worried about inflicting further pain, and
she made it clear that she wanted nothing to do with me. Less
than halfway home, Francesca and I switched seats.

I checked on Jane in the morning and again after work the
next few days. She was getting around surprisingly well using a
single crutch and seemed to be in good spirits. The dance company was rehearsing new material, which they videotaped for

her to study, and she was confident that she'd be able to catch up. It was going to be a six-week convalescence, I reminded her.

"No, I don't believe that," she said. "They don't know what they're talking about," wincing, "those so-called doctors."

"Give it time. What else can you do?"

"I can stop listening to the likes of you, Colin. H.I.M.T."

"Himt?"

"Halted in mid-transformation."

"You're going to tell me more, aren't you, whether I want to hear it or not."

"Most perspicacious boy. Hobble with me to the front of the class. You were on your way. And I'll tell you where, to save you having to ask the obvious: you were well on your way to becoming the person you were meant to be."

"Really. What stopped me?"

"I told you, no stupid obvious questions. You have to promise me."

"I do. I'm shut, I'm Silent Sam. Why don't you take a load off. Elevate it or something." She was trying to cut slices off a loaf of bread while balancing on her good leg. The knife was too short and hadn't the necessary serrated edge.

"If you don't stop nagging, you'll remain in the dark. Not a good place to be. Toast or plain?"

"Toast. I was halted in development because…?"

"You were halted in *metamorphosis* because."

"Fine."

"Because … you made the fatal error…"

"Yes?"

"Oh, Colin, why are you making me say it? Can't you read my mind?"

"I don't want to change. I don't see why I should."

"All bourgeois, suburban, blind, grown-up-stupid mole-rats must change. It's a rule."

"I'm going to make you say it."

"If you do I'll cry. I'll twist my knee and fall in a heap on this grungy linoleum floor. You'll have to pick me up and you'll throw your back out in the process."

"Say it."

"No."

"Yes."

"You're in love with me and I won't have it. I can't have it."

"Why not?"

"The stupidest, stupidest questions!"

"You can't love me back."

"Something like that."

The toast was burning. It was a terrible moment. Neither of us wanted to move. The smoke alarm went off and still we didn't move. When I did it was to open the door and run into the hallway, down the stairs and outside. I didn't know where I was going. I had never felt more wretched or crueler. She probably couldn't reach the alarm to disable it, not without standing on a chair and risking further damage to her knee. Her roommates were at rehearsal. I imagined her hopping back into the kitchen, unplugging the toaster, turning it upside down in frustration, shaking it to dislodge the charred remnant. Throwing it against the wall. Opening a window to let the smoke out. But these would have been my reactions, not hers. This was nothing but my imagined, petulant, anguished, self-pitying tantrum. Knowing Jane, I could be sure she had that alarm turned off and that toaster righted in less time than it took me to run like a wounded antelope out into the street.

Those who can't accept rejection attract a kind of pathos almost too unsettling to describe. They begin, after the initial shock has worn off, by acting as if the moment of rejection never happened. I went back to Jane's apartment the next evening, after a sleepless night and a day at work during which I did more to scuttle the project Mr. Saukville and I were working on than I did to complete it. Jane was out, said one of her roommates, a new face—they were always changing. Out? Yes, she said, a friend had come by to pick her up. Where had they gone? She said she didn't know, picking up her keys and shoulder bag. She hadn't asked.

"I'm on my way out myself. I'll tell Jane you stopped by." Was it a man? Yes, she said, he was someone who used to dance with the company.

"She wasn't wearing a long red scarf around her neck, was she?"

"No, she wasn't," she said in a pitying tone, whether for my weak attempt at humour or my obvious lovesickness I couldn't be sure.

One weekend Chandra and I drove to Lac Memphrémagog, where she and Max had built their house, and where she stabled her horse at a nearby farm. Max was travelling and Beth had gone down to New York City to see a Broadway show with a girlfriend. It was early in the affair—Chandra and I had spent four or five lunch hours together—and when she called she sounded almost shy. She had arranged for a neighbour, a retired woman with no grandchildren of her own, to babysit. The boards, as they say, had been swept clean. She made it seem as if she had just that moment decided to call and spirit me away, "if all's clear at your end, Colin." She knew full well that such was the case. This was not a woman who left anything to chance. It was she who had put the idea in Beth's impressionable mind to take in the theatricals. "I've heard that *Rent* is fabulous. I wish I could go myself. I'd go with you, but my marks have to be in first thing next week and then there's my paper for the Learneds. Why don't you call up Cecilia and make a junket of it? The packages are a dream, I've heard. Nothing left to chance."

When I thought about Chandra's planning and manipulation, I was impressed by her skill, but it was disconcerting that I could be just as convincing a liar as she was.

She did her best that weekend to teach me how to ride. Neither my mount, a near-blind swaybacked grey mare, nor I showed any enthusiasm for our limited partnership. Our time in the beginner's ring was short, unsuccessful and not to be repeated. Just as I believed downhill skiing and skydiving were for people with death wishes, so too was horseback riding for those naïve enough to think that the quadruped understands what we require of it or cares enough about us to carry out our requests safely.

It was a pleasant getaway, my equestrian shortcomings notwithstanding. We stayed two nights in a motel the limitations of which we hardly noticed, so heightened was our sense of illicit thrill. For pure concentrated ability to focus, Chandra was nonpareil, in bed and out, that is when she was employing her considerable powers of concentration. When she was not, little could lift her from the wheel-rut of annoyance. In an instant her companion could become intensely boring, her surroundings, regardless of what or where they were, vexing. She had envisioned the two of us trail riding up to a remote cabin, the key for which she had procured from the stable owner, but when she realized that I would rather drink bleach than spend time astraddle the broad back of a coarsely carpeted beast of burden, she let that famous focus of hers be atomized. When I tried to interest her in a rented video to watch in bed, she looked at me as if I'd suggested we move to Nashville and become a country-and-western duet.

"Put your clothes on," she said.

"What?"

"Come on, move. Now! I'll explain on the way."

She'd remembered seeing a notice on the announcements sign of a church we'd passed earlier. The sign had said something about a recital and she was almost certain she had read the word, "dance."

"Oh, great. We have a fifty-fifty chance of walking in on a bunch of six-year-olds' ballet recital or their grandparents' social night."

"At least we'll be doing something," she said.

"Are you saying that the hopeless romance and acerbic social satire of *The Graduate* is nothing?"

"You're such a little Dustin."

I held my tongue. It was enough to see her snapped back into alert mode, all moving parts meshing again.

It was a big old United church with a newer hall built onto it, the white vinyl siding of the hall in contrast to the pink granite of the sanctuary. The performance had begun. Gingerly we opened one of the double doors leading into a gymnasium-style hall. The place was almost full. I wanted to back out, but she led the way up to the front row, where two seats in the middle of the right side were empty. I felt all eyes in the room trained on us. Chandra had the look of a child at her first circus performance. She took off her jacket quickly. I struggled awkwardly with mine, not wanting to draw more attention than I already had, and in doing so was even more distracting to the people seated behind us than I should have been. The result was that Chandra, recognizing the performer before I did—there had been no name posted on the sign, simply, "Dance Recital"—took hold of my hand and squeezed hard.

Jacoba Wyndham had once without warning cancelled a performance in London, before the Queen, in favour of a hastily organized one in a refugee camp in Kosovo. It only increased her cachet. I'd heard a rumour that she was living in a large yurt outside of Sydney, Australia and that she had given up dancing indefinitely. Yet here she was, in North Hatley, Quebec.

My first thought was that Chandra had arranged this. She assured me after the performance that she hadn't.

"I kind of wish Beth had been along with us to see her, she would have loved it."

I shook my head in disbelief. Only Chandra could so completely close the various compartments of her life that way, each one watertight with no passageways connecting one to the next: Max: Cabin 1A; children: 1 B and C; Colin: 2A; — no, 2D, we don't want to stack the men, do we!—career: 3B, etc. And so to her it was conceivable that the wife of the man with whom she was having an affair should accompany them to watch a performance that she, the wife, more than most of those in the audience, could enjoy and appreciate. "Too much of life is lost on those unable to appreciate it," Chandra would say. Of course Beth, a dancer at heart but issued the least dancer-like body, should be there to see this great artist.

What does fidelity have to do with it? And while we're at it, I could hear her say, let's talk about this loaded word, shall we? Infidelity. What if you don't accept the premise of marital monogamy? It's like, what if you're not religious? What then does one do with the word "sin"? Does it become irrelevant and meaningless?

Well, Beth wasn't there, I was, and when I saw Jane I didn't recognize her immediately. I knew Jacoba Wyndham to see. She had had enough exposure in arts-channel documentaries and in newspapers, with profiles of her life and criticism of her aesthetic, that my sincere reaction was, "Cool." We were getting to see this icon, here of all places. Then, a beat and a half later, recognition and remembrance, and I became flustered, my neck and face beginning to flame, my heart to bang against its bars, ears filling with a roar.

Her costume was a white straitjacket over black floor-length evening gown. She moved in such a way that her impediment was not noticeable unless you were looking for it, because her gait was straight-legged and erratic like the movements of a primitive automaton. Her feet were bare. The trademark stiff leg shot out parallel to the floor, in front, out to the side, as if independent of the body it was attached to, and the toes, those grotesque little hammers I used to massage to remove stiffness, cramp and soreness, were splayed like the claws of a cat held against its will. Like that first one, in the old drill hall, this performance was at times too much to bear and I closed my eyes or looked down at my feet, thinking, Coward, sit up and give her your attention, she deserves that at least. Let the past be past. Her stage persona, so different from the private Jane and yet trailing threads of antecedence from her brief time with Red Bugatti, was still not distant enough for me to be neutral, at ease and unclamped from my still intense regard for her.

After the show, her handlers moved her quickly through a back exit, and people in the audience remained seated or milled in the aisles, bumping the metal folding chairs off their alignment, murmuring to themselves and each other, mumbling their incomprehension. This was not the way they were used to feeling in this space, violated like this, ears still ringing from the industrial cacophony played too loud, their minds still processing the meaning and impact of the dance, although few of these white- and grey-haired folk would have used the word "dance" to describe the way she had moved her body in their sight. Many were there for the experience of being close to such notoriety—word must have spread through the community—and had they been younger they might have tried to claim an autograph or a quick word at the lip of the stage, something, some stardust to rub off on an aspiring artist.

She looked older than she was. Greater concerns than mine had toughened her face, her limbs. She was on a different trajectory, aging in cat years, absorbing the world's toxic residue, its excrescence, using up her body in the service of artistic defiance. If anything could be said to be a sin it was this consumption, this burning away of her youth, her innocence, impetuousness, ingenuous fresh hope, the girl who had tilted her mirror to direct lemony sunshine into my eyes, burning my retinas, blinding me, giving me new vision.

I remained seated while Chandra stood. Having processed the experience, cataloguing it for optimal retrieval, something she could work into a lecture, she was ready to move on to the next fun thing. I was angry at having been ambushed in this way by my past and at not being able to be an objective observer, inasmuch as anyone watching one of Jacoba's dances can be said to be objective, for she implicates you, tricking you the way the slickest confidence artist makes unsuspecting saps his accomplices. Together you steal the floor and the walls, then wait, breath held, eyes skyward, for the ceiling to fall.

"That beats watching Little Big Man trying to act, wouldn't you say, Colin?"

"Why did you do this?"

"I swear I had no idea," she said, and I believed her. It didn't do much to calm me down. "You used to date her or something, didn't you?"

"Or something."

"Too bad she rushed off so quickly."

I grunted an affirmative sound.

"Come," she said, tugging at my arm to make me stand, "don't be grumpy. Come back with me, come back to our iniquitous den, and I'll frame you with my black-stockinged leg."

She got me to smile, to forget again for a little while, to play and be simple and indolent and indulgent. We did start watching *The Graduate* that night in the motel room but fell asleep before the climax at the church.

After our re-enactment of *le dernier dejeuner* of Isadora Duncan's children, as if we'd heard the same whispered caveat, we failed to make plans for the next month's theme. Some months passed. One day Beth bumped into Max at lunchtime outside Ben's delicatessen. It was an odd exchange, according to Beth. Distracted, Max revealed that Chandra had not gone anywhere in weeks, that she was spending all day at home "catching up on her reading." Novels, of all things. Chandra, a Milton specialist, used to boast that she never read fiction, that it was a decadent self-indulgent genre. Now she was reading and re-reading two novels, John Irving's *The 158-Pound Marriage* and Ford Madox Ford's *The Good Soldier*. She was going around the house all day in bathrobe and slippers, muttering, "four-sided prison" and "infernal minuet."

Fall and winter that year she rarely left the house. She neglected her teaching, precipitating the hiring of a replacement for her, and began writing emails to CBC radio and to politicians. She kept saying that something catastrophic was coming. She didn't know what it would be or where it would hit. Nobody listened. "I've been out there. I know," she said. She held a short-lived vigil outside the American consulate, standing for a night and a day on the sidewalk across the street and holding a sign that read, "Atone." People asked her what in particular she was protesting, but she wouldn't answer.

She kept all her emails. Max found thousands of them in her office at the university, printed out and stored in file folders arranged by date. Most were addressed to public figures and to the CEOs of various companies. In a vague, rambling way they expressed her suspicions that a global conflagration was coming. She must have gotten Jacoba's email address off her website, because included in the files was a letter to her and this short reply:

Dear Professor Nazreen:
Thank you very much for your query. I'm not exactly sure what it is you're warning me of, but I appreciate the thought all the same. I don't know if I agree with you about the "demise of art at the hands of the cult of the personal." If you're saying we have to rescue art from the average

person, then I couldn't disagree more. If anything, more people should be encouraged to express themselves through dance or visual art or music or drama. I mean, think about it. What if we did? What if we reorganized the world so that we were all performers as well as audience members? What if, instead of living to the tired-out drumbeat we label, "Normalcy," we lived each moment as if in a performance? Watch your children play sometime. They sound delightful, by the way.

You're absolutely right about the dangers of militarism and imperialist expansion. We have to draw the line at warfare and violence, unless the art demands it or is corrupt without it. My credo has always been, "Do no harm."

Yes, I do remember Colin, very well. Please give him my warmest regards. We did some growing up together.

Thank you for asking about the knee. What can I say? It's there. I work around it. Or, rather, I work with it. The injury has defined my style to a great extent. I would be a different performer without it. As for the circumstances surrounding the injury, I don't know why Colin told you that, but he must be thinking about someone else. I hurt it in a downhill skiing accident. That's a very strange story he told you.

Thanks also for suggesting those titles to read. As for my performance schedule, ever since the security incident a few years ago in Nauheim, I no longer publish such bulletins.

Thanks again for your interest. Be well and be good to yourself.

She signed it, "Jacoba." Not the full name and not Jane Burden. The Jane I had known no longer existed. Maybe she never did exist. We looked for other emails, other forms of correspondence between them, but found none.

"We did some growing up together." Can any two people truthfully say such a thing? Jane and I were together a short while before growing into different people. If you stay together long enough, you see who the other person is becoming. It's not so much a transformation as a gradual unearthing. Or maybe it's a gradual earthing-over, not necessarily a lesser process when you think about it.

One day I bumped into Tighe Burden on Greene Street. He was helping to transform an Italian restaurant, one I'd thought about going into for lunch that day, into a Prohibition-era speakeasy. The production company's white trailers lined both sides of the street. Thick black power cords snaked along the edge of the sidewalk, crossing the pavement under sturdy little plastic ramps. Down an alley, powerful arc lamps lit a dingy side entrance. Tighe was coming out the front door as I stood at the bottom of the stairs looking up and wondering where I would eat now. This sort of setback never used to bother me. Until recently the sight of a movie set could make me smile like a kid and think about the make-believe being spun there and the famous American actors who might be wandering between takes into bistros on Crescent Street.

"Yo, Colin, who died, my man?"

By way of answer I almost told him about Chandra. Instead I said I was looking for a place to eat. He happened to be heading for the catering trailer and said I was welcome to tag along. The company always spread more food than the crew could eat, and since no "names" were there that day nobody would mind if I "bellied up to the trough." He found me a visitor's tag and slung it around my neck.

He filled a plate and we claimed two empty folding chairs set up outside one of the dressing room trailers. No one gave me a second look. It was a slow day on the set. The lighting techs were having a difficult time pleasing the cinematographer, who was convinced that the room, in order to be authentic, had to have the feel of a smoky cave. Tighe's job was to construct a series of sliding wall panels that could be quickly changed to disguise the nature of the illegal club. He was most proud of the bar, which could be lowered until its surface was flush with and indistinguishable from the floorboards.

Exhausting the subject of work, we talked for a while about Francesca, who was expecting their third child, and Beth, who had begun, in the last few months, after practically moving in with Max and the kids to help cook, clean, buy groceries, and drive people to their various lessons and sports games and therapy sessions, to talk with a guarded enthusiasm about adoption. Tighe said, "That's good, man, that's a real positive move. Cause, like, kids take you out of yourself. When people ask me what I do now, I tell them, one, I'm a dad, two, I build sets, and three, I manage the club. In that order."

"That order."

"Damn straight. Most important job in the world is to make healthy people. The rest of it is dressing."

"People are pretty resilient. Kids are." I was thinking of Lori and Vaughan Nazreen, who were adapting slowly to life without their mother, shuffling back to normalcy.

"Oh, it doesn't take much. That I know."

"Much to...?"

"To strip the threads, man, screw a kid's head around so bad she can't function right."

"She? Are you thinking about Jane?"

"No." He folded his empty paper plate in one big paw and leaned forward preparing to stand. "No, just, you know, general case scenario."

"Right. You have to get…"

"Back to the sweatshop. You know it. I'm gonna be here till two in the morning if I don't rev up. Nice to see you, Colin."

I thanked him for lunch and told him to give my best to Francesca. He'd almost told me something. Part of me said, Drop it, it's none of your business, but another part, the one that was thinking about Chandra and her correspondence with Jacoba, wondering what she thought the dancer could tell her, wanted to pry.

"Hey, Tighe?" He stopped walking and turned around. "If you ever need to talk…"

"Thanks. I will. Appreciate it."

"You've got my number."

"That I do."

"So what did happen? To Jane, I mean." A look passed over his face, only for an instant, and I wondered if this was the look he got when he was preparing to deal with a customer who had had too much to drink. "I thought maybe you were starting to tell me something about her."

"You have yourself a good day," he said, turning, walking back up the stairs into the restaurant.

I figured that was the door closing tight on the subject of Jane Burden until, two days later, the phone woke us. It was Tighe. He'd been drinking, not enough that he was slurring his words but enough to make his speech slow and deliberate. Yes, he said, I'd been right. He had indeed been referring to Jane. Something had happened to her, something no one outside of his immediate family knew about, not even Francesca. He'd sworn an oath to Jane and his father that he would never speak of it, but he couldn't keep it inside any longer. It was an acid that had eaten through its container.

From bed Beth gave me a questioning look. "Just a sec, Tighe." I covered the mouthpiece. "It's Jane's brother," I whispered. "He and Frankie had a fight. He's had a few. I'll try to talk him home." She burrowed under the covers and I took the phone into the dining room.

In the darkness, quickly becoming chilled, I regretted having pushed with my questions into Tighe's weakened container. This has nothing to do with me, I thought. It was a romantic notion to think that I still had a connection to Jane, that I mattered in the least to her, that what I'd experienced that summer was anything more than a fiction.

"Listen, Tighe, we don't have to do this now."

"I think we do, Colin."

"Why?"

"Why. Why. Good question. Because if I don't..." He went quiet.

"What? If you don't, what? You still there? Tell me what you called to say."

"She...she was always incredible about coping. You know?"

"Jane, you mean."

"Even when she was little, she had this way. It was like, I don't know exactly, like she could turn into whatever she needed to be. Good girl, party girl, ice queen, loudmouth.

Whatever. I could never do that. I had my one thing, big Tighe, big dependable moose. Nobody...nobody thought I could feel bad inside, because I was always big, lovable and tough."

"So, this thing, it didn't just happen to Jane. It happened to you, too."

"I guess you could say that. Our mother, her and Dad were fighting a lot. Dad was seeing this other woman, she's out of the picture now, and he couldn't decide if he was going to leave us to live with her or break it off or what. Our mother kept at him, demanding an answer and he couldn't tell her. He needed more time, he said. 'Stop bothering me, woman. I will deal with this in my own way. If you had any respect for me you would back off.' But it was making her crazy. He was away so much for business, more now than ever, and all she could think was that he was with her. This went on for a long time. Months. Long time for a kid. I was maybe twelve, thirteen. I remember wishing that she would go away and he would come back, she was so strung out miserable, bringing the misery down on everybody. Just go, I wanted to tell her. Give him what he deserves. Walk out. That'll teach the bastard.

"He phoned one day and asked to speak to me, wanted to meet me downtown to talk, said he had something important to say, so I jumped on the Métro. He was at this swank bar, more like a men's club, with leather armchairs and old portraits on the wall. He was dressed in a new suit. Even then, at my age—I mean, what kid pays attention to what his parents are wearing?—I was impressed. He looked like a real smooth operator. I guess that's what love does for you.

"We sat at this almost private table in part of the room that had its own glass doors, and he closed them. 'Tighe,' he said, 'I've come to a decision and I wanted to tell you first.' 'You should tell Mom first, don't you think?' 'No, it's important I tell you first, son, because you're almost a man now and you have to be strong for your mother.' 'You're going away.' 'That's right,' he said, 'I'm going to live with the woman I told you about. I love her and it's best that your mother and I...what I'm trying to say is that you're going to stay with your mother and Jane will come live with me.'"

"Was that all right?" I asked.

"Hell no, it wasn't all right! What kind of question is that, Was that all right?"

"I meant did you handle it all right. Did you cope?"

"That year I grew like ten inches taller and bulked right out. People who used to pat me on the head, now I was patting them on the head. And strong. I thought I could do anything. I mean, cope? Cope is nothing. I thought I could solve everything. Thing is, our mother, when she heard about our father's brilliant solution, the magic saw-the-family-in-half trick, she went berserk. No way was she letting him take Jane, even around the corner. He got a legal separation and then a divorce. He had a good lawyer who convinced the judge that our father's plan was the best one, since our mother refused to cooperate. Refused to play his sick game, was how she put it. 'Go, just go,' she told him. 'You've got your whore, I give you your freedom. What do you want with my little girl?' 'Jane needs a stable mother,' he said. He convinced the court that her drinking made her unfit. I never quite got the logic. Apparently it was fine for me to live with her, somehow I was immune, but Jane was impressionable, had more to gain or lose."

"I can see that," I said.

"Good for you, because I never could and neither could Jane. All we could see was two adults squabbling over what was best for them. A boy for her and a girl for him. Even-Steven. As I said, it was a mess. It took a court order and the police to pry Jane out of our mother's grip. It was ugly. Screaming, Jane crying, Mom being restrained by this cop who used way too much force. Dad was outside waiting in the car on the street. He didn't even come inside. I'll never forgive him for that, for not being there and getting his hands dirty, hearing the noise. He was the one who started it all."

Beth got up and went into the kitchen. She reappeared with a glass of water. "Colin, it's so late." I made a helpless gesture and nodded my head. Soon, soon. This was important.

"So she wasn't content to live apart from Jane."

"You got it, Pontiac. Dad's lawyer had conveniently filed a restraining order preventing Mom from coming within so many blocks of him or Jane, and this was too much for her. Some women would've given up, let it defeat them, or accept it and get on with their lives."

"I don't know too many who would, Tighe."

"Ya, well, Mom was not one, she was the extreme opposite. All it did was make her more determined than ever to get Jane back. So she did some sleuthing, hired a detective and found out where they were living, which was in Outremont, and one night didn't she up and sneak in the house and kidnap Jane. The police came in the morning with a social worker and took the kid away to a foster home, and she stayed there for like a week until Dad could convince the family-court judge that he had been the injured party—him!—and Jane should come home. Which she did, but not until after a week of thinking she was never going to see any of us again. You can imagine what that does to a kid."

I let out a murmur of understanding.

"This happened a couple more times. Mom hanging around Jane's school at dismissal time, taking her for a milkshake, another time to a movie, Dad getting wind of it, calling the friggin' gendarmes and this time getting her cited for violating the writ. Couple hundred dollars in fines did nothing. She comes back more determined than ever. But also I see something new in her eyes, an emptier desperation. She stopped caring about herself, stopped eating, didn't change her clothes or wash her hair. That was when I learned how to cook. Everything. Got myself up and out to school on time. Made sure there was supper for the two of us, even though half of it usually went into the garbage. I thought, If this is what being married is like, no thank you.

"That went on, I don't know, not too long, until we learned that Dad and Jane were moving away, we didn't know where, exactly. The woman he had taken up with didn't seem to be in the picture anymore. She had probably had it with all the legal wrangling and the abductions, Mom waking everybody up in the middle of the night, smashing bottles against the side of the house him and Jane were renting at the time. Now, thinking that she wasn't going to be able to see Jane anymore, she went dead almost. What's the word? Cat-something."

"Catatonic."

"Right. I thought she'd gone completely nuts for a while there. Then all of a sudden she's normal. It's like whatever connection was loose got tightened. She fixed herself right up, took care of the way she looked, got her hair done, got a prescription for sleeping pills, started working at the Musée. Everything seemed good again. I missed Jane and my father, sure, what kid wouldn't, but I also believed that this wasn't going to last forever. One day we'd be back together, the four of us, the way it used to be.

"I was in Boy Scouts that year, I remember. All my friends in school were, too. Geez it was fun. When I was doing Scouts I forgot about everything going on at home. We were planning a big overnight camping trip, everybody getting hyper thinking about it, trying to calm each other down with list-making and assigning duties, but I was still buzzing when I got out of the meeting, it was at my old school. Mom was waiting for me in the car. Usually I didn't talk much. This time, though, you couldn't shut me up. I had to tell her everything we had planned, every cookout, every canoe trip, every game of Capture the Flag. It was good, I guess, because I didn't notice just how distracted she was as she drove and didn't notice that we went right by the turn-off to our street. Soon we were in a part of the city I didn't recognize and I asked her where we were going. To get Jane, she said, and I think I started to cry. She reached across and gave me a slap back-handed across the face to make me shut up. Which I did. I just sat there biting my lip.

"She had used her detective to find Dad and Jane again and had gotten word to her somehow that she was coming to see her. It was urgent that Jane get out of the house at a set time and wait for the car a few blocks away. She wasn't allowed to say anything to Dad. I don't know exactly what she told Jane. Her life was in danger or something like that. Anyway, when we came down their street and drove past the house, there she was waiting with her little blue suitcase in her hand. She stepped back into some bushes when she saw the car. We pulled up and I rolled down the window to show her my face. She didn't take a second to look up and down the street, just made for the back door, which I had reached back and unlocked.

"I remember she looked scared slouched down in the back seat. Mom didn't say anything. I reached my hand back between the seats to touch Jane's. She said, 'What?' and slapped it away. I think maybe I needed the reassurance more than she did."

Tighe paused again. His breathing was heavy into the mouthpiece of the phone. A sip and gulp, then the release of breath like a gasp. Dead air for five seconds, ten, twenty. I didn't say anything.

"I knew something weird was up. You sense it. You feel it like something caught at the back of your neck, itching the crap out of you. It felt good to have Jane there. I thought, okay, three is fine. We can make do. My father, I was letting him go, it was like I was the one driving away from him, not Jane. You read about boys trying to knock their fathers off the hill, replace them, like it's some kind of rite of passage we all have to go through. You're not a man until you can beat your old pop at an arm wrestle sort of thing.

"What I remember is this two-sided feeling, like, one, I was thinking about what it was going to be like to be grown up like my father and maybe it was all right for him to be starting over with another woman, maybe he was better off without us dragging him down and reminding him of all the sad stuff. And two, helpless, because he wasn't there and he usually drove the car and where were we going now?

"She wasn't slowing down for stop signs or traffic lights. Ran a couple of reds. I mean, scary, right? Not speeding up going through the intersection like you'd expect. She was refusing to accept that they even existed, those red lights, not for her. Lucky for us the traffic wasn't too bad that time of day, but shit, narrow misses or what. It still wakes me up sometimes. You ever have dreams like that?"

I told him I did. I have one about falling to earth from a great distance, waiting to hit, but lying in bed while it was happening. Not surprisingly, Tighe's was about driving at high speed through red lights into busy intersections.

"She got us out of the city and headed over the bridge to the West Island. At Beaconsfield we turned toward the river. It might have been Pointe Claire. All I know is it wasn't familiar. Quiet streets, lots of trees, nice sidewalks, front lawns and hedges sort of place. I thought, sure, okay, maybe this is where we're moving to live now. We passed a school with a big playground, plenty of grass and running room, not like the cramped pavement of the school I was going to at the time. Baseball diamond, hoops, I liked that. I convinced myself that this was what we were doing and that we'd go back to get our clothes and furniture later.

"You think you got it all figured out, even when you're a kid. You know you don't know everything, but that doesn't stop you from thinking that what you do know makes sense. We were coming close to the water and I could see some lights from the city, the lights of cars going over the bridges. Sailboats, a marina. Maybe we we're going to live on a houseboat. I'd always thought it'd be cool to live on a boat. That's what I was thinking then, changing my hopes and expectations to fit the change in scenery. Jane hadn't said a word. I looked back and couldn't see her face very well. Her legs were going like she had to go to the bathroom. She might've been asleep.

I think I asked my mother if this was where we were going to live. She kept driving as if she couldn't hear me.

"If we were going to live on a houseboat—and it sure looked like that's where we were headed, because we were inside a big marina complex now and driving along a private stretch that led to all these docks—we'd need electricity hooked up for heat in the wintertime. I wondered if we would have to pull the boat out of the water or leave it there. If we let it get frozen in the ice, that might damage the hull. Maybe the hull was built super strong to withstand the pressure. I wanted to sleep in a captain's bed with the raised wooden side designed to keep you from rolling out during heavy seas. A friend of mine built captains' bunks for his kids. I pictured keeping my clothes in the drawers built in to the bottom part of the bed. That appealed to me, still does. I don't mind small spaces as long as they're designed good. Funny thing for somebody my size to say, right? But it's true, I like the feeling of being tucked in.

"I remember it was fall, school had started and Scouts, so it was maybe late September, early October, getting nippy, the air. Nice time of year, maybe my favourite. Francesca and me, we like to drive up on Mount Royal with the kids and have a picnic at Beaver Lake. You ever do that, Colin?"

Yes, I said, we did, all the time.

"It's too tough a climb for them, my nippers. I usually get roped into carrying them. They're light as feathers. I can take both of them on my back and hardly notice it, they're that little, my girls. They're growing up too fast. You turn around, they're up to there on you. You know what I mean? Blink and you miss it.

"Anyway, there's other cars parked on some of the docks. All these white masts rocking back and forth, the plinking sound of ropes and wires slapping against hollow things. Like all these boats are talking impatiently to each other. When you heading out again? What you rubbing up against? Sounds like Styrofoam, it's squeaking so much. He fix that cracked keel on you yet? How does a kid know he loves boats so much when he's never been on one? Don't ask me. All I know is I was into them instantly. I wanted to get out of the car and step down into one and squeeze down into a cabin, press my face up against the glass of a little round porthole, maybe see underwater when the waves splashed high. And we could go anywhere we wanted. Head out on a good day. Up the seaway to the Gulf, around to who knows where. The Maritimes, Boston, New York, Florida. The freedom of it, the whole idea—how does something like that take a hold of you in an instant? Where does it come from? It must have been hiding in me and I never knew it. A boat. Sails. Something about floating, not being in a car, not having to stop and buy gas and drive alongside a million lunatics who think they're in the Grand Prix. I could take classes by two-way radio. We could sail around the world and I could go to school wherever we happened to be. Or not. Learn some other languages. What a feeling. Getting on toward night, it's dark, we're finally stopped on one of the docks, the whole scene is like out of a movie it's so new and strange, and fuck if I'm not planning the rest of my life around one of these sixteen-footers.

"Jane roused and said she had to go to the bathroom. I think, in her state, for her to say that out loud meant she couldn't hold it any longer. I'm jolted out of my daydream. Mom is sitting like she's waiting for something, a signal, maybe. Both hands gripping the wheel tight even though we're idling and in Park. At least I thought we were in Park, until she takes her foot off the brake and we start rolling forward, headed for the end of the dock. It's concrete, solidly built with substantial pylons or whatever you call them that the lines are tied to. These people who moor here, they must have money. Only rich people can afford to buy boats like these. The rental cost of keeping your boat there. I know how it is now. Did I, back then? I can't say for sure. I do know that whatever feeling I was having, that boff daydream about living on a boat and sailing around the world, when Jane spoke, like the bubble I was in broke and I knew we didn't belong there. Don't ask me how.

"Jane said again how she really had to go, she wanted out, and the car was picking up speed even though I don't think she had her foot on the gas. I looked at her, then ahead to the water, to her again. No change of expression. Stone rigid. Mom, Mom, I say to her, Jane has to get out. Not, Stop immediately, you crazy nutcase psycho, pathetic obsessive loser, self-destructive suicidal mental case. Jane has to go to the bathroom. Nobody else is on the wharf. There might've been people in the boats themselves, but I don't remember seeing any lights on.

"Something made me roll my window down. Maybe I was trying to get out or thinking about jumping out. Just as my hand stopped, not able to get it any lower, she hits the gas, like stomps on it full throttle, and we kick ahead, laying rubber like a dragster until the tires catch. The front wheels hit the raised edge of the dock, the impact is this jolt that brings the rear end up off the ground for a sec and then we're over. The funny thing is it's not like one of those rides. You ever been on that log ride at La Ronde? La Flume? Your stomach rises into your throat for a couple seconds, then you hit bottom and all the water splashes over you, especially if you're sitting in the front? Well, it didn't feel nothing like that. It was this slow-motion feeling. We're over, the front of the car goes down, we hit the water, start to sink. The water is coming in the window fast, holding us in. The whole car fills up in no time. I remembering breathing in some water, choking, coughing it out, taking a breath before the air pocket disappeared, and undoing my seatbelt.

"Somehow, don't ask me how, I pull myself up out the window and I swim to the surface. It doesn't take too long. The water's maybe ten, fifteen feet deep and the car's on the bottom. Not much of a current there. We're in this protected bay. I start yelling for help and before I've stopped yelling and crying I hear a splash in the water and then another, close by me. Two men on another dock must've seen the car go over and they come running over. Dive in. I try a duck dive to go down to the car again, but it's too dark to see anything. I have to come back up. It feels like I can hardly keep my head above water. Somebody's arm comes around my chest from behind and I'm being pulled toward the dock. He gets me to grab hold of the ladder. Can you get up? Yes, I think so. I tell him Jane is still down there.

"I try climbing up the ladder, but got no strength left, so I loop my arm through and float there, waiting for I don't know what. It's too long a time. There's people now above my head. They're asking each other what happened and is anybody down there. Beams of light move across the surface. I try to get up the ladder again. Somebody spots me from above. A life ring on a rope drops beside me. I put it over my head and shoulders so it's snug under my armpits and then they're pulling me up. Fresh catch. Look everybody, caught me a live boy! I don't realize I'm cold until they lay me out on the wharf and put a jacket over me and I start shivering, my whole body shaking uncontrollably. Somebody says, 'He's in shock.'

"I try to ask about Jane and my mother, but my teeth are chattering too much. I hear a siren. Strong red light flashing. An ambulance backs down the dock until it's close. The back doors open. '*Bouge pas, p'tit, sois calme*,' a man says, wrapping me in a heavy blanket. They lift me onto a stretcher, it rises up on wheels, and I get slid into the compartment. It's a nice feeling. Snug, like I was talking about before. The lights are on and I start looking around at the equipment. It all looks important. Everything has something written on the side in French. One of the attendants gives me some water, asks me if I'm hungry. No, I say. Where's my...? Where's my...? But I can't get it out. Don't worry, he says. They're okay. They're in the other ambulance. I don't remember nothing else. I guess I passed out."

It was eight on a Saturday morning when Max came by in a rental truck, and we drove first to his office to get some boxes of personal effects. His hair, still black, was returning in soft, wispy patches. As he unlocked the office door, he said, "Of all the people she knows, Chandra will miss you and Beth the most. She wanted me to ask Beth not to come today. Did you know that?"

"Nothing would have kept her away, Max."

"Oh, I know, and I told her that. She was adamant, though. I asked her if she felt it was just too hard to say goodbye, take too much out of her. She said no, it wasn't that exactly. She said she was afraid that if she saw Beth again she might not be content to go. She said something about it being messy, her wanting to drag a piece of this world away with her. Funny."

I didn't think it was funny at all. Max grew quiet and his breathing laboured as we carried cartons down the corridor from the office to the elevator. The upper level of the mall was beginning to fill with shoppers.

When we arrived at the house, I got out of the truck and began to direct him down the steep drive. The slope and design of the laneway demanded three tight turns, a difficult enough manoeuvre in a car, and I had to keep sending him back up to make new approaches. He looked like he was becoming bewildered, as if he had been awakened by my voice, only to find that he was not in bed but seated at the impossible wheel. He'd hired a man with a backhoe to line the entire driveway with large boulders, and these now stymied the truck's progress. I said as much to him. What I said—and I knew as soon as I'd said it that it was a poor choice of commentary—was that I wondered what had possessed him to make the approach to his house impassable.

He climbed down from the cab, leaving the driver's door wide open and the engine running, brushed by me, stomped down the pavement and slammed his way into the house. A man named Tim, who was married to Angela, one of Max's colleagues, brought the truck the rest of the way down.

Beth was sitting with Chandra on her bed, helping her sort through various piles of papers.

"What did you say to Max?"

When I told her, she said that the best thing I could do for the moment was to mind the children, the Nazreens' as well as two who belonged to Tim and Angela.

Chandra's brother, Gary, who had flown from Colorado to drive the truck once it was loaded, was trying to keep the children occupied in the living room. A large blue cartoon genie was singing and changing shape every few seconds to an inattentive audience. Tim and Angela's youngest, Manny, decided then that he wanted to see his mother, and began to cry inconsolably when Gary wrapped his arms around him to keep him out of the kitchen. Manny's wails triggered a similar response in Lori and Vaughan Nazreen, who darted past me in an end-run around the couch. This pulled the women, Angela wrapping china plates in newsprint, and Beth sifting bills, wills, and homemade Mother's Day cards, away from their work, the exasperation wry on their faces.

Hearing the heavy rear door of the U-Haul roll up, Gary left to help Tim load boxes. I ducked down the stairs to the basement. Midway down sat a shallow box containing a dozen each of seed packets and empty plastic medicine bottles. I picked it up and brought it into the basement, where Max was hunched over a red toolbox open on the floor.

"What do you want done with these, Max? I thought someone might trip on them."

"I know exactly where those are going," he said, taking the box and placing it beside the tools.

"Tell me where to begin, then."

Everything stacked against one wall was to be loaded onto the truck, while all else was garbage. Armed with this distinction, I began carrying the larger items, a floor lamp, a set of four kitchen chairs, a child's bicycle, upstairs. The children were colouring on large sheets of newsprint spread on the kitchen floor while Angela and Beth put cookware into boxes and dry goods into plastic grocery bags.

"There's an empty chest of drawers ready to go in Chandra's room," said Beth.

Chandra was asleep on her back on the wide bed, the stacks of envelopes and manila files arranged on either side of her. She was able to concentrate only for short stretches now before having to rest. The papers around her were barely disturbed by the rise and fall of her breathing. I sat gingerly at the foot of the bed. Her deep olive skin that had once glowed, regally, beneath black eyes and a noble nose, so arrogant, always so right, was now like parchment. Her mane of thick black hair, tossed at me more than once in teasing condescension in symposia and departmental meetings and dimly lit restaurants, was now a cropped white cloud. The pupils of her eyes seemed visible through onionskin lids.

Beth said, "Colin, Tim says he has room for that dresser now. Do you want help with it?"

I stood abruptly and the room grew dim. She got me to bend down on one knee and lower my head.

"You've been going at it too hard, mister. Why don't you loosen that?" She unbuttoned my collar. "I bet it's pressing on your carotid sinus."

After a few minutes I regained my head and set out to prove my fitness, despite Beth's warning, by moving the dresser out to the truck all by myself.

The rest of the day passed as if I were watching a grainy film of it, including my own efforts, projected onto the bare walls of the house. The family renting the house arrived in the midst of the upheaval to swim in the lake, and changed into their suits in the bathroom. When they announced that they had forgotten their towels, Max dug through already packed boxes to find some for them. During this time a woman arrived to look at the kitchen table and chairs Max was selling.

"I really like the set," she said, "but I have no way to get it home. Can you deliver it?"

"No, I'm sorry, I can't," said Max.

"Most places deliver."

"I am not most places."

"Well, I just thought when I saw that big truck parked outside..."

"Madam, you go outside and look in the back of that truck. Look at how much bloody room there is in there. If I had room enough for a table and four chairs, I would be sending them on to Mile High City, now wouldn't I?"

She left without purchasing anything. Chandra called Max into the bedroom to chastise him for his rudeness and he absorbed her censure patiently. Nothing she said, whether it was that he had tied an antique serving board closed so that it was in danger of being scratched by the cord, or that he was being a tyrant for not having arranged lunch yet, or that the flight to Denver he had booked for her was all wrong because it left in the morning and she would never be able to nap on the wretched airplane in the morning, diminished his attention to her. Nor did he reduce himself in obsequiousness. Never did he reply that bond-weakening utterance, "Yes, dear."

When I saw him again, Max was holding a glass filled with a thick, brown liquid that resembled chocolate milk. The drink, Chandra's Sludge as Max called it, was a bitter concoction that came in the form of a brown powder in a small plastic bottle, the same type of container I'd found with the seed packets in the box on the stairs. The cure was a combination of four wild roots and barks, all common and native to North America, dried and pulverized. To mix the solution, the powder first had to be boiled in water for a number of hours, strained through a clean cloth, boiled again, and then cooled. Its name derived from that of a Canadian nun who had adapted a native Indian recipe to cure a number of her colleagues of breast cancer early in the century. Each twenty-eight-gram bottle cost fifty dollars and lasted about a week. Until recently the Sludge had been a point of contention between Beth and the Nazreens.

"If you keep ignoring my advice, I can't be your doctor anymore," Beth would say. Chandra kept drinking the Sludge and Beth kept driving out to the lake every evening to see her.

Because the renting family was bringing in its own refrigerator, Max and Chandra's had to be moved into the basement as the final act of the day. This news came not from Max but Gary, who seemed to be just waking up while the rest of us leaned, sweat-stained and drooping, against various counters and doorjambs in the kitchen. Angela was down at the lake with the children. Beth closed the vertical blinds against the early evening sun, and then stood with her arms crossed watching Gary work with a large screwdriver.

"There's a good part of your weight right there," he said, leaning the door against the sink. All the food had been removed and either thrown away or placed in plastic bags with the two families' names on them. Beth's and mine, the smaller, contained the food the children would never have eaten: jars of chutney, curry mixes, cans of mushrooms, sardines, pungent cracker spreads. The other, Tim and Angela's, contained breakfast cereal, cookies, bread, four boxes of lasagne noodles, jelly mixes, juice boxes, raisins, and chicken noodle soup.

Gary marshalled us around the empty shell and we shuffled with it to the top of the basement stairs. Gary and Tim took the heavier bottom end and proceeded down backwards. At the bottom of the stairs the doorway was not wide enough for two to pass through at once. Tim took the weight as Gary crawled under the refrigerator and through the door. During this transfer the pair grunted and swore and laughed through gritted teeth as if this were the activity they had hoped to be doing all day. Tim then had to wait until Max reached him on that side before he could take his share of the load again.

"You'll have to let me take it the rest of the way, Max."

"No," said Max, "you are my guests. This is my burden. I have to..."

Gary swore at him to give up his place.

"I'm trapped here until you move," said Tim. "Gary can't hold that whole back end much longer."

Max let Tim take the weight and he stepped back up the stairs. On the other side, expecting another step but finding none, I stumbled and sidestepped quickly to regain my balance. As I did so, I stepped onto the edge of the box of seeds and empty medicine bottles. The contents flipped out, the seeds rattling snake-like, the plastic bottles bouncing with hollow pongs around my shoes. My arms gave out and the side of the appliance I was holding toppled slowly. As Tim tried to correct the imbalance, Gary sang out new profanity, and the whole thing crashed to the floor.

"How did those get back there? I moved them out of the way," I complained.

"I know exactly where they're going."

"No, you don't. You haven't a clue where those are going. Somebody could've been hurt. Wake up, Max. Just wake up."

Tim and Gary righted the appliance and pushed it into a corner of the basement. Beth came downstairs and helped Max pick up the scattering of seeds that had burst from their packets.

"They're to go all around the property. Around the boulders. Soften the rocks a bit. For memory and luck. I've known for a long time now where I want them to go. I just haven't found the time to plant them."

After that we wandered around the house in the falling darkness, picking up toys and crayons and bits of paper, looking for more to do. The truck could hold no more. Chandra's rocking chair would not fit, and so she gave it to Tim and Angela. Max told us to feel free to take anything that had been destined for the trash, but there was now a quickly descending sense that we had only a little time left in which to depart, that to stay was to risk being locked inside something dark and airless. We said our goodbyes quickly as if we were going to see the Nazreens the next day, and then walked up the driveway past the moving van to the road above, where the cars were parked. I got in, moved the driver's seat back, and reached across to unlock Beth's side. She opened the door but did not get in.

"Wait for me, please. I won't be long." I assumed she wanted to say goodbye to Chandra again. I rolled my window down and listened to the sound of her receding footsteps. From the dark came amplified sounds: water lapping at a dock, a dog barking from across the lake, tree branches rubbing overhead. The screen door opened and slapped shut. I waited for the same sound that would signal her return.

Finally I got out of the car and walked down the driveway, feeling my way more than seeing from one of Max's boulders to the next. Around the final turn the truck loomed, grinning with dim eyes. No lights were on in the house, but from a point beside and just below it, on the slope to the lake, came an irregular flash of light, and I walked around the house toward it.

Max's landscaping plans had included an extension of the line of boulders along both sides of a wide path that led from the front corner of the house diagonally down through a series of terraced sections to the beach. Max and Beth were moving up from one rock to the next. Beth held the shallow cardboard box and a flashlight that she kept trained on the ground where Max sliced open a mouth of soil with a shovel. Beth handed him one of the empty Sludge containers, which he dropped into the hole and tamped down with the toe of his shoe. After she sprinkled in some seeds, he removed the blade of the shovel and stomped twice to close the gash.

They were doing it all wrong. The seeds were much too deep. Max's technique was better suited to the planting of seedling conifers than to perennials. It would take a miracle for any of those flowers to show themselves in the spring. This furtive attempt to carry out his plan by darkness was comical but salvageable. I opened my mouth to tell them I was there and to set them right. All I could get out was, "Beth. I was worried."

"About me?"

"Yes, I..."

"You shouldn't be. Do you want to help?"

"Help? No, that's okay. I'll just watch."

When the last of the packets was emptied, the three of us hugged. I apologized for yelling at Max, who said that he would miss us and that he wished we could move to Denver with him. We said we wished we could, too. We told him we would visit as soon as we could.

The Woman
in the Vineyard

WHEN TROYER CALLED to say that he was going to be in the city a few weeks and needed a bed—nothing more, he promised, I would hardly be aware of his presence—I offered him my modest guest room. He had taken one of my writing workshops and was someone I had recommended for residencies and grants. I suppose I considered him something of a protegé.

At the time of his arrival I lived alone. I spent my days in my attic office, my evenings reading and listening to music. In that indefinite period between the breakup of my most recent relationship and any desire to begin a new one, I was uncharacteristically serene. Problems that used to upset me I dealt with in a workmanlike manner, as if it were not my but my neighbour's front lawn that had to be trenched in order to free the sewer pipe of tree roots, not my but a gremlin's fault that a clogged gutter had led to an ice dam and leaking roof. Solitude, although not a state I wish for myself for the remainder of my days, does bring with it clarity of mind generally unattainable by those entwined in intimate relationships. A day or an entire season can take on a felicitous shape, sprung from within rather than through negotiation. On the other hand, during that time of celibate bachelorhood I was more likely than before to invite company, more likely to chance rejection if only to stave off boredom.

Troyer arrived when he said he would, emerging from a taxi after what seemed, as I watched from the living room window, an unusually long time. He explained that he had had to use his bank card to pay for the ride from the airport and had forgotten his identification number. His credit card balance was over its limit and so he wrote the cabby a cheque. I remarked that in this city the taxi drivers usually took only cash. "You must have a trustworthy face," I said.

"Oh, but I do," he replied. "Everyone tells me that. I can't count the number of times I've dined out on the mere assumption that I am an honest man."

He travelled light, carrying only a leather weekender grip and a good umbrella. The carry-on was in the style of bag doctors used to tote when they made house calls. This one had an inner sleeve for his laptop. He was otherwise unencumbered. He said he didn't maintain an apartment anymore. When he taught his one semester out of three per year, he rented a college dorm room. The other eight months of the year he lived abroad. Paper correspondence, of which he received very little by then, went to his office at the arts college where he had tenure or to his literary agent. It seemed an ideal, attractive life, the freedom of it immensely appealing. He went from friend to friend all around the world, trying never to overstay his welcome. I meant to ask him how he decided when to move on. He had to be sensitive to his hosts, their personality, their ability to accommodate the writer, and their circumstances at that point in their lives. As it turned out, he left before I could learn his trick of never staying in one place so long that he began to smell like yesterday's fish.

I should add that I have not loved everything this author has written. We met before Troyer became published. At that time I enjoyed being a facilitator as much as I did a teacher and took it upon myself to introduce him to editors at publishing houses where I was known. Unfortunately none of these contacts accepted his work, and he published his first collection of stories independently, online, in what seemed a regrettable instance of desperate vanity. In most cases, after the self-published author has paid out more money than the book will ever recoup in sales, and after he has distributed a copy to every member of his family, the urge to write subsides, the fire dying to a weak ember, and the *auteur soi-disant* gets on with leading a more realistic life.

Troyer, however, did not fit that model of defeat. A newly established literary agent happened to read his ebook and within minutes of finishing the collection had signed him as his representative. In almost that brief a period they had a contract with a reputable literary publisher to release the stories in print and to publish his novel-in-progress when it was completed. This pathway to publication has become the norm rather than the exception. The entire industry, its very aesthetic, has been turned on its head. How readers choose to consume their quirky fiction, stories in which cardboard cutout characters say silly or outrageous things and act with risible predictability, is their prerogative. Troyer, to his credit, was not being untrue to his nature when he wrote his frothy accounts of young, cosmopolitan, urban professionals hooking up, breaking up, crying on each other's shoulder, laughing about childish matters, and exhibiting an astounding lack of civic engagement and personal responsibility.

We would see each other first thing in the morning and not again until late afternoon. He liked to spend his mornings out and about, visiting galleries and museums and writing a few hours in a library or coffee shop before meeting a friend or colleague for lunch. He seemed to have no end of contacts in the city, despite never having lived here. I, on the other hand, have been here all my life and can count the number of people I see regularly on the fingers of one hand. I say this merely to illustrate the difference between Troyer and me. Too much socializing puts me off my work. Even having him under my roof caused me to change my habits and consequently my output, which has never been voluminous. To look at the situation objectively, the unhappy truth was that his presence, however limited, affected me to the point of distraction. I asked myself, was this jealousy? Was I committing that most pathetic offence against art, the personal comparison? I suppose I was. The man was younger than I, had been writing for fewer years, and yet had achieved more. More books published, more critical attention, more appearances at literary festivals and on television and radio, more money earned. In the meantime, those whose opinions I trusted told me that I had a reputation for integrity, literary quality and anti-commercialism. The writer's writer, a particularly dubious distinction. See what that buys you at the grocery store.

Because the results of my culinary efforts are unpredictable, Troyer and I would often eat out at the end of the day, alternating between three Asian restaurants I like and can afford. My house guest was to his credit agreeable in this and in most matters generally. The secret to his ability to live and travel cheaply, I could see, was this highly consistent bonhomie. He went along with you, he sat still in the middle of the boat, he listened while others spoke, his glass always charged ready for the next toast. It was his quiet genius, really. Had he not been a novelist he would have made a successful diplomat or spy.

We were eating Korean sashimi and drinking hot sake when he recounted a story from his latest trip abroad. He had stayed at a French retreat, an artists' colony that had once been a monastery, near the village of Vacqueyras. The administrators of the institution maintained the simplicity of the former religious order, asking visitors to keep to themselves except during meals, refrain from making loud sounds, and respect the natural beauty of the grounds, which ran to many acres and incorporated a large vineyard. A celebrity vintner, his expensive, limited-quantity wines highly sought, grafted new varieties of grape onto established vines of Grenache and Syrah, harvested the fruit and paid the colony a handsome fee, the income helping offset the cost of accommodating the artists.

The winemaker was none other than Heinz Werner Glick, the filmmaker. Glick hired locals to see to the day-to-day work of pruning the vines, checking for blight, forcing the fruit to work for its water. Sometimes the auteur showed up on the property, as much to be seen as to see to his crop. He was known to enjoy the impact his presence made on the painters, composers, choreographers, dramaturges, actors and writers who might be trying to work. It was even thought he did so to throw people off their creativity. Troyer did not want to believe that this giant of post-reunification German cinema could be so deliberately disruptive. On the other hand, he said, not to test the hypothesis would have been a lost opportunity for someone who depended on the subversive tendencies of the psyche for the material of his stories. And so, learning at breakfast one morning that Glick was there that day, Troyer set out to put himself where the man would have no choice but to speak with him.

If you happen to be familiar with Glick's oeuvre, you know that such little schemes of convenience rarely turn out as planned. A woman obsessed with her child's music teacher destroys her marriage, reputation and career, as well as the nerves in her hands, while learning to play the piano. The very investigative body he established to root out graft and influence-peddling arrests a politician who had presented himself to the electorate as a reformer pitted against corruption. A legendary professional cyclist pushes his grandson to pursue the same rigorous pastime, with deadly result. Synopses reduce a work of art to a mere wisp of itself and many feel Glick has been unfairly branded a pessimist, and yet the curdling of hope does seem to be one of his dominant themes. Some who believe in karma might suggest that the negativity expressed in his work has prevented him from achieving the masterpieces of some of his contemporaries and has kept him out of the inner circle of prizewinners. My house guest might not have been thinking about such matters while he ambled towards the vineyard. Still, I wonder if he could feel his intention turning against him with every nonchalant step he took in that direction.

The filmmaker was standing on an access road that ran alongside the vineyard. The road was paved in brilliant white quartz gravel, which the monks had arranged to be brought from many kilometers away. It was a highly prized surface because it produced little dust, thus reducing the amount of water needed to clean the harvested grapes before they were crushed. Troyer was dazzled by the scene: the shining path, almost blinding in the bright summer sunshine; the deep green and purple masses clustered low and hugging the undulating contours of the landscape; Glick, who had Turkish and

Hungarian in his family background, standing, dressed all in workman drab, his instantly identifiable uniform that could also cause him to be mistaken for Fidel Castro, his black beard aimed at the sky, gesticulating angrily; his interlocutor, a trim, athletic-looking woman in her late forties who was dressed in running shoes and lightweight track suit, a headband holding her hair off her face, shifting her weight from foot to foot while listening. Or pretending to listen. Troyer thought he saw her attention stray. The slightest shift of the head, a loss of shoulder alignment.

I picture Troyer attempting to approach the couple soundlessly, his intention hampered by the brittle crunch of gravel underfoot. My onetime house guest is a small man. I would say he is the right weight for his height. He is pleasingly proportioned, if I can make that observation without it being construed as anything more than an aesthetic judgment. A film camera would capture this man's tidy, compact body and economical movements and call it the encapsulation of grace. I noticed, the few times we walked together, that no matter the length of his stride, his feet struck the ground directly in line with his center of gravity. He would lean forward, spine straight and aligned with his neck and legs. It was the subtlest suggestion that he was falling, each step a preventative act. The effect, then, of his curving approach across the lawn and along the snow-white path, must have been for anyone watching from a distance reminiscent of the approach of a hunting cat moving upon stationary game.

The woman dressed in running gear, Sylvaine Delacroix, was at one time an actor. She and Glick had been married many years earlier during a difficult time of poverty, child-rearing, competing professional desires and demands, and the erosive toll these circumstances took on the union. She appeared in many of his films. I won't say that she starred in them. Her scenes tend to place her in static poses with minimal dialogue and are distinguished by a strong tension between her body's evident desire to move and the physical restrictions placed upon her character. In one such memorable film she is naked standing navel-deep in fast-flowing icy water. As still as she is, after a quarter and then half a minute watching her we would swear she is being carried along by the current. The effect is achieved not by the movement of the camera, the change of angle or strength of lens magnification but by the alteration of light playing over and across her. Light and shadow animate her, the product of cloud flow we feel more than see. Every pore of her exposed skin puckers into gooseflesh. Her arms are held out to the side so that her fingers only just touch the surface of the stream. Our perspective is so tight on her that her surroundings are indistinct. We think of her as being in a mountainous region, although we can't be sure.

In another film she sits while riding in a series of public-transit vehicles. In each bus and train car she is held immobile within the tight pack of passengers sharing the space. The abutting shoulder of the man seated beside her, the bony hip of the woman standing in the aisle and steadying herself while holding the overhead strap, the large baby-carriage and its wailing occupant cutting the character played by Sylvaine Delacroix off from escape. Knowing now that dance was her passion and knowing that as an actress she was more than Glick's pawn, was in fact his enigmatic muse, I think of these early works as cruel exercises bordering on torture. The filming of a single scene can demand the intense attention of an entire day. Shooting, re-filming, changing perspective or endeavouring to reproduce the precise details of the previous take, Glick sacrificed everything on the altar of his art. Was his treatment of his actors, Ms. Delacroix in particular, a justifiable crime perpetrated in the name of a greater good? He was her husband. Did he cease to be married to her while he peered through the lens of his camera at a person in distress? And what use is such a question to someone in a darkened theatre watching the performance?

It turned out that Glick had not been aware that his ex-wife and former muse was staying at the monastery. Their meeting beside the vineyard was as far as he knew the result of chance. Troyer had no way of knowing this, not until much later. He drew near, coddling his assumption that Glick had waylaid her and that Glick was intent on undermining whatever practice, planning, training, meditation, creation of new work or combination of any of these she happened to be engaged in. Tit for tat, I believe, was Troyer's simplistic term for what he as third wheel was intending by way of intervention. He should have kept his distance. This is my assessment, not his. The writer remains on the sidelines for good reason: we lack the ability to take part in life and not mess it up more than it already is. Although we might have the inexplicable power to peer into the future, we tend not to recognize all that a moment holds, its entire significance, until we have had time to turn it over many different ways in our minds. Transformative memory for us takes the place of hindsight; it isn't so much that we look back to see an event for what it was as it is that we rewrite history to make it what in our estimation it should have been.

The woman saw Troyer first, the change in her eyes, the flicker of distraction signalling to Glick that this carefully blocked scene was about to be disrupted. The German, I have read, is notorious for his sudden storms on the set. The slightest interruption can trigger these outbursts. Actors, honoured to be working for such a legend, a genius, know that by doing so they put themselves within striking distance of his rage. These tantrums are reportedly dramatic, cinematic, even beautifully wrought, as if he had spent time planning their execution, matching them specifically to the moment and the perceived infraction, the crime against art, as he has been known to characterize these usually understandable and often unavoidable work stoppages. A sneeze, a forgotten line, a wardrobe malfunction, the weather, a shift in the light, the intrusion of the larger, unregulated world.

As Troyer tells it, anyone witnessing the moment would have thought that this unassuming pair was suddenly beset by a wild, hungry beast. The way they turned and their defensive postures made for a reaction incommensurate with the writer's arrival. It was otherwise a pleasant day, the air fresh and warm, the sunshine bright. The distant hills seemed to gesture to them as the ancients believed the gods reached down to intercede in mortal affairs. The vineyards exhaled an intoxicating *garrigue*. A scene less suited to fright and contention could not be imagined.

What did he want? Why was he bothering them? This was voiced not by the man, who had made his name slinging such challenges, but by the woman, who had, it seemed, left her submissive, pliant persona behind. How dare he sneak up on them in this way? It was at once the perfect inversion of what Troyer expected and the perfect effect he was after. Instead of the filmmaker deliberately undermining the bubble of tranquility in which the retreat lay suspended and protected from the fractious world, here was Glick defended as the purported victim of the same sort of mischief.

Troyer introduced himself, offering sincere apologies and explaining that he had only wanted to meet them, to simply say hello and give thanks for the films, copies of which he assured them were among his most cherished possessions. It was enough to defuse the woman's anger. Glick looked on, Buddha-like, saying nothing. He and Troyer shared a glance that Troyer took to mean that he should not be upset by her flash of pique. He had wandered into firing range and had been the recipient of misdirected ire.

"Yes, well, I am sorry also," said Sylvaine Delacroix warily. She thanked Troyer for his interest and said that she hoped to see him again but without their making a plan to meet. It was what you said to be polite when what you really wanted was to see the person's back becoming smaller. Glick gruffly offered similar conciliatory words, not quite apology since he had not been the one to wheel so viciously on Troyer but in the vein of no-hard-feelings, with a hearty handshake to seal the moment. The writer left the scene hastily. It was not quite "Exit pursued by bear," but Troyer admitted to a similar feeling, the metaphysical equivalent of hot breath on the back of his neck. Glick had been unperturbed. Rather, he let Troyer see how amused he was, a brief glimpse of the cards in his hand. It was Delacroix, strong, sharply defined, difficult, who figured in the writer's imagination now. As he walked away he was preoccupied with one question: when would he see her again and alone?

It is entirely plausible that Sylvaine Delacroix had conspired to be at the artists' retreat when her ex-husband was also going to be there. The reason? Confrontation, curiosity, revenge, longing, masochism or any combination of these. In today's most successful erotica, women let themselves be used as playthings by powerful men. What Glick created in his films was the opposite of this. It is in fact the antithesis of pornography. He is on record as saying that his goal always, his vision for the work of art, was the visual, kinetic record of a soul in torment, the victim of an indifferent world. She, Troyer believed, was tormented not by the cruel demands of an exacting artist but a monstrous neglect.

Perhaps I make too much of Troyer's intrusion and the couple's reaction to him. These are people aware of the tacit rules of social intercourse, after all. Against expectation, for example, one refrains from humiliating a stranger, someone perhaps never to be encountered again. The paved surface gives more to the runner than does the sandy beach. Because they better reflect our image and our intention, the firmer path, the better known quantity, the friend and the sibling take the greater pounding. Thus are we harder on those we know and love than we are on those with whom we form weaker emotional attachments, often because we can't separate love from desire, appetite, expectation, narcissism. Any image displayed in love's mirror, however familiar, is still a distortion of the actual. Troyer's intention in interrupting the former lovers dissolved rapidly in the acid bath of social convention. That said, I do think it led to something wholly unintended, a work of art that might not have come about otherwise.

In Troyer's fictional depiction of the encounter, as described in his novel, *The Woman in the Vineyard*, the Glick character, now a playwright, takes the novelist in hand as he might take an ingénue unsure of her emphasis, her lines or her character's motivation, his blacksmith-large arm and paw pulling her to him, comforting her paternally. The interloping scribe finds himself hustled off stage-left, as it were, not quite the bum's rush but close. The writer knows he is being hurried away. It is all right, it fits his desire: the playwright is the one he wants to speak with alone. He apologizes to the woman, in the novel a stage actress, assuring her that the last thing he wanted to do was to cause distress. She mumbles something dismissive, fixes the playwright momentarily with a searing look, and walks quickly off.

While he was staying with me Troyer worked on a suite of stories begun while he had been resident at the former monastery. They were set elsewhere, in Buenos Aires, the most recent city he had visited before going to Provence. I have confessed in these pages my lack of enthusiasm for much of this man's writing. I suppose the reason for this boils down to one thing: he employs the exotic as backdrop to the same story told repeatedly. A man travels the world in search of identity and acceptance. He seeks it in Taipei in the same way and with essentially the same result as in Chicago, Bruges, Nairobi or Istanbul. Cultural reactions to his hero, always the same figure, vary according to attitudes peculiar to the location. For the most part, however, because he tends to blend innocuously into whatever landscape surrounds him, acceptance is a relative constant. An entourage of young, rich, hedonistic drifters assembles to embrace him. Troyer, like most of us, leaves such immersion as Lawrence Durrell's in Alexandria, Paul Bowles' in Tangier and Henry Miller's in Paris for more daring writers.

My theory, for which I have no support beyond intuition, is that Troyer is a spy. He knows how to travel and where to stay without drawing attention. He is an accurate recorder of the sort of detail I tend to skip over in my writing: the shape of a face, the quality of the material in an outfit, the exact name of a hue. It is as if he were trained to see things at their most concrete. His identifiers peer below the surface, peek under the disguise. Good novelists do that well, though a mediocre storyteller will burden a novel with minutiae at the expense of narrative momentum. To further promote my unproven hunch, my house guest has been everywhere there has occurred a significant global event, the ousting of Morsi in Egypt, for example, and the recent bombings in Madrid and Mumbai. He was there only days before each. What it adds up to I can't say for certain. His presence neither prevented nor contributed to the events in question, as far as I can see, and I have tallied at least ten such instances. It used to be called skullduggery. Now it seems to be the way everyone operates. My first wife used to accuse me of being a crackpot conspiracy theorist, the sort who sees a clandestine government plot underlying every act of terror. I won't deny it, although in the ensuing time since 9/11/2001 I no longer make room-clearing statements. I still believe most of us have no clue about what our governments are doing in secret.

We were dining at a fashionable and expensive restaurant, Troyer's treat to thank me for my hospitality, when he told me more about Heinz Werner Glick. Content that he had achieved what he had set out to do, which was to "pull a fast one" before the same could be done to him, the writer began talking about the one film of Glick's he knew well, the one considered his best and which again featured Sylvaine Delacroix. The actress and the filmmaker were newly married then, as he recalled, and were very much, very publicly in love. They became adept at harnessing the power of publicity, any such attention attracted to their benefit, in the American style that is so pervasive now. This included the staging of loud embarrassing rows in restaurants and the publication of salacious rumours about the state of their union and the probability of infidelity. In one such press release, authored anonymously, it was suggested that she had become so enraged over one of her husband's many dalliances that she hired someone to have him killed. It was a falsehood, they assured the reading public in a magazine profile published in Milan, but not until the rumour had accomplished what they had wished it to, which was a heightened interest in their recently released film.

The plot was based on a true story, a famous murder in Zurich. An heiress was charged with killing her husband, a much younger man who it was believed had married her for her fortune. The murder was deemed an act of passion, the police assembling evidence to suggest that the woman had discovered her husband's true motive and was afraid that he was planning to kill her. Complicating the case was the fact that his body was never found and the method of murder mere conjecture. Young lovers out for a midnight bit of boating on the lake testified that they saw the heiress's yacht at rest nearby and heard the splash of something large heaved over the side. It was the young woman in the small boat who insisted she saw a body-sized bundle hit the water. Her paramour, oars in hand, was looking at her and away from the yacht.

The accused was able to provide an alibi for her whereabouts at the time of the supposed disposal of a body. Her maid had brought her some herbal tea in her bedroom at around 11:30 that night. The mistress of the house, her lawyer argued, could not have travelled across the city and then aboard her boat to the spot on the lake where the witnesses claimed they saw and heard something suspicious in time to have been directly involved. Given that she was of petite stature and unable alone to lift a man's corpse to drop it overboard, her accusers pursued a more likely explanation, that she had hired a killer and given him or her the means to use the yacht.

It would not have been an intelligent thing to do, the defence countered. Her boat was easily identified by its name, *Das Rastlose Mädchen.* Furthermore, the captain of the yacht had also been home at the time of its alleged use and knew nothing about the vessel having left its berth that night. The yacht was returned to its regular mooring unharmed and apparently untouched: no fingerprints other than those of the captain, the heiress, her husband, the deckhand, the galley cook and a few guests, all of whom could account for their whereabouts that night, turned up when the police dusted all surfaces.

Troyer has been able to live comfortably teaching part-time, writing his fictionalized travelogues, which he launches regularly and at a handsome profit to his publisher, travelling and enjoying the life of a peripatetic intellectual. He admitted to me that he considered his greatest failing his inability to avoid sticking his nose into the affairs of others, especially if the intrusion promised fodder for a good story. His initial urge, to interrupt the grandstanding of the German filmmaker, soon became intense curiosity about the man's relationship with the actress-turned-dancer. Unlike his fictional main character, he was intimidated by Glick, and so chose instead to engage the woman and to learn from her the particulars of her recent encounter with her ex-husband and the reason why they appeared to be so upset with each other.

The dancers in residence at the retreat, a group of five plus two choreographers, were all from different places and companies. The nature of their work made it difficult to create in isolation, and so together and with the addition of some young dancers from the region they developed new work and honed their skills. Much of the work involved physical conditioning and body awareness. Practitioners from the world of yoga, T'ai chi, sports medicine, drama and the musical arts all led workshops aimed at helping the dancers become stronger, more flexible, more expressive and more receptive to the demands of new work.

They had the use of a large indoor space, a former granary converted to a dance studio, its stone floor covered by a more forgiving surface. Light entered through high small windows near the ceiling, and two of the walls that shared a corner were entirely mirrored. A reliable pianist accompanied the sessions. Troyer noted this woman's ability to sight-read and to intuit from minimal suggestion the choreographer's wishes for variations in the music. Other residents like Troyer, working outside the discipline, were encouraged to watch these practice sessions as long as they made themselves inconspicuous and their numbers remained small. The morning he slipped in and claimed a chair, he was the only spectator in the room.

Sylvaine was working with a male dancer on a tricky manoeuvre that had her rolling in a controlled motion across his back. During the instant they came together in the move, he stood with his backed humped and his arms hanging down almost touching the floor. His instruction was to stop for a single beat and no longer. Approaching him from the side, obliquely and almost blind, since one instant he had to be elsewhere and the next in place, she had to time her part of the intersection flawlessly. Her roll took the form of a back-to-back move, spine-aligned-with-spine, a quick on and off.

Her legs had to be straight and held parted in a rigid V-shape throughout, feet held at right angles to the line of her legs. Conversely her arms had to be so relaxed they flopped, apparently boneless.

When they practised from a stationary beginning they were able to complete the step to the choreographer's specifications. Leading to the intersecting roll, each dancer performed several intricate moves that were themselves demanding and not easy to remember. The young man achieved his lead-up steps fluidly with a natural cadence that gave him the right timing. The former actor, on the other hand, was struggling. Troyer could see her thinking about what she was doing. It showed in her face. Because she could not see her partner those few seconds before they came together in the roll, she began to balk, pulling up short or glancing over her shoulder for reassurance.

"No!" shouted the choreographer, a woman with a short fuse. "It has to be blind. Trust your instinct," she commanded. "If you fall, you fall. You do know how to fall, don't you? Does she speak English? *Comprenez-vous, mademoiselle?* Yes? Take a short break, please, and compose yourself. Perhaps we should try this with another girl." She turned to her assistant, a slip of a boy with a clipboard, and said something in a low voice.

Every rehearsal reaches a point beyond which further work is counterproductive. The dancers broke for the day. Sylvaine was towelling off and donning her warm-up gear, wrapping a light scarf around her neck to keep from tightening up, when Troyer approached her. Did she have a few moments to chat? He wanted to make amends for so rudely interrupting her and Glick the other day. And, he confessed, he was intrigued. Could she assuage his curiosity and tell him what it had been like to act in the films? He told her that he had been an ardent fan for years. "Please," he said, "if you don't mind, would you explain this dramatic change in your professional life?"

She regarded him coolly. "Who are you, again?"

He told her, sensing she did not care to know.

"I don't trust writers," she said. "They take so much more than they are prepared to give."

"I like to think that what I write becomes a gift to whoever reads it."

"Then you have a naïve concept of gift giving, Mr. Troyer. Every novel is baked from the ground bones of real victims."

Despite the lacerating sting of her criticism he remained diplomatic. He reminded her that he was there, as was she, to work creatively, and not as a journalist or a prying paparazzo. He was no vampire feeding on celebrity, contrary to what she might have decided about him.

Eventually she warmed to him. They walked between the outbuildings. The stones of the barns and vineries were sun-bleached, the whitewash on the dining hall and dormitories newly applied. They came to the vineyard where Troyer had witnessed the couple conversing so intently. She liked to walk the rows, she said, up one and down the other. It helped her visualize the elements of the dance she was learning.

"When I walk nowhere in particular, buffered from the larger world as in a maze, my mind takes flight. True, it lets me review the work, the demands made on my body, but more than that I make contact, energy connections. I feel a power enter me, up from the ground and in through the soles of my feet. I become like a lightning rod. Have you ever experienced such a thing, Mr. Troyer? Your body becomes nothing more than a conduit."

Yes, he said. It happened sometimes when he became lost in his writing, when he would become suspended in an eternal now, an unmoving, unchanging moment of creativity during which nothing existed beyond the screen, the words having appeared magically, put there by an unseen hand.

As they entered the section devoted to Glick's hybrid grapes, she admitted to what he had suspected, that she had contrived to be there when the German would most likely be checking the progress of his crop.

"It isn't what you think," she said, bending to a crouch to inspect a plump bunch growing near the ground. "I don't want anything from him, nothing material, that is. I surprised him in the same way you surprised the two of us, Mr. Troyer. Something in the cant of your head and the trajectory of your approach, not direct like an arrow but oblique, curving—it told me you were up to something. You wanted to be *le sabot jeté dans la machine*. It's not right?"

He admitted to it. For as long as he could remember he was someone attracted to the misdeeds of others, particularly those in power who abused their position, be it legal, financial or moral. For example, Glick liked being the storm cloud that blocks the sun at the garden party. Well, Troyer vowed, such a disturbance would not go unanswered, not as long as he could play the role of balancing avenger.

"Interruption in the form of correction. How protestant of us," she said. "How boring."

That couldn't be all of it. She didn't care one way or the other whether or not her former Svengali liked to be the mischief maker disturbing his fellow artists' shit.

"You are a more interesting man than you make yourself out to be, Mr. Troyer, but ultimately avengers are sad lonely characters. Wouldn't you agree? They think they are right-ing wrongs when really nobody thanks them for what they do, and often they become scapegoats after the act. The pun-isher can't bring back the murder victim, nor can he restore fully the original item stolen, since it will from that point on always bear the memory of the crime. And revenge for what? An overly active ego? My God, without ego great art would never be made."

Her harsh assessment of him hurt. With a few choice words she had reduced him to a petty agent of dubious jus-tice, while at the same time suggesting that if he wasn't a more interesting, complicated man than he seemed at first glance to be, she was going to be sorely disappointed.

In the twenty minutes they walked together through the vineyard, Troyer forgot about everything, his writing project, his reason for interrupting Heinz Werner Glick, his critical suc-cess and modest sales, and gave all his attention to this wom-an, with whom, he came to realize, he shared a remarkable number of traits. They were both people not fully actualized unless in service to a power greater than themselves. In Ms. Delacroix's case, she was a being of rare talent unable to exert her skill unless interpreting the vision of another. Troyer—and I recognized this in him early, from that first writing work-shop in which he was my tentative student—could not write unless he was thinking about the way his stories were going to be received. The work reveals this with embarrassing clarity. His is a conditional voice, one that continually clarifies, justi-fies, makes sure at every turn that not only do we understand his point, we are allied to him in that understanding. It could be his most annoying trait, that assumption, more accurately a presumptuous claim, that we are as glad to see him on our doorstep and hear him ringing our private doorbell as we are happy to read every contrived, derivative thing he has issued into print.

I should point out that I felt this way about Troyer and his writing until I read *The Woman in the Vineyard*, his most recent novel, which, incidentally, he dedicated to me. Even without his touching acknowledgment of the part I played in the book's creation, I would have come to a radical re-evaluation of the man's worth. I mean, of course, his place in literature; his worthiness in personal terms demands more space than I can devote to the question here. And yet, can the man and his work really be separated? Moreover, how can relative worth be assigned to a human being? We are born into a world, in this country at least, that assumes we are all equal regardless of circumstance. No life is of greater value than another. Only what we do and make sit comparable to other actions and products, and even that valuation arrives fraught with difficulty.

I am trying to determine what about *The Woman in the Vineyard* makes it so markedly better than anything Troyer has published to this point. I think it has to do with making himself, or whoever stands in as Troyer, an elemental figure stripped of all but one function, and because of this someone emotionally vulnerable. His main character is a playwright in love with a woman who has spurned his advances and who also happens to be an actress, not a star although someone who could become one. Unwittingly, the playwright creates a drama tailor-made for the woman, a part that draws on her peculiar strengths, the way she moves and uses her voice. Knowing what Troyer has told me about Sylvaine Delacroix, I immediately recognized her in the character of the actress.

Contrary to expectation, the jilted playwright has not created this vehicle in order to promote the actress in question. Instead, he has done so to ruin her career, writing a part so demanding that she can only fail in the attempt. She is on stage for every scene but two of a three-hour play, with almost as much to say as Hamlet. On top of that she must perform a number of exhausting feats of physical endurance. If he cannot love and be loved in return, he will ensure that the object of his affection never enjoys the attention of anyone she might wish to embrace, so defeated in spirit will she be.

You can guess what happens. The unintended result of this nefarious scheme is that the Sylvaine Delacroix-inspired character rises to and exceeds the expectations of the role. She gives the performance of a lifetime. Instead of being undone by it, she comes to define herself by the role. The play becomes a long running, record breaking, critically acclaimed hit that travels the world for years afterwards, with her reprising her character many times during her career. Conversely the playwright is punished by not being able to write anything comparable or even worthy of being staged.

On the basis of such a synopsis the reader would be excused for dismissing the story as being a rather thick morality play. What makes it intriguing and Troyer's novel so remarkable is the way he uses the actress to reflect so much about motivation in the modern age. She chooses to accept the poisoned part because, unknown to the playwright, she too wants to experience career death. She believes that her true calling is to be a modern dancer and that before she can effect that change she must commit ritual suicide. Hardly remembering the playwright or his protestations of love, she sees only that her agent has delivered the very thing she has been craving, a part that would leave her so humiliated it would be as if she had died so that she could be resurrected a different person. A born-again dancer. Her suspect reasoning was that the only way to become a great dancer was to fail catastrophically as an actor.

What neither she nor the playwright could see was that she was in that punishing, mortifying role the embodiment of everything the audience craved, a character in worse straits than they, a woman so bent on self-annihilation that her pain becomes the most highly prized entertainment imaginable, a person who in losing personhood becomes shorthand for end-times consciousness. In the few dark days remaining, it says, let us laugh scathingly at the victim, thereby alleviating for a brief time our corrosive fear. Let us usher in the last chapter of the world by taking delight in the suffering of others.

Anything the world knows about Heinz Werner Glick has come by way of conjecture drawn from his work. In his film based on the Swiss murder, for example, Sylvaine Delacroix plays the part of the young lover in the rowboat. In the real-life story the young woman was a maid serving in the household of a very rich man, a banker thought to have made his fortune storing large quantities of purloined Nazi gold. Notably his biographer asserts that Glick was the child of a lady's maid serving in a large German house before and during the war, and the suggestion is that he was the offspring of a dalliance between the maid and her employer. She was allowed to continue living in the house, working as before and letting her son be raised as a member of the man's family, a brood of seven other children. What was the addition of one more to a progressive home buffered by wealth and relatively untouched by war?

This did not mean that within *die Familie Glick* little Heinz was treated as an equal. He was still a bastard, a product of the lower class. He was made to do the bidding of the other children, who could be diabolically creative in the ways they found to torment him. The head of the household, the banker, was a haughty, emotionally distant man whose attention seemed always directed elsewhere and most often towards his work. His wife considered the maid's continued presence and her very existence an affront barely countenanced. Her dirty little boy would be made to know his place.

Heinz feared the woman as a child fears witches, hags and the sorceresses of fairy tales. The other Glick children were cared for by a nanny, their exposure to their mother limited to mornings and evenings, when she would shower them with effusive attention. Little Heinz had only his own mother, who never had time to herself let alone time to spend with him. She worked from the moment her eyes opened in the morning until the instant she fell exhausted, often still wearing her uniform, into bed late at night.

In the film, Sylvaine's character, the maid in the rowboat, becomes a key witness in the prosecution's case against the heiress. Glick's vision, no doubt fuelled by his own childhood memories and his mother's difficult position, becomes the nightmare experienced by the maid. Only she has seen the bundle the size of an adult body hit the water, although her boyfriend says he heard the splash. She is the one who remembers the name emblazoned on the yacht's stern and under cross-examination maintains her assertion that she had no prior knowledge that the vessel belonged to the heiress. She has not been fed that information, she contends, nor coached in her responses by the prosecuting attorney in the case. She becomes the state's best chance to win a conviction.

Glick places Delacroix in the witness box for almost the entire film and for most of her time on screen. She stands throughout. The lighting, her restrictive clothing, tightly draped, binding, the box-shaped stall that contains her, and the oppressive questions are all meant to hold her in place. Unremittingly the defence counsel makes her restate the details of what she saw. Her good character is called into question. What resentments did she have against her employer and the moneyed class in general? Was it not true that she had a baby out of wedlock, that the baby's father was her present employer, and that the boy had been taken from her? How intimately did she know the young man who was rowing the boat that night? Was it not the case that she had been planning to break off her engagement to him, because she was romantically involved with the heiress's husband?

"That was the plan, can you deny it? You weren't floating so close to the yacht that night by accident," the defence challenges. "You were there because you thought your lover was up there on that deck, that he was very much alive, and that he was disposing of the body of the heiress. You couldn't stay away as you should have."

"No!" she cries. "That is absurd." She is in love with Gunther, the rower. She knows nothing about the heiress or her husband.

The lawyer will not let up. "Are you telling me that you have heard nothing about their troubled marriage? Servants talk to one another, households communicate, this is a tight community. Gossip takes wing. After all, what else do you have for entertainment if not salacious speculation concerning the illicit affairs of those from whom you take a salary and to whom you owe your well-being?"

The interrogation, from both sides, continues unabated for hours. It takes the form and quality of torture. Sylvaine's character slumps and writhes. Incomprehension, humiliation and exhaustion contort her features. Surprise gives way to outrage, which ebbs to disbelief, fear and finally defeat. The inconceivable asserted often enough becomes the probable. Students of the film find that the remarkable thing about it is not so much the ordeal of the role, the countless hours of physically and emotionally draining scene-takes on that claustrophobia-inducing set, but the sense, achieved with spare, minimal dialogue, that such trials as this one happen every day and that they are mundanely commonplace. A young woman, her will draining away along with her repeated claims of innocence, is browbeaten into capitulation. To watch it is to experience the slow death of a magnificent animal in the bullring. Delacroix from the beginning of her acting career had a dancer's supple strength and balance, that majestic posture, the neck of a swan. To see her being used in this way, brought to her knees stab-by-stab, is hypnotic. Were we in the audience able to intercede on the victim's behalf we might not have done it, so stylish a rape does the film depict.

I am acutely aware that this account places layer upon layer between the reader and whatever truth is to be had. This is Troyer's story as told by me. He relates what Ms. Delacroix told him and what he has gleaned from the films. On top of this we have my relationship to Troyer, once that of mentor and student, now a reversal of roles, he having become the more successful because the more adventurous. The final layer is Troyer's novel. I know too much about its antecedence to judge it impartially. I should be able to; believe me when I say I can't. The story is ruined for me. Think about it. It is morning, I am awake, just, the coffee is freshly dripping into the pot, my world for a blessed but too-brief time is without perturbation, and then he is there, at my side, speaking *in medias res* about this infernal encounter of his.

It fed his imagination, engendered his book and informed every waking moment of his stay with me. Did we speak of anything else, of ideas or global events or the writing life? I assure you we did not. What we explored, what he continually pushed into the foreground for investigation, was this co-dependent relationship of Glick and Delacroix. My role was to remain mute except for the occasional clarifying question. Troyer was not satisfied to let the unknown remain so; he despised enigma. The films, although entry points, were insufficient. He recounted what he had learned from each of them, a dozen at least, as if trying to unravel a tangle of lies. It became oppressive, it bored me to distraction. Unable to redirect the conversation once we got snagged on the subject, I contrived to avoid the man whenever possible. I forged outrageous excuses for my absence. A writer who closes his ears to narrative deceives his instinct. It became an escalating source of discomfort, exacerbated by the fact that we arrived at and passed, by two days, then three and four, the day he was supposed to depart, without his acknowledging the delay. The story of the woman in the vineyard took over his entire consciousness, it seemed, leaving no room for such mundane matters as work schedules, travel itineraries, or the courtesy of leaving his host in peace, returning me to the solitude I so craved.

I have come to the conclusion, after separating my personal complaints from the larger story, that the completed matrix points to a single idea, that of liberation. Sylvaine Delacroix could not begin to free herself from the ties that bound her—her past with and work for a man who cast her in highly restricted roles, her vocation, her gender's traditional acceptance of subservience to men—until she effected a radical change. In exchanging the acting life for that of a dancer, she appears to have doffed one set of chains only to don another. This was puzzling. How could she be said to be freer in one than in the other?

Troyer was no help answering this question. He concerned himself only with the details of the story. The way his mind works, ideas get in the way. Nothing should impede the narrative. It must be simply that this happened followed by that, without explanation. Each reader creates an individual, subjective context. Troyer likened himself to a detective solving a mystery, whereas I wanted him to give me a framework of ideas upon which to examine the implications of the fiction. Throughout his visit we remained thus, separate in disagreement.

Those who have been enslaved and freed come to a junction at which they must confront their abusers, in person or symbolically. Somehow they must make peace with the past. The consequence of not achieving forgiveness and of not letting the memory of the crime fade and disappear, is illness and early death. Of this I am convinced. As Troyer kept mucking through the fragments of what he thought he knew about Sylvaine Delacroix and Heinz Werner Glick, and as he made the waters not clearer but increasingly choked with the sediment of his research, he was blind to the obvious reading of the story. The actress-turned-dancer was confronting her tormentor in an act of self-preservation. Whether or not he admitted guilt in the matter was less important than was her brave demonstration of survival. Why is this so clear to me, when the one who was there, who interviewed the woman and psychoanalyzed the man, who heard or dreamt their separate confessions, failed to see it?

Troyer took a three-day side-trip during his stay with me. A friend picked him up in her car and drove him to her cottage on a secluded lake an hour's drive north of here. On passing the open door of his room the first morning of his absence I looked in and saw that he had left his laptop and bound journal sitting on top of the desk beside his bed. Before he left for the cottage he said that he had begun writing his novel, going so far as to say that he found my house highly conducive to his creativity and that he would be sure to recognize me in the acknowledgments in the published product. Something about the way he said this stung more painfully than it should. He knew that it had been twelve years since I'd published a book. I could not help thinking that he was giving me a backhanded gesture of thanks, that it was less an acknowledgment of my help than it was the running up the flagpole of a banner announcing his comparative success. Someone less confident in his station might have been devastated by it.

I am not proud of what I did next, although I don't consider it worthy of guilt or punishment. It was my house, after all. When he returned I told him what I'd done. He deserved to know, both that I had violated his privacy and, to my thinking the more salient point, that I knew now that he was a fraud. He had essentially stolen the plot of his novel from Glick and Delacroix. Without the real case of the heiress and her yacht, without Glick's connection to that story by way of his childhood nurse, without Glick's subsequent film, that is, his artistic approach, embrace, alchemical manipulation of the material, what would Troyer have had? Nothing. Add what he had appropriated of what Delacroix had told him about herself and Glick, and you have what amounts to theft.

I was the least surprised of anyone to hear Troyer characterize *The Woman in the Vineyard* as homage. Imitation as sincere flattery, etc. It made me close to nauseated to contemplate.

My confession to him, that I had read the notes and early chapters of the novel without his permission, swiftly put an end to his time of free room-and-board with me and, not a surprise, an end to our acquaintance. He would publish an angry, bordering-on-vicious attack against me in a national newspaper, the subject being my influence on a generation of younger writers, a "pall" that he argued did more to harm the state of our national letters than to promote it. When he called my "so-called school" of novel writing "antiquated, self-indulgent, quasi-intellectual pap that stews in its own complacent juices and turns out stories so plot-thin and boring that from even the most reactionary pulpit they are condemned for their soporific dearth of action," I did not give him the satisfaction of a reply. I understood this to be the residue of an abiding anger still simmering after what he considered my violation of his sacrosanct privacy. This is understandable, I suppose, coming from someone who continues to believe that a private life is desirable and necessary. We live at a time when to keep something to oneself is the same thing as throwing it out with the trash. In fact, I don't even believe his sniper's ambush of me in print had much at all to do with me reading the equivalent of his teenage diary. I think it had everything to do with his fear that I was going to steal his already pilfered goods. What can

I say about that except that he is entitled to his opinion, this is still a place where freedom of speech is upheld, and little minds produce small thoughts.

It is far more rewarding to return to the stories that caused all the fuss in the first place. In the historical record, the eye-witness testimony of Glick's boyhood nurse did nothing to incriminate the heiress, whose lawyer made quick dismissive mincemeat of the young woman, of both her account of events on the water that night and her reputation. As the trial drew to a close the jury could not even be sure the yacht in question had left its mooring that evening. Nothing corroborated her testimony except for that of her fiancé, Gunther, who arguably would have said anything to support her, and so nothing prevented what she said she saw from being discredited wholesale.

Not content with exoneration, the wealthy woman set out to destroy the nurse, now ex-nurse given that she was fired as soon as the not-guilty verdict was rendered; the rich close ranks in such instances. Even Gunther abandoned her, breaking the engagement within the month following the end of the trial. The rumour continued to circulate that the nurse had been romantically involved with the heiress's young husband before he disappeared. Glick grabs hold of this gossip in his film. In a breathtakingly short time the young woman finds herself alone and destitute, unable to secure even the most menial work. Whether or not she left Zurich is a matter of conjecture. In some accounts she became a beggar stationed every day outside the gates of the heiress's mansion. In others she becomes a prostitute and in a few years the proprietor of a notorious brothel, and she takes her revenge upon the heiress by effecting the death, by venereal disease, of her only son. In yet another version the ex-nurse travels to a distant canton, where she becomes a successful merchant who eventually buys the heiress's industrial and banking empire out from under her.

Here is the point at which Troyer and I diverge with respect to this fictional amalgam of possible truths: where he was content to repackage what was already there, I craved significance, deeper meaning. There had to be more, for example, to Troyer's interview with Delacroix. She was dismissed from rehearsal that day she and her partner tried unsuccessfully to execute their difficult move, the blind back-roll. Inured to being treated harshly by her director, she shook her head apologetically as if to say that it was all her fault. Her partner assured her that he was as much to blame as she was for their failure, if not the greater cause of their timing problem. He was a ruggedly handsome man with a long, sculpted face, large hands and prominent veins in his arms and legs. He was strong enough to lift her all manner of ways, and his rhythm and ability to anticipate and react were impeccable. In short he was not the problem. Even onlooker Troyer, whose knowledge of the art form was at best elementary, could see that the male partner was where he should have been at every beat, doing what the choreographer required of him. It was Delacroix who was off that day. Troyer believed that she was distracted by Glick's presence, by something the German said to her before Troyer so inexpertly sneaked up on them.

They walked, Delacroix and Troyer, through the rows of grapes. If she told him what she and Glick said to each other earlier, Troyer did not tell me. What he did relate were the sensations he remembered from the twenty minutes they spent together, the way the light played on the distant hills, the smells—juniper, pine, rosemary, thyme—seeming to originate in the ripening fruit, the colour and visual texture of the gnarled vines.

"Sometimes," she said, "I feel as old and twisted as these branches." This is a quotation from Troyer's novel. Whether or not she said this to him is immaterial, I believe, at this point. If she did not say it she most certainly should have. It pins her precisely in that moment, holds her up to the light. Still a youthful woman of early middle age, she felt ancient. Not defeated, not weak the way the elderly become, but tough and deeply rooted. One can be weary and still vigorous, one's body more able to endure than it had been in younger days but lacking the explosive ecstasies of brimming youth. As an artist she had made herself an increasingly reliable vessel. Her vintages could be anticipated with excitement. They could be counted on. Was this artistic death, predictability without brilliance? In a sense she had come to see herself not as an artist but an artist's prop, a highly developed, finely calibrated instrument. Thus, to fail, to be unable to do what the artist wanted of her, as in the dance studio that day, would have left her puzzled and frustrated.

In Troyer's novel the Glick character, the playwright, is defeated by his own plot to ruin the woman with whom he is still in love. Heinz Werner Glick, conversely, gave no indication that his relationship with Sylvaine Delacroix contributed to anything but a prolonged period of successful filmmaking and theatre. And in the time since their divorce, he wrote and staged an opera based on the life of Silvio Berlusconi, the disgraced Italian prime minister and billionaire media mogul. His films, in German and English, have earned significant praise and won international prizes. Stills from his body of work formed the basis for a visual-arts exhibition that drew large crowds in Europe and North America. He is often photographed with his new love, a statuesque fashion model who, not surprisingly, had the lead in one of his recent films. The couple is sometimes seen with his eleven-year-old daughter, Io. The paparazzi seem unable to capture them in anything but happy poses. On the surface, then, he appears to be the opposite of the blocked artist. And although Delacroix did not become defined by a single gruelling role, she did become a significant modern dancer and, later, when her body finally did stop responding as it should to commands, a choreographer of note. It almost doesn't matter that Troyer interrupted them in the midst of an argument the specifics of which are probably never to be revealed.

In the months following Troyer's departure, I continued to work in solitude, publishing little and seldom, content with sifting, with making circular passes through well-rifled drawers. But that moment, Troyer's ambush, continued to nag. What do former lovers fight about in the hot, close moments after one has surprised the other? They don't argue about large matters. My intuition tells me that whatever pain resides in them is buried deep and it takes considerable coaxing to draw it out of hiding. For that, one talks with a therapist. No, I think it has to have been about something relatively small, inconsequential. Glick, anxious to gauge the progress of a new hybrid grape, was annoyed at having been delayed in doing so. Anyone, a stranger or a former lover, would have set him on edge. I imagine him saying, "I'm busy, I'm in a hurry, I haven't time right now. What is it, is Io all right? You look fit. What are you doing here, are you working? Dance, what do you mean, *dance*? You're an actor. I made you into one. This is ridiculous. Puppet? I never treated you as such. I can't stop you throwing away your talent. She is well, then? Gretchen can't wait to see her again."

This is all preliminary banter until the reason for the confrontation is stated: Delacroix has been invited to join a dance company that travels widely most of the year. Glick has not been returning her calls. His assistant, rather, has not been passing her messages on to the filmmaker. The crux of the matter—contrary to what I suggested earlier, this is hardly a small thing—is that she needs him to take Io to live with him for an extended period, a year and possibly longer. Mother and daughter, to this point best friends and inseparable, have been fighting of late. It is inevitable, the result of hormonal changes, burgeoning selfhood, the pushing against boundaries, the testing of personality, new muscles. The girl is growing up quickly. Yes, she answers him, it would indeed seem to be a time when the girl needs her mother. The truth is that Sylvaine needs to do this, she must, now, or shrivel and blow away on the next strong wind. Can he not understand that?

He did, evidently, since soon afterwards Io was living and travelling with her father and his girlfriend. I can't begin to approximate the mind of an eleven-year-old girl except to acknowledge or merely wish for her to be aware and happy in her altered circumstances, to see how lucky she is to be the daughter of such a brilliant man and of a talented woman perceptive enough to know that for her continued good health Io had to break out of her mother's orbit for a year. I am fascinated to have seen this very thing worked out in Glick's most recent work.

By now you must think I write only by way of a filter formed by the creative work of others. Troyer's novel, Glick's films, Delacroix's performance as described in X's review. It is, I admit, the way I engage with the world nowadays. It does restrict the quality of my output to a rather narrow scope of observation and commentary. Have I become nothing more since Troyer's stay in my house than a critic? I do wish I could write a simple and profound piece of fiction that does not buckle under the weight of self-consciousness. Leave off interpretation, I hear myself saying even as I continue in this quest for meaning.

This all came to a head not long ago when I was approached to write a theatrical adaptation of *The Woman in the Vineyard*. According to his publisher, Troyer tried unsuccessfully to adapt his novel to the stage. This struck me as strange, given that his book is about a playwright, an actress and the play he fashions for her to perform. To be fair to Troyer, we can be too close emotionally to our work, the product of our often blinkered imaginations, to manipulate it beyond our initial vision for it.

My first reaction was to refuse to do it. Admittedly I am someone who usually says no and, after considering the request, changes his mind. Here, for what it's worth, was my thinking at the time of being asked. First, why should I help a man for whom I felt something stronger than annoyance but milder than animosity? A man who with his most recent book had achieved something I had not, that is, commercial and critical success. A protegé whose acknowledgment of my contribution to his professional development was nothing but a stinging nettle. A colleague, someone I considered a colleague, who thought of me only as that creep who paws through his guests' belongings while they are away. A man who called himself a literary artist yet lacked the imagination necessary to transcend such petty notions as personal privacy. Who could not bring himself to embody my point of view long enough to understand my reasons for wanting to know more about the subjects of his writing project.

Once I was able to let go of these negative valuations of Troyer the man, I found it easier to approach his novel as someone with an objective purpose, i.e., adaptation, in mind. It was going to do me and my career no favours to continue to hold a grudge. And if Troyer hated me for what he considered an unforgivable violation, well that was his unfortunate egg to coddle. I had a book to read and turn into a play.

According to the editor I spoke with, Troyer himself had recommended me for the project. I won't pretend I wasn't flattered, despite the frostiness of our parting. So much of what we think of as divinely inspired masterwork, the painting that commands a million dollars at auction, the film that tops every critic's list, the book that refuses to fall out of print, was made because somebody asked for it to be made. No ego is so insularly resilient that it does not need stroking. Not even Heinz Werner Glick dismisses genuine praise. It was gratifying to be asked.

Troyer uses a tripartite structure of scenes between which he moves in telling his story. Of course, they are larger than mere scenes, they are episodes, but for me to envision the novel as a play I needed those three points on the triangle to be constant and static. The first is set in a nursery and involves the close, loving relationship of an eight-year-old boy, the future playwright, and his nurse, a 19-year-old girl he thinks of as both mother and lover. The second is situated in a rowboat on Lake Zurich. In the boat are the nurse and her boyfriend. As he rows, languidly dipping the oars, he tells her about the dream he had the night before.

He is bent low while picking ripe grapes for the wine harvest when he feels the light touch of a hand on the back of his neck. He stands and turns to see a grown woman who has the bald head and undeveloped face of a baby. Nevertheless she speaks in an adult voice, addressing him as though she has known him all her life. This does not strike him as strange. She tells him that she must show him where she has buried his music. Again he considers this in no way out of the ordinary. Gunther is a composer, Troyer tells us. I have no way of knowing, without researching the question, whether or not the real Gunther was a composer of music. From the subjective position of a reader presented with an unfamiliar story, it strikes me that his vocation and the mention of music in the dream are too convenient not to have been fabricated. Then again, what should composers dream about if not the product of their work?

When Troyer was still speaking to me, before he left in an indignant huff over my innocent act of curiosity regarding his writing, I asked him about the dance move Sylvaine was trying to perfect with her partner. Had they been able to accomplish it? He said that he didn't know. He left the place the next day. My first thought was that he wasn't much of an investigator. What journalist worth his byline up and goes home so soon into a story? In his defence I admit that Troyer was not there to delve into the lives of this intriguing former couple, he was there to write fiction. Given the matter and form of what he produced while in residence there, however, I do still think he fled the scene too soon. The imagination needs distance and time enough to allow the real to be transformed, that much I will concede. But what did he miss by leaving so soon? What might his novel have become?

We agreed that the woman he had met and I had watched in Glick's films was not someone who would have let such an insurmountable thing as a tricky physical manoeuvre defeat her. She was a model of perseverance, I said, letting the remark be taken for a subtle gibe should he be so perceptive as to recognize it as such. I don't believe he did, for he continued to speak earnestly about that frustrating rehearsal and their subsequent stroll. Throwing herself into the move only to fail repeatedly was difficult to watch.

"I looked away," he said. "It was too painful. Her partner was doing everything he could to help her without destroying the integrity of the choreographer's vision. It was her fault they weren't nailing it, no doubt about that. Poor thing. You could see all the years of formal training in him even though he was quite a bit younger than she was. She was operating on instinct, raw talent and the force of her will. It would be like entering a milk-delivery van in a high-speed car race. You might have your accelerator pedal pressed to the floor, but that isn't going to cut it."

I reminded him of his hasty exit. What about his obligation to the story? I didn't even mention his curiosity, which he must have had to suppress.

"Well, yes, you are one hundred percent correct," he replied congenially. "A writer does not flinch, let alone avert his eyes. You said something to that effect in your creative writing course, if I'm not mistaken. So here's my thinking, and all I can hope is that you can see it my way once I've told you: the person I saw while I sat on the sidelines in that mirrored studio was my sister.

"She was eight years older than me and all she wanted to do was sing. Did she have a voice? She did; so does a frog or a blue jay. Our father loved her so dotingly that he refused to let anyone tell her the truth. He would rather lose his hearing than say anything to hurt her, and so he continued to pay for expensive singing lessons with a renowned opera singer. My sister must have been competent enough by then that this woman took her on as a student. I can't imagine anyone being so cold-hearted as to take my father's money knowing that the student was sure to fail. All I remember is the sound of what to my ears was a strained, reedy, unpleasant noise that would go on for a prolonged period behind closed doors.

"Was it cruelty on our part not to tell her? Was it only that I was too young to appreciate the kind of music she wanted to sing? Had she improved, these questions and their answers would have been moot. She didn't improve, and I wasn't the only one to innocently say so. Even our father conceded the futility of the endeavour. And so one day he took his daughter aside to break the news to her that money had become tight and he could no longer afford to pay for her lessons. 'It's because I'm no good, isn't it, Daddy,' she said.

"'No, no, you are marvellous,' he said. He was such a bad liar. She knew right off that the whole song and dance about the money was just his way of letting her down easy. To her credit she didn't make a big deal of it. She was her papa's daughter in that regard, able to smile stoically in the face of adversity and say it didn't hurt a bit when really it did hurt a whole hell of a lot.

"She would have been in her final year of high school then. Her plan had been to study music at university and go on to become a famous opera star. She'd done the research, setting her sights finally on a small, prestigious liberal arts college in New England. Her marks all through high school were stellar, high 90s across the board, and she played on her school's field hockey team. On paper she was the perfect candidate for a scholarship. She'd even won an award in a national essay-writing contest, her entry something about the mathematics of Bach. I mean, talk about the cruelty of the cosmos. Human cruelty—I was going to say that it pales in comparison, but you get what I mean, don't you? Think about it. All her life, ever since she was a little girl with dreams bigger that a wish for the latest fad doll, she wanted to sing on stage. And this is what plops on her head from above.

"When she admitted to herself that a career as a vocal performer was closed to her, she lost interest in everything. Her marks in senior year plummeted. She quit playing hockey, stopped doing anything physically active. She had always been a large girl, not corpulent but solid, another factor contributing to her self-image and her goal of being the next Maureen Forrester. Now she hid in her room, eating and becoming fat. She used to hang out with a gang of friends, boys and girls in equal number, as I recall. They stopped coming to the house to see her. It was like watching a great sorrowful balloon expand, not to take flight but to sink into the earth and disappear.

"How much was it about letting go of life's handholds and sliding to her regrettable, pathetic end and how much the result of unavoidable circumstance? We could have saved her. All it would have taken was the blunt truth told early. Telling a child she can do anything, accomplish whatever she sets her sights on, is the most irresponsible thing a parent can do. It makes me burn and weep, it really does, to think about my beautiful sister, her spirit broken."

"What does she do now?" I asked rather stupidly, not having heard any of Troyer's narrative clues.

"She doesn't do anything, she's dead." He looked at me as though I'd desecrated her grave. "She got diabetes, which led to heart disease. By the time her cardiomyopathy was diagnosed she was beyond saving."

I was sorry and I told him so. But this did not sit right somehow. If he had asked me to read a story with this in it I would have red-flagged the offending passage. More information, please, I'd have written in the margin. A person does not live very long with diabetes without having seen a doctor, who presumably would have taken a good listen to Troyer's sister's heart and lungs, given her obesity and sudden sedentary state. How long a period were we talking about, from first instance of despondency to death? I couldn't ask a grieving brother such accusatory questions. I guess I might have, but then I'd have been calling into doubt the veracity of his story. And that was a line I was not going to cross, not in his presence, that is.

Having made his point about Sylvaine Delacroix, and having left behind a thick smear of unimpeachable sentiment, Troyer went off to visit his friend at her cottage. It left me alone to mull over the man's entire story to date, an account I had no reason until that moment to question. I was bothered first by the fact that he was willing to use his private family history to illustrate what amounted to a minor point, the relative unpreparedness of the actress for her new career. One question ignited the next. For example, would Ms. Delacroix not have to demonstrate her professional fitness, her suitability for the developmental work she would be undertaking at the artists' retreat? Competition for space in such programs runs high. She would have had to send an audition tape along with the endorsement of reputable experts in the discipline. This wasn't Saturday morning, take your kid to the Y and sign her up for introductory ballet. Didn't he say that she had recently joined a touring dance company? I was becoming suspicious not only of this part of Troyer's byzantine story but the entire conceit.

I should have been able to separate what I thought of Troyer, my expanding doubt concerning his trustworthiness, and what I had to work with in adapting his novel. A fiction writer, they say, is someone who tells the truth only on the page. Why, then, should I have harboured such compunctions to the point of being obsessed and unable to work? The man was at best a distant acquaintance. It wasn't as if he was a friend who had betrayed a confidence, shattered a bond. Emotion need not have played any part in this. I had his book, which I'd dissected in my attempt to put the details, the events of his narrative, into a simple linear structure. There they were, and are still, spread before me across the large table in my office. For the longest time I moved the photocopied pages, some whole, some reduced to a few words, as I might arrange jigsaw-puzzle pieces while looking for connections. Whatever I tried to construct either reproduced the approximate novel or leaned towards an oral account. Of the two records, what Troyer told me over the course of his stay makes for the more memorable story. I think this is the sticking point of my problem: putting aside the question of trust and truthfulness and judging by purely literary standards, I believe that what he told me over the course of his stay is the better book, if I can use that term to compare the two.

I decided to put the adaptation on hold until I knew more, not about Troyer's novel—it I had pulled apart, digested and regurgitated—but the people on whom he'd based his characters. I secured a small travel grant and convinced the publisher who had commissioned the work to throw in an equal amount. It was an audacious bit of salesmanship, if I may say so. There might have been some embellishment, some fiction-alizing of my intentions and vision for the project. In any case it was going to be enough to get me across the pond to the very artists' retreat where Troyer's story began. My thinking was that if I could stay there a few days, as a writer needing only peace and solitude, sleeping in one of the rudimentary cells, taking meals in silence, walking where Troyer, Glick and Delacroix did, seeing and touching the vines of plump grapes, gazing out on the purple undulating hills, I might chance upon an approach to the project I'd hitherto been missing. And if being there should tell me more about the trio and their brief encounter, so much the better. At the very least I knew that Glick had reason to visit there periodically, and should our paths not intersect I hoped for a way to contact him once in residence. Finding the filmmaker, my reasoning told me, I should then be led to his former muse. Being still-active art-ists, they would doubtless be involved in work or be looking for their next project. Their fields depended on collaborative work. I would find people to talk to, to ask about the subjects of my search. I had no desire to see Troyer again. I did want to expose him, however, to my detective efforts and to the world. At the time of planning my trip it did not strike me as counter-productive to lay bare the hidden truths about an author whose published work I was adapting to the stage. I didn't think that effecting the first would scuttle the second, proof that naivety is not restricted to the young.

I thought about the third point of my triangle, the form upon which I was trying to structure my play. I would say it is the apex, the staged courtroom, where we the audience can see beyond the frame of the theatrical set to include all action taking place backstage and in the wings. Here, centrally, is dramatized the prolonged testimony of the nurse, whom we have already seen taking care of the playwright as a young boy. Behind the scenes the playwright tries to subvert the performance. He orders sounds and music to be played at the wrong times. He amends the script from one night to the next. He has her wear ridiculous outfits, hides her regular costume. Maddeningly for him, her performance only improves.

Inside these adjoining sides I hang Troyer himself or the character I name Troyer, a writer in retreat at a French artists' colony. This, as you might guess, is my addition, one not found in Troyer's novel, the title of which he presents, somewhat lamely I thought, by way of a dream her lover tells the nurse while they are out spooning in the moonlight on Lake Zurich. When I read that the first time, I laughed angrily. The woman in the vineyard, I felt, was central to the entire conceit. To hide Sylvaine Delacroix in that way was dishonest. It approached the criminal in its fraudulence. A dream? Come on, I said to no one. What reader even halfway perceptive was not going to pick up on the artificiality of such a clunky device?

And yet I couldn't ignore it. Troyer had made the conscious decision to translate his encounter with the enigmatic Ms. Delacroix into a simplified artistic language removed from the personal. Had I not heard what I consider to be the real story, the dream version might not have upset me so. I had no choice but to include it in my adaptation, although to do so ran contrary to my instinct. So much depended on the integrity of Gunther's dream. If it held up, if it supported the structure and was integral to the whole, I would include it.

Some of Troyer's version, published in the pages of his novel, follows:

How ardent, his piercing look. He made her feel self-conscious when all she wanted was to drift peacefully on the placid water. His intentions were unmistakable: only her acceptance of his proposal would do. Otherwise, he claimed, aloud and in a stream of letters, he was lost. She liked him. She liked several other young men who had also made their attraction to her clear if not in so feverish a way as had Gunther. But this Miss Kern, Monika, dipping her hand into the first, warmest layer of the glacier-fed lake, wanted a different sort of passion, one without so many words. She would know it—she would know *him*, rather, when he stormed into her life. Until then, after six and a half days a week tied to that nursery in a stifling household where nobody said what they were really thinking and everything had to be just so and her charges considered her nothing more than a large child herself, an evening out in a quietly drifting boat was all she needed.

"May I tell you about the dream I had last night?" he asked after a particularly intense love-stare elicited no response from her.

"By all means," she replied. "I will interpret its meaning for you."

He was walking through a vineyard, he said, the plants of which stood so tall that he could not see over them on either side. The rows were not laid straight but in a maze formation, so that before long he could no longer tell where he was in relation to the entrance. "I knew I had entered through an arbour thick with pink and white roses. Where that gate stood now was anybody's guess."

Around a corner he felt someone touch him on the back. Turning, he encountered a woman who was nude except for a necklace of rose thorns. She had the lean, toned body of a dancer and she smiled at him beatifically. When he asked, "Are you an angel?" she did not respond. As he approached her she receded, although she did not appear to move her feet. In the reality of the dream this was not puzzling to him. She turned around and began to run away. Without having been told, he knew that she wanted him to follow her, and so he did. He had not run this way, with unconscious abandon, for many years, not since childhood. It was like flying, his feet barely touching the ground, and he breathed easily, not in the least winded. No matter how fast he ran, the distance between him and the woman remained constant. What was more, she was telling him things he could hear clearly as if they sat tête-à-tête on a love seat in a hushed room.

She promised that if he caught her before they left the labyrinth of plump, bountiful grapes that were ripe for harvest she would be his. But if he failed he would be put to death. It was only fair, she assured him. Again, this stipulation struck him as being perfectly reasonable. He did not ask how he might be killed, he didn't have to, for he knew that if he did not catch the dancer soon he would be crushed along with the grapes in a gigantic wine press. Increased effort brought him closer to her. The tight turns of the maze came sooner and sooner as he careened around corners, his clothes catching and tearing on jagged protrusions of the twisted vines. It was as if the tendrils were animate and trying to grab hold of him. They wanted him to fail, they craved his death. If he died then they would not.

Meanwhile, still sprinting, he could no longer see the woman. As he ran he tried leaping high to peer over the top of the maze. With each jumping stride he remained airborne longer. She had vanished. He could still hear what she was telling him, however. It was her story, one of great devotion and suffering. She was in thrall to a powerful, cruel master who made her do unspeakable things for his perverse pleasure. Her only relief came once a day for one hour, during which time she was allowed to stroll alone through his maze. She was not permitted to talk to anyone she might encounter there. She was committing a punishable sin by talking to Gunther, who called out to her, "Stop running. Why are you fleeing? Let me bring you away from this prison."

She replied, "But don't you see? It isn't a prison, it's my life, it's what I was destined for, how I'm meant to live."

I read a newspaper article recently about a group of physicists and mathematicians who are seriously exploring the possibility that all human consciousness is the product of a computer simulation and that the proof of this might lie in such anomalous phenomena as our dream life.

While I waited to board my flight to Paris I watched a woman in a burka hustled away by no fewer than six security personnel. It happened swiftly with little sound, and none of the other people seated in the gate's waiting area seemed the least bit perturbed by the arrest. I tried to read my book but couldn't concentrate. It made me think about security and justice and the freedoms we have given up like so many unquestioning sheep.

I wish I could tell you I got on that plane, flew to France, found answers to my questions, filled all the gaps Troyer left behind, came home and finished turning his enigmatic novel into a play. To tell you the truth I abandoned the project.

I could say I lost my nerve or I lost the thread or I stopped believing it was even worth doing. Each statement is right in its own way but not completely right. The closest thing to an explanation I can give you is that like a car I ran out of fuel and discovered that all the gas stations were closed. I have been a fabulist for so long, living inside stories, I am no longer confident I can find the exit. And so, forgive me if I stop here and think awhile, to figure out my next move and the subsequent ones and, ultimately, how I'm meant to live.